*the fifth*
# SEASON

# the fifth
# SEASON

*A Novel of Suspense*

# Don Bredes

THREE RIVERS PRESS
NEW YORK

Published in the United States by Three Rivers Press, an imprint of the Crown
Publishing Group, a division of Random House, Inc., New York.
www.crownpublishing.com

Three Rivers Press and the Tugboat design are registered trademarks of
Random House, Inc.

Library of Congress Cataloging-in-Publication Data
Bredes, Don.
The fifth season : a novel of suspense / Don Bredes.— 1st ed.
1. Police—Vermont—Fiction.  2. Mass murder—Fiction.  3. Vermont—Fiction.
I. Title.
PS3552.R363G76  2005
813'.54—dc22
2004023141

ISBN 0-609-60688-3

Printed in the United States of America

*Design by Lynne Amft*

10 9 8 7 6 5 4 3 2 1

First Edition

*For Dounia*

. . . the best way out is always through.

—*Robert Frost, "A Servant to Servants"*

# SUNDAY

# 1

The dawn broke clear again on the eighth of April, ending the longest stretch of bad weather anyone had seen in these parts since the Ice Age, sixty-three straight days of snow and sleet and rain. The sun that crested Canada Ridge that morning found me on my east sidehill, opening my cold frames to its first rays. I had one hundred flats of market produce out there—lettuces, herbs, and crucifers—all looking paler and leggier than I liked. The break in the weather would be fleeting, and I wasn't about to waste a second of it.

I took my breakfast (tea, yogurt, half a cantaloupe, and the last of Friday night's onion focaccia) out to the picnic table under my mother's budding lilac, where I ate listening to the white-noise roar of Ricker Brook in the softwoods below my greenhouse. The flooding down along the river would only worsen today. Already a long stretch of the county highway that skirted the shore of the lake from Tipton into Quebec was under three feet of water from the fishing access to Perry Crossing.

Having my view back again was a true gift. More than two months had passed since I'd been able to see from my hill over the ragged spruce woods and the village steeples all the way across the lake to the worn silhouette of Mount Joseph, ten miles off. The mountain's façade was in shadow at this hour, but its dome gleamed against the sky. At its foot the lake surface looked like paraffin, yellow-gray and dappled with patches of snow.

I picked up my bird glasses. By law, all the fishing shanties should have been off the ice a week ago, and yet one remained—

particle board, with a sheet of corrugated Plexiglas for a roof. Larry Tetrault's, if I had to bet. When that shack went through, he'd get hit with a thousand-dollar fine from Fish and Wildlife plus the cost of dragging it up from the bottom—only it would be his girlfriend, Trudy Barrett, writing the check, since she was the one in that household with a steady income. Still, if he got right on it, Larry could at least snake a cable out there and save everyone concerned a lot of trouble and expense. I made a note to give him a nudge around noontime, when you could usually count on his being both awake and sober.

I had intended to spend this fine day transplanting squash and tomatoes in the greenhouse, and for a few blissful hours it went as planned. The soft, moving air threaded with the pungent aroma of the tomatoes was a tonic. All morning, even with the doors open at both ends, I couldn't hear a thing over the tumult of the brook except, now and then, the burble of a red-winged blackbird in the marsh, celebrating the sun. It wasn't until I was walking up across my soggy lawn for lunch that my spirits took a plunge at the sound of a woman's voice floating down from my answering machine in the kitchen: Ella McPhetres, our town clerk. She had a mission for me.

It was Ella who'd recruited me for the post of constable the year before, she and my half-brother, Spud. The town had been without a constable ever since Clyde Greeley remarried and moved to Springfield five years earlier, simply because no one among our two-hundred-and-some residents was remotely qualified for the job—no one, that is, until I came home. I was perfect. "And there's nothing to it," Spud promised me. "A little light peacekeeping's all it amounts to. Plus, you could use the stipend. You can't keep cornflakes in the cupboard on what I'm paying you."

That much was true. Spud and his wife, Brenda, ran the high, rolling dairy farm a mile past my mother's cabin. I'd been putting in a hand there when Spud needed one—sugaring, haying, pruning Christmas trees—as long as he could afford to pay me a little something, not to make him feel beholden. I took on the farmwork more for its social value than for the money, anyway—same reason I stood for constable, to keep myself in circulation. The stipend was two grand a year.

I hit Play.

"Hector, this is Thad Rowell up on the plateau. I got something real unusual here that I think you'll want to take a look at. Maybe you could call me when you get this . . ." He paused to listen to someone else in the room, a woman who sounded agitated, though I couldn't make out what she was saying. "OK, second thought, I'll call the sheriff. Thanks anyway."

By all means. Call the sheriff.

"Hector? Vaughn Higbee. I apologize for calling so early on a Sunday, but I was hoping to catch you. I need your help. Could you get back to me right away, please? Today? Thanks."

Higbee was a professor in the humanities department at the state college in Allenburg—wealthy Sierra Club type, raised a few steers on the side. He'd lost his second wife in an accident the summer before, and I had great sympathy for what he'd been through. Just the same, if he was calling me again about the condition of his road, as I supposed he was, there was very little I could do for him. As he already knew.

"Oh, Constable! *Help* me! I'm so *frightened*! There's this great big yellow thing in the sky, and I don't know what it is!" Wilma. Calling from her car. I could hear the radio playing beneath her flutey laugh. Wilma and I had been seeing each other for about six months. Smart and nervy and strikingly pretty, she was a prolific reporter for our local daily, the *Allenburg Eagle*. "Listen up, you recluse, you'll love this. You know Thad Rowell, farms up on the Bailey Plateau? His rabbit dog came trotting out of the woods this morning with a human *hand* in its mouth. Rowell called the sheriff, and Petey and the boys have just uncovered an abandoned vehicle and a bunch of human remains up in the old Space Research compound. I'm on my way there now. It's—let's see, it's eleven-sixteen. Be there or be square. Oh, and I have lunch all packed, so I hope you get this in time. If not, your loss, I'll just see you tonight at the convent. Over and out. Wait—what else did I want to say? Oh, yeah. Happy birthday! Hah! Thought I forgot, didn't you?"

When she and her husband parted ways last fall, Wilma moved into a spectacular apartment on the third floor of the old Notre Dame Convent, a limestone landmark just north of Allenburg on a long rise above the Passumpsic River. Wilma's rooms had been the mother superior's suite—arched casement windows with a view of the river and the town, a rooftop patio, a fireplace with a marble hearth—and she was the building's only resident. The first two floors were dental offices.

"Hector? Thad Rowell again. Hey, if you're around, maybe you could do me a favor. See, I got this dead hand here that my dog found out in the woods. The state medical examiner was supposed to come pick it up two hours ago, but he hasn't shown up, and I was hoping maybe you could come out and take possession of this thing. Sorry, I didn't know who else to call. Thanks."

The last message was Ella McPhetres's. "Heck? Ella. You know I hate to trouble you on the weekend, but Judge Larrabee has just issued a relief-from-abuse order for a local woman. I tried the sheriff's office, but they're all otherwise occupied, so you're it. Call me as soon as you get this. I'm home all day."

I punched in Vaughn Higbee's number.

"Hector! Thank you for calling back. What a day, huh? Look, I don't want to beat around the bush here. This is the deal: if our road doesn't get taken care of by the end of the day tomorrow, I'm going to sue the town. There it is. If not A, then B."

"Might be easier if you'd trade in that old diesel of yours for a Hummer, something with a little clearance."

He was in no mood. "I don't want a damn Hummer. I want the same services that every other taxpayer in this town gets. I'm right and you know it, Hector."

"Yes, and I know Marcel. You bring a lawsuit and you'll make his day." The town's road commissioner, Marcel Boisvert, was Vaughn Higbee's father-in-law. They'd been at odds for years. "As I said last week, Vaughn, you have to give him time. He'll come around eventually."

"Yeah, he'll die eventually, too. I'm through waiting. You know how many mornings he plowed me into my garage this winter? Now the old bastard's making his five-year-old grandson slog in and out every day through a mile of mud. You're the law in this town, Hector. What if we needed an ambulance out here? You want that on your conscience?"

With all the spring rain on top of the winter's burden of snow, we were in the middle of a brutal mud season, and nowhere was it worse than out through Greenwood Hollow, where Vaughn Higbee and his boy were living in the 1840 red brick Greek Revival mansion that he and Kathy Boisvert had spent a fortune refurbishing. All the while I was growing up, the Greenwood place hadn't been much more than a boarded-up shell. We used to go dig for old bottles there, out behind the tumbled barn. Today, slate-roofed and fitted out with fancy appliances and central air, it was still known in town as the Greenwood place, never mind that no Greenwood had hayed those fields since Eisenhower was president. Vaughn's commute between the hollow and the state college campus in

Allenburg was long enough, but for a week now he'd been having to leave his car at the four corners and walk into the hollow, carrying his briefcase, his groceries, and his five-year-old boy, Marc.

Marcel Boisvert was a direct descendant of the first Abenaki landholders in the valley and as untraveled and hard-hearted as the granite monadnock that overlooked it. An expert outdoorsman, he was regarded as the best deer hunter in the north country. Every November he'd bring home a ten- or twelve-pointer from Maine's deep woods, where the biggest whitetails could still be taken. As Tipton's road commissioner, he was valued for his mechanical skills and respected for the sixty-hour weeks he routinely put in. But he was a somber, uncompromising man, and he maintained our 890 miles of public thoroughfare according to an intricate collection of grudges and prejudices, which no one in this town could influence. Least of all me.

Marcel's daughter Kathy met Vaughn Higbee when she was a junior at Allenburg State. She fell for his unruly ponytail, his irreverence, and his scholarly passion for Abenaki culture. Vaughn was smitten by Kathy's beauty and wit, and her Indian blood. Twice her age when they met, he was in the middle of a divorce from a queenly equestrienne, a Connecticut blueblood nobody here had much use for, according to my mother. Long before the split was final, she and their two teenage girls loaded up the horses and moved back to Darien.

Just a day after her graduation, resolute in the face of her father's outrage at the prospect, Kathy married Vaughn and moved with him into an Airstream camper they'd installed under the dooryard maples on the derelict sheep farm in Greenwood Hollow. The place had come to Kathy on her twenty-first birthday, a bequest of her grandfather, Philo. Kathy and Marcel stopped speaking after that, and Kathy found she was forbidden to set foot on the home place whether he was there or not. Whenever Shirley drove out to the hollow to visit her daughter, it was understood she would pretend she was going shopping or to a church meeting.

Over the next few years Kathy and Vaughn turned the old Greenwood mansion into a showplace, and Kathy earned her master's in counseling, which led to a good position with the state's Department of Social Services, but it wasn't until she gave him a grandson that Marcel came around. Little Marc was a peach-skinned cherub. With his mother's big violet-blue eyes and blond curls, he was one of those babies you can't stop looking at. Gifted, too, as it turned out, speaking whole sentences before his first birthday.

Ella McPhetres always maintained it was the helpless love they shared for that baby that drew the family together again. Just how they managed to mend the rift no one knew, but the next October Kathy and Marcel went bow-hunting once again as they'd done each fall before she'd taken up with Vaughn, and all five of them began spending the holidays together over one of Shirley's fricasseed turkeys or maple-cured hams. Shirley's special joy was the baby. She looked after him on weekdays while Kathy and Vaughn were at work, and somehow managed to persuade Marcel to invest in a swing set and a jungle gym, which he set up in the Boisvert backyard.

Last June, Kathy and Vaughn flew out west for a hang-gliding vacation, leaving Marc with Marcel and Shirley. Kathy was killed out there, decapitated by a guy wire. The entire town was stunned and heartbroken. Marcel was consumed with grief. After the funeral service, he shunned the sight of Vaughn and his small grandson, but it wasn't until months later, when the snow began to pile up, that Vaughn realized the road crew had all but stopped keeping up the spur into Greenwood Hollow.

I glanced at the schoolroom clock above the fridge with the

thought that if I could catch Marcel at home for his noon dinner, Shirley's presence might provide a buffer. Most men were more tractable when their wives were in earshot. "I'll talk to him, Vaughn. That's all I can promise."

"That's all I'm asking. Your family goes back in this town, Hector. He puts stock in those things."

I didn't bother to contradict him. "I'll talk to him," I said again, "but in return I'd like you to drop this lawsuit business."

"Sorry, Hector, I can't do that. Look, all I'm after here is fair treatment. Whatever I need to do to get it, I reserve that right."

"This isn't about your rights, Vaughn. It's about whether you have the grace not to saddle the town with attorneys' fees by bringing a lawsuit you know you can't win."

"You're not hearing me. I'm giving *you* a chance to do the right thing here. You and the select board. Hire a new road foreman, I don't care what you do, but my road gets graded by Tuesday or I'll see you people in court." He broke the connection.

I was standing there staring at the profusion of yellow wildflowers on the Wilderness Society calendar that I'd put up over my mother's pine secretary, trying to remember who else I was supposed to call, when the phone jangled in my hand.

*"Hello!"*

"Hector? Is that you?"

Naomi. My ex-wife. A gassy sweetness welled up under my ribs. I'd heard nothing from Naomi in almost two years, not since the morning she walked out of our bungalow in Truro with a suitcase and the baby.

"It's me."

"Are you all right? You sound funny."

"I'm fine. What's wrong, Nay?"

"What do you mean, 'wrong'? It's your *birthday*!"

I said nothing.

"Sorry, Hector. You know me—I called on a whim. Say the word and I'll get off."

"Something's wrong. What is it?" I wanted something to be wrong. She was living in the desert north of San Diego, where she and her new man were raising avocados. That's all I knew. I pictured her outdoors, in shorts, tan, barefoot, sitting on a redwood bench in a patch of coarse turf shaded by glossy trees. I'd never been to California.

"No, really, everything's great. In fact, just yesterday we were at the aquarium, and I had this very powerful sense of—"

"Stop, Nay. I don't want to hear about it."

"Right. I'm sorry. I'm sorry if I screwed up your morning, Hector."

"My morning!" Try the last five years.

"Afternoon. Whatever it is back there."

I just laughed.

"OK, I'll sign off. I miss you, Heck, that's all. Have a happy day."

I stood for a moment staring at the phone and then hurried out into the day before the damn thing could ring again.

2

My Power Wagon splashed and jounced down the long, rutted hill to the T at the defunct sawmill, where I turned onto the Common Road a mile or so west of the village. Ricker Brook raged along beside the road, full of ice and debris. A lemony mist shimmered out over the fields.

There was no traffic moving in the village, just a couple of cars I could see pulled up in front of Sullivan's store. I passed the library, the old brick bank building, now empty except for an insurance office, and the eight white wood-frame houses along the west side of the common, their east-facing windows like scraps of gold foil in the sun. Swinging north onto the Lake Road after the Presbyterian church, I found the way blocked by two orange sawhorses. A sign, hand-lettered on a piece of box board, read, ROAD CLOSED—NO THRU TRAFFIC.

I wove between the sawhorses. The Boisvert farm lay about a mile east of the village on the High Settlement Road near the edge of the ash plain. The High Settlement Road met the Lake Road about one hundred yards before the state fishing access. There the next half-mile of pavement disappeared under a sea of frothy, coffee-colored water.

As I motored past the town garage and equipment yard, I slowed for a look through the open gates and spotted Marcel's black Ford 250 parked near the door of the Quonset garage, so I turned in.

He was crouched under a droplight in the garage, working on a jammed sand spreader. Hearing my shoes in the grit on the floor, he threw a brief glance toward me, then turned without expression back to his work.

I watched him for a minute, hoping he might come up with a neutral word to offer. No such luck.

"Good afternoon, Marcel."

He nodded.

"You know, on a day like this a fella might be tempted to imagine we're all done with ice storms."

He looked up, shading his eyes with his wrench hand. With the bay door open behind me, I was backlit by the sky. "Not if he was working for me. Worst winter for ice I ever saw."

"That's for sure. Worst spring for mud, too, the way we're going."

He pursed his lips. "I know it. Ira Moody's been out a week with the shingles, and I had to give the Blake kid the time he had comin'. Add to that the goddamn grader was broke down most of March."

"You had some trouble getting parts, Ella told me."

"Parts had to come from Michigan. By dogsled, I guess."

"She's fixed now, though, isn't she?"

"Till she isn't."

"Marcel, do you suppose tomorrow you might spread a little material on the spur into Greenwood Hollow?"

His hands went still. "He come cryin' to you, didn't he?"

"Come on now. Anyone can see you've been neglecting that road into the hollow."

"I've been neglecting it, have I? What do you know about it?"

"I know that when Kathy was living out there, that stretch was passable all year round."

He swung his wrench handle into the side of an acetylene tank. The clang echoed overhead. "You trying to tell me how to do my job?"

"No, I'm asking you to have some heart. For the sake of the community, if nothing else. Vaughn's going to sue the town if that road doesn't get graded, and I can understand why he's out of patience."

He stood. "You know what? Reg would be ashamed of you. You're a *disgrace* to the community."

My father and Marcel grew up together. Reg had been constable at one time, too, though I had no memory of it. He died of barn lung when I was ten. "Listen, Marcel, whatever it is you've had against me all these years, this little situation here, this has nothing to do with it. I'm trying to mediate, that's all."

"Mediate?" He snorted.

"I'm asking you to spread a couple loads on the Greenwood Hollow road. They've been walking in for a week."

"First off, I don't know that a couple loads wouldn't just make things *worse*. Second, I been out straight for nine weeks. Like I said, Moody's got the shingles, and I got Kevin Blake taking off every other day to help his dad sugar. Which is why you find me here on a Sunday busting my knuckles when I ought to be at church." He stooped down for the wrench handle. "Let me tell you something. There's two sections of that road where it's choked so bad with alders you got nowhere to put the snow. Three years I been meaning to get that brush cut back, get them ditches cleaned out, and here we are. Didn't get done. Nobody told me we were about to get the snowiest February on record."

"Think about the boy, Marcel. He's five years old, and he just lost his mother. He doesn't need this hardship."

"Hardship! When my dad was a boy, there was two families living up in that hollow, and them kids *walked* to school. Every goddamn day! Thirty below, they *walked* to school. Don't give me this hardship crap."

"Just think about it, will you, Marcel? I want to believe you'll do the right thing after you've taken the time to think it through."

"You high-handed shit," he said, jaw tight.

I paused in the garage doorway. "You know we can't afford a lawsuit, Marcel."

"Well, then, *he's* the one you should be talkin' to about the sake of the friggin' community!"

I lingered a moment in case some persuasive rejoinder might occur to me, but it didn't happen. I nodded and left.

Thad Rowell and his brother milked two hundred Jerseys up on the west side of Arrow Lake, a couple of miles inland from the

Prentiss Point overlook. They farmed the high, open dairy country from Longview Bay to the border, territory settled by their Scottish forebears in the 1820s. They'd gone organic some years earlier—even raised their own grain—and it had been paying off for them.

Thad greeted me outside the milk room on the sawdust path he'd laid down across his yard. He told me he'd been keeping the hand in a sap bucket packed in snow, as instructed over the phone by the state medical examiner. "Griswold. Marty Griswold. You know the fella? Said he'd be here by ten, and here it's going on one. Think he got lost?"

"No, what happened is the sheriff found the rest of the body. Griswold probably went straight to the scene."

He nodded. "Space Research?"

"I believe so."

"That's where I told 'em." He pointed toward the black woods across a field covered in corn stubble and broken swaths of snow. "One of my rabbit dogs I got no time for was missing since Friday night. This morning I'm out back burning trash and I hear her bell. I look up and here's Judy trotting across the field. You could tell by the way she held her head that she had something. At first I thought it was a glove she picked up someplace, like a welder's glove."

"Isn't that compound all fenced in up there?"

"Well, it was at one time, but that facility's been abandoned over fifteen years, Hector. Nobody was too pleased when that fence went up in the first place, either."

"I suppose not."

"Looks like a war zone, if you been in there lately—buildings trashed, windows all shot out, graffiti and shit all over."

"Who owns the property?"

He shrugged. "Some Canuck. So—you want to see this ugly thing?"

I followed him through a small doorway. He lifted off the white plastic sacking he had draped over the bucket.

The hand was gray, desiccated, and flecked with leaf mold, the nails like lumps of wax.

"Looks like it was chopped off," Thad said. "What do you think?"

"I would agree. At the carpals."

"So it musta come from a murder victim."

"Most likely."

"And the killer was trying to keep him from being identified."

"That's a safe bet."

I opened my pocket knife and probed. The hand had been out in the woods for months. In a protected spot, too, or else the voles and beetles would have recycled it. The two punctures in the heel of the thumb were courtesy of Judy the beagle. Otherwise it was intact. It seemed quite possible that forensics would be able to recover some decent impressions after softening the fingers in solution for a few days.

"If you're headed on up there now," Thad said, nudging the bucket with his toe, "maybe you could take this thing along with you. Save them boys a trip."

"Better not, Thad. If the ME said he'd be here, he'll be here. I wouldn't want to cross him up."

He sucked a breath through his teeth and looked back toward the house. "It's just . . . She's been after me to get it out of here since breakfast. It's got her all creeped out."

"I understand. If I see Griswold, I'll mention it."

The Space Research compound was an eight-thousand-acre tract of rugged woodland that straddled the border, most of it in Quebec. It was bought in parcels during the seventies by Gerald Bull, a Canadian genius in aerodynamics and ballistics, whose lifelong dream had been to build a cannon powerful enough to send a satellite into orbit. The little town of Tipton (and the even littler town of Brainard's Cliff, just across the line) was where he decided to construct his supergun. Bull's Space Research Corporation was a state-of-the-art facility for munitions testing and manufacture, comprising machine shops, radar tracking stations, telemetry towers, and firing ranges. Its primary product was conventional ordnance—premium mortar shells and tank rounds—which he marketed abroad. He put his profits toward the supergun.

With the blessing of both the Canadian and U.S. defense departments, Bull's enterprise thrived for a span of years, and Tipton reversed its decades-long decline. Space Research brought in two hundred employees. The tax base doubled. The town floated a bond to add six classrooms and an auditorium to the village academy, and there were plans to refurbish the community recreation field and improve the lakefront with a pier and a picnic area. In the spring of 1981, however, following the change of administrations in Washington, Bull found himself charged by a U.S. attorney with arms trade violations for selling weapons to the South Africans. At first he was astounded, and later he was humiliated when his no-contest plea resulted in a six-month sentence in a federal prison, after which he abandoned the compound in Tipton and transplanted his munitions business to Belgium.

The road up to Space Research was unplowed but steep enough and pitched to the south so that most of the snow had melted out of it. Fans of dark gravel marked where the vehicles before mine had jounced across the washouts that gullied the surface. I drove in past a boarded-up U.S. Customs blockhouse, across a wide parking area, and on to where the road veered uphill again into the snow-filled woods.

Four vehicles were parked this side of a concrete drainage culvert—two white-and-red Montcalm County sheriffs' cruisers, the state medical examiner's gray van, and Wilma's rusting wreck of a Mazda sedan. The state police, apparently, had already left.

I followed the muddy trough in the snow past the main office complex, a Mediterranean-style assembly of white stucco cubes with large window openings and connecting walkways suspended over a marble-chip courtyard. Thad wasn't kidding. The interior partitions had all been bashed in and burned, and the courtyard had become a dump for worn-out appliances, bedsprings, tires, car batteries, scrap wood, anything some bum didn't want to pay to have hauled off or recycled.

The hike in wasn't long, but the footing was pretty bad. By the time I could hear voices, the sun was halfway to the horizon and a cold wind was cutting through the woods. Yellow crime-scene tape rippled from tree to tree. I spotted Wilma first—her cloud of ginger-gold hair—on the other side of a ravine. She made a wave. I waved back.

Twenty feet down the ravine, a faded blue Toyota pickup was lodged in a stand of hemlocks, tailgate first, windshield and headlamps smashed. The hemlock boughs that someone had laid as camouflage across the hood and cab were piled to one side in the snow. A stream of meltwater chuckled along under the rear wheels.

Sheriff Petey Mueller stood spraddle-legged in the loose snow, his gray uniform trousers soaked to the knees, hands clasped behind his back, talking with the state medical examiner, Marty Griswold. Griswold was squirrelly and bristle-headed, in a quilted vest and green wool hunting pants with leather braces. Two of his technicians in jumpsuits were labeling Baggies and packing them into a steel locker. On the far side of the truck a couple of Petey's deputies, Delmore Osgood and Lew Pfister, were fooling around with a metal detector.

"About time, Constable!" Wilma called out. She had on her calf-high Bean boots and a red plaid thrift-shop bird hunter's jacket, which she liked for its big game pockets.

Petey glanced at me over his shoulder. "Look out now, boys. Here's the Harvard man come to tell us rubes what we're doing wrong."

Petey and I had been friends since high school—we'd played side by side on the football team, his tackle to my tight end. He was up for reelection in the fall, and I supposed he knew I'd been approached to run against him. I'd declined, but Pete was worried about his prospects anyway. With good reason, too. He was conscientious enough, though over the last few years, as he'd put on too much weight to play an active role in law enforcement, he'd been compelled to rely on his full-time deputies—Delmore Osgood, Lew Pfister, Arnold Blow, and his brother-in-law, Maury Gentler—who were a mixed bag. Maury Gentler was another fat man. Because of his bad knees, Pete kept Maury posted at the metal detector in the Montcalm County Courthouse lobby. Lew Pfister was a grizzled long-haul trucker who'd gone on disability after losing an eye in a battery explosion. Arnold Blow, once a town cop in Delaware, was the most experienced and capable of the lot, but he was chronically depressed and alcoholic and currently on medical leave. Delmore Osgood was a local boy, tall and well built and impressive in uniform, but also dull-witted and impulsive. He'd been in trouble often in his teens, breaking into summer camps, deer jacking, DWI, vandalizing cemeteries, and more, which ended only when his guidance counselor talked him into joining the army. A few years after that, Delmore came home from the Gulf War with a reputation as an ace tank gunner. Somehow he had managed to parlay his wartime exploits into a deputy's gig.

I skidded down into the ravine through crusty snow and leaf litter.

Pete introduced me to Griswold.

"I've heard some good things about you," I said.

"Likewise." Griswold's handshake was limp.

"Troopers didn't stay long, did they?"

Pete yawned. "Yeah, some memorial service they had to get to. Pretty obvious what we're looking at, though. Me and Tierney are together on that." Rob Tierney was a state police detective who worked out of the state's attorney's office in Allenburg.

"Which is what?"

"Stolen vehicle and a homicide. This pickup here disappeared off a used-car lot in Pinkley, Georgia, Halloween night. Plates were stolen off a Tennessee vehicle a couple days later. Victim's male, Caucasian, about six foot, medium build, thirty to forty. Took a charge of number-four shot in the back. Marty's putting time of death at around five months ago."

"You remember the Granite Hills Bank job," Griswold said. He pulled a pint of spring water out of his vest pocket and unscrewed the cap.

"I sure do."

"Looks like this is them."

The November before, some bruiser with shaggy reddish hair, a southern accent, and a cut-down shotgun held up the two tellers of the Granite Hills Bank branch in Shadboro. Witnesses said he ran back to a blue pickup that had a light-colored license plate and a second man at the wheel. They took off toward Tipton and weren't seen again. The next day the state's attorney and the state police announced that their suspect in the robbery was a habitual offender named Malcolm Waller, who'd slipped away from a state prison work detail in north Georgia the month before the holdup. Connecticut state police happened to stop Waller and another desperado on Thanksgiving Day outside a Quality Inn near Danbury. There was an exchange of gunfire, a trooper was hit in the leg, the fugitives got away.

"So you have these badasses runnin' for the line," Pete said. "And you have to figure Waller's the one with the shotgun, 'cause his buddy's doing the driving. Well, soon as they get out here and ditch the truck, Waller computes he doesn't need a wheel man anymore, so *boom,* he lowers his profile and doubles his proceeds both at the same time."

"Looking out for number one," Delmore Osgood said, loud. He was lighting a cigarette while Deputy Pfister packed up the metal detector.

"Then he slips across the line with about six K in U.S. currency and poof, he's gone," Pete said. "Worst kind of fugitive, too—smart, vicious, and nothing to lose."

"He chopped off the guy's hands," Delmore said. "Which it's a good thing he did, or else we wouldn't be here. You know Thad Rowell, right? Dog of his nosed up one of the hands and brought it back home."

"Right," I said. "I stopped by the Rowell farm on the way out here."

Pete frowned. "You did? What for?"

"Rowell asked me to." I turned to Griswold. "Looked to me as though you ought to score some prints off those fingers."

Griswold grunted.

"What else have you come up with? Besides the number-four shot."

He puffed his cheeks and blew. "A disarticulated skeleton. Traces of viscera with ribs. Most of the vertebrae, scapulae, sternum, and some of the bones of the extremities . . ." He looked at his clipboard. "Also a tooled leather belt with a chrome-plated Mack bulldog buckle, two cheap street shoes containing some tissue, and several types of fabric and fibers. Not bad, considering the time frame. Though I wish I had the head."

"Some animal make off with it?"

"It was forcibly removed. Below the fourth cervical."

Above us, Wilma's cell phone chirped.

Pete rolled his eyes. "No place sacred."

"Yes," Wilma said brightly, "it so happens I am. Aren't you clever?" She put the phone to her chest. "Hector, you have a call. It's Ella."

"Hold it." She was about to toss it to me. I pulled myself up the bank, grabbing at the hemlocks.

"Tracked you down, didn't I?" Ella was pleased with herself. "Listen, did you get my message this morning?"

"I did. Relief-from-abuse order. Slipped my mind, Ella, I'm sorry."

"It's for Shirley Boisvert, Hector."

"Oh, Christ."

"She reached me this morning from the phone at Sullivan's. Seems Marcel's been putting the boots to her. Little as that woman gets out, who would know? I picked her up and drove her to the emergency room. The doc there called in a victim's advocate—one of these gals from Women Helping Women—and here we are."

"Right, good. So who has the papers?"

"I do. This advocate drew up a statement, court clerk called it in to Judge Larrabee, and now Shirley has a court order to have Marcel removed from the house, if you can believe it."

"Marcel was born in that house."

"That's what I'm saying. But it's Shirley's home, too, obviously, and she has the right to live there without being abused."

"I understand. Where is Shirley now?"

"She's staying here with us until he vacates."

"You're a saint, Ella. Is she all right?"

"Not too bad. Split lip and bruises. Mentally she's not doing that great, though."

"How do you mean?"

"Well, you know, she's always been a damn curmudgeon. Now she's all jittery and depressed."

"Can't blame her for being depressed."

"Who's blamin' her? This whole town's been depressed for weeks. It all starts in the pituitary."

"The what?"

"The pituitary. That gland in your brain that goes blooey if you don't get enough sun."

"Right. I'm on my way, Ella. Should be there within the hour." I handed the phone to Wilma. "I have to go back to the village to serve some paper."

"Now, I take it."

I nodded.

"What's it about?"

"Marcel Boisvert. Relief from abuse."

She sighed. "That's a shame. I've got iced champagne, Beluga caviar, and a fresh baguette down in the trunk of my Mazda."

I laughed. "That's lunch?"

"Today it is. What's more," she said, "I have a crimson silk camisole to slip into."

"Don't tell me that."

"But a man's got to do what a man's got to do."

"Hold that thought."

"I've been holding it all day," she said.

Petey Mueller was struggling to leverage his bulk up out of the ravine, clutching at trees for handholds, sliding back. Delmore and Lew were far down the trail. Ahead of them, Griswold and his techs were out of sight.

"Need a hand, Pete?"

He didn't answer. We waited for him.

"*Hooh!*" He bent to catch his breath, clutching his knees. His flushed face made me wonder whether he had a defibrillator down in his cruiser.

He straightened and bellowed, "*Delmore!*"

"*Whaaat?*" Osgood called back. They were some distance away now. We couldn't see them through the trees.

"What in the hell is your all-fired *hurry?*"

# 3

Ella's was a rambling cottage about five miles up the west shore of the lake. Spacious and rustic and cozy-looking, with its deep eaves, irregular cedar-plank siding, and a huge fieldstone chimney, it stood on a short rise above the water on open land that had been in Ray McPhetres's family for three generations. His grandfather had built it in the 1920s as a fishing camp. Its many small-paned windows were all flanked by functional green shutters.

Ray had owned a concrete and gravel plant on the highway halfway between Tipton and Allenburg, a solid business that his son Tom took over when Ray died of stomach cancer ten or fifteen years ago. Having lived with Ray for thirty years in the stark, sixties-modern structure of formed concrete that he had built on a barren hill overlooking the concrete plant, Ella couldn't wait to get out of it once Ray was gone. She had her father-in-law's old camp in Tipton insulated and fitted with an oil furnace, and moved right in.

Her long driveway curved uphill though a stand of paper birch, crossing an undulating meadow that Ella had brush-hogged every year or two to keep it clear. It filled with lupine every summer. The house stood on a promontory that offered broad views in three directions, west over the meadow to the far-off Green Mountains, east across the middle of the lake with Mount Joe in the center, and north up the gap toward the plains of French Canada. Behind the house to the south, a short path descended through a softwood stand to a sunny green cove, where Ella kept a diving raft in the summertime.

Ella's grandson, Burt, in shorts no doubt for the first time this season, was out shooting hoops in the crushed stone driveway with his best buddy, Nick Olson—high school freshmen, just starting to put a little muscle on their angular frames. At the sight of my Power Wagon they froze, Burt clutching the ball to his breastbone. They'd been arrested the summer before, these two, after breaking into the academy one night and smashing up Myra Dill's eighth-grade classroom. They weren't bad kids, as the select board understood, although Ella was disgusted and embarrassed by the vandalism. She'd been caring for Burt and his older sister, Stephanie, since their mother ran off to the roadless reaches of Alaska with her lover, a heavy-equipment operator who had been working for Ella's son, Tom. Tom had turned right around and married his bookkeeper, who wasted no time making the children's lives miserable, as stepmothers are wont to do.

I parked my truck on the side of the drive, so as not to be in their way.

"Relax, you guys," I said. "You've paid your debt to society." The school committee had them in that building all of August, painting and scrubbing.

The boys didn't speak but looked down down at their sneakers and darted glances at each other.

I didn't see Ella's gold Voyager. "I guess your grandmother's not around, eh, Burt?"

"Yeah, her and Stephanie went for pizza."

I gestured for the ball. Burt bounced it over. It was soft. I slapped it down a few times, shuffled, keys jingling in my jacket pocket, stopped and jumped, from fifteen . . .

Front of the rim. My back, I noticed, was sore after a day on my feet.

"You got moves, Mr. Bellevance," Nicky Olson said. He fetched the rebound and flipped the ball back to me.

I jumped and fired. Around and out. "Looks like that's all I've got, is moves," I said.

"Allenburg took states his senior year," Burt said.

"You told me," Nicky said.

Burt passed me the ball.

I redirected it to Nicky. "Ancient history."

It was the best time of my life. Which I took for granted, of course, heedless youth that I was, with four years of college hoops ahead of me and dreams of being drafted by the Celtics. If Bill Bradley could make it to the pros out of Princeton, hell, with any luck, why not me? My career ended a few months later, five minutes into the second game of the regular season, in Ithaca. Somebody slipped and cut my legs out from under me while I was in the air, and I hit the hardwood neck-first. That was where my luck came in, such as it was: I wasn't paralyzed. Though I didn't walk for fifteen weeks.

Burt said, "They ought to be back right off, if you want to wait. They left an hour ago."

"I'll do that. Is Mrs. Boisvert in the house?"

He nodded. "She isn't the friendliest."

Ella had narcissus blooming in her white-painted window boxes, dozens of them, and off under her fruit trees there were crocuses and snowdrops gathered like troupes of fairies. The main house was surrounded by lilies.

I rapped three times on the doorframe, then walked in through Ella's impressively cluttered porch to the kitchen entry, where I loosened my laces and stepped out of my muddy boots.

Shirley Boisvert sat on a stool at the sunny pine counter with a can of Mountain Dew in front of her, *All Things Considered* on the radio. She wore overalls and a faded green workshirt with the sleeves rolled up, a few turquoise beads on a silk cord around her neck. Broad-shouldered and angular, she was in her early sixties, with prominent cheekbones, long creases on either side of her mouth, and piercing blue eyes like Kathy's. Her iron-gray hair was cut in a pageboy with a middle part.

"Mr. Bellevance," she said, twisting to take me in.

"Good afternoon, Shirley. You're looking sore there, I'm sorry to see."

She touched her wrist to her swollen lower lip. "He cuffed me. Six stitches' worth. Knocked my bridge out of my mouth. And when I went to pick it up, didn't he take his foot and shove me into the wood box. Doctor said I might have a cracked rib. I'm awful tender."

I leaned over the counter for a look at her face. "You've been icing that, I hope."

She drew herself back from me, straightening on the stool. "It ain't the first time I been smacked."

"How are you feeling now?"

"Not too good, if you want to know. It don't help, either, being stuck out here with a bunch of crazies."

"Shirley, one way or another we'll get Marcel out of the house. But before it comes to a head—are you sure you want to live there by yourself?"

"Hell, I'm all by myself there the way it is now. He don't come indoors except to eat and sleep and use the facility."

"What set him off?"

"What set him off?"

"Why did he cuff you?"

She inhaled and looked away. "I don't know what it was. He's strict in his ways, Marcel. You do something against his instructions, you got to face the consequences."

"Marcel runs your life, does he?"

"Always has. I'm used to it." She massaged the skin under her eyes. "Worst thing is he won't let me see my grandson. I barely set eyes on him since Kathy died, where before I was over there just about every day. She wasn't paying me. It was a family arrangement."

"You looked after Marc while they were working."

"From when he was just eight weeks old. But now that Kathy's gone, Marcel won't let Vaughn step foot on our property."

"He blames Vaughn for what happened to Kathy."

"Course he does. Stupid goddamn hang-gliding. She only went and done it because of Vaughn." Shirley rolled her can between her hands. Her bare forearms resting on the countertop looked hard as ax handles, the elbows dry and callused. "If Vaughn wouldn't have put her up to that nonsense, Marc would still have a mother. *And* a grandmother. Now he's got neither one." She looked up. Her upper lip curved in where the bridge was missing. "That boy needs female attention."

"Shirley, if you'd like, I'll try to arrange for you and Marc to have some time together."

She stopped fiddling with the can and looked at me. "You could do that?"

"I can try. As long as you're free and available, why not?"

She glanced around in consternation. "But I couldn't have him *here*. These kids of hers, they're a couple of garbage-mouth *dinks*."

"They're just teenagers, Shirley. Let me ask you once more, are you sure you want to go back to the farm?"

"Where else am I gonna go?" She felt her mouth. "My *teeth* are back home, my *pills,* my *photos*—everything. My *eye*glasses. My clothes. This counselor—Lucy Pratt—she told me, get him out of the house, that's the best thing. He's supposed to do what the judge tells him to do."

"Do you think Marcel will do what the judge tells him to do?"

"If he knows what's good for him. It's my home, too!"

I sighed. "OK. I don't know if he'll leave tonight, so you just stay put until you hear from me."

"Wait— *You're* gonna do it?"

"That's why I'm here, Shirley. To pick up the papers."

"Shit. She said they were gonna get the *police*." She rubbed her chin. "Jesus Christ, he ain't gonna listen to *you*."

"If he won't listen to me—"

The kitchen door flew in and banged against the wall.

*"Fuck you!"* Stephanie yelled, backing into the house. She was a big-boned girl in black nylon shorts, a studded denim jacket, and chestnut dreadlocks. "I'm *going*! They invited me and I'm *going*!"

Turning to find she had an audience, Stephanie glowered and stomped through the kitchen into the dining room in her high, thick-soled leather work boots, mud clots skittering across the floor, untied laces slapping on the stairs. "And I do *not* want any of your fucking *pizza*!"

"Not so fast, girl!" Ella shouted. "You bring those clodhoppers back *down* here, you *hear*? *Now*!"

"See?" Shirley hissed. "What'd I tell you?"

Ella had caught the storm door with her foot. She was cradling two pizza boxes, a bag of sodas, and a large handbag. I relieved her of the pizzas.

"Thank you. Lately we are having a lot of trouble accepting the fact that we are only fifteen years old."

The aroma of oregano and garlic and peppers reminded me that I'd eaten nothing all day but an apple. I set the boxes on the counter. "What's the issue?"

"The issue? The issue is Stephanie is *not* driving up into Quebec tonight with a carload of wild-ass boys. That's beyond discussion." She caught Shirley's stare from the end of the counter. "I'm sorry you had to be a witness to this, Shirley."

"County road's flooded at the crossing," Shirley said. "Anybody going up to Canada's gonna have to drive all the way around the mountain."

I said, "Teenagers'll make your life miserable, Ella, if you let them."

"Tell me something I don't know." She grabbed a DustBuster from its wall mount next to her coat closet and began vacuuming up the scattered clots of mud, like a shorebird feeding. "They're going *drinking*, Hector! The girl just turned fifteen! What's more, some of these boys aren't even *boys*—they're twenty, twenty-two years old!"

"No, you're right, you're right." I was recollecting my own underage forays to the beer joints up across in the Townships, how little concern we had then for what our mothers said we could and couldn't do. Girls, of course, were a different matter altogether.

"As long as Stephanie is living under my roof, I'm responsible for her, and I take that seriously. Just the same, the arrangement's going to end in a hurry if she starts defying me. This house is not a crash pad. The state can put her in foster care—for as long as that would last."

"Any child of mine ever swore at me like that," Shirley said, "they'd be picking bar soap out of their molars for a week."

Ella's glare said they'd already touched on this subject.

She turned to me. "You're here for the papers. Hang tight." She skated through the room, pushing her feet into her scuffs as she went.

"See?" Shirley said to my back.

"See what?"

"Why my stomach's all in friggin' knots."

"Shirley, I'd say you're fortunate Ella offered to take you in."

She was rapping the pine counter with the soda can. "I know that. It's just . . . Back when we was raising kids, we took *care* of them. We were a *family*. And families stood by each other. There wasn't any of this day-care nonsense. There wasn't these kids walking into the schoolyard and shooting the teacher and half their classmates, either." She rose and rammed her stool in under the counter. "I swear I don't know what kind of society this *is* anymore. These kids today, they don't get guidance! They don't get love. They get sent out of their own home and stuck all day with a herd of *other* kids, starting when they're just *babies*. These kids are growing up with no sense of family, no sense of morals, no self-respect, no love! People say *guns* is the problem, but I was raised around guns and I know it ain't that. I'll tell you what it is." She thumped the can on the counter. "It's *television*. And *computers*. It's pornography and drugs, and I'll tell you what *else* it is, it's parents that don't give a goddamn where their kids are at all day or who's looking after them, if anybody is, and what kind of crap they're filling their brains with. Society today teaches parents to think of their own selves first. They get it hammered into them that they're supposed to get out and work and buy possessions and stimulate the friggin' economy. It's *brain*washing. We got to get back to the days when the mother stayed home with the children, when the mother loved the children and took care of the home! But now we got all these mothers sending their kids off to the day-care center so they can go chase the almighty dollar. It's just sickening."

"Shirley, you know, most families today can't make ends meet on a single salary. The way things are—"

"See, that's just crap. It all depends on your choice of lifestyle—what you're willing to do without. How many TVs do you need? How many computers? Shoot, they got 'em for free down at the library. I'm telling you, if Marcel and me can get by like we do with all of our insurance and medical bills and every other damn thing, then anybody can do it."

Ella came back through the dining room with the court documents, glancing warily from me to Shirley and back.

At this, Shirley whirled around and threw open the door to the basement—where I supposed Ella kept a spare room for guests—and charged down the stairs, house slippers clapping the treads.

Ella shut the door. "She's a pistol, isn't she?"

"She's a woman who knows her own mind. Something to be said for that."

The copies were on scrolled-up fax paper from Ella's home office machine. I tried smoothing them flat against the edge of the dining table.

"I don't mind telling you I'm not looking forward to this, Ella. I've butted heads with Marcel once today already."

"Oh God. Don't tell me—Vaughn Higbee."

"He called you?"

"Twice this weekend. He ought to face the music and move out of Greenwood Hollow, if you ask me."

"I think he ought to just go out and buy a big SUV."

Ella shook her head. "All I know is, as long as one of them keeps trying to break the other one, I won't have any peace."

"Marcel needs time, that's all."

"Think so? Wait till you read Shirley's affidavit. He threw her down and *kicked* her. He needs professional help, Hector—which you and I both know he ain't going to get. The least he can do is take a rest. Go spend a week at deer camp. He's got vacation saved up. He should use it."

"Good idea. I'll make that suggestion."

"We get Marcel out of the picture, and I might just talk Kevin Blake into grading that spur."

"Perfect solution. Marcel may need a day or so to make up his mind, though."

"You put it to him clear and direct, I think he'll go for it. Fact is, he's got to." She leaned closer to me. "The other thing is, I don't know how long I can keep Shirley out here." Her lipstick was flaking. The alcohol on her breath surprised me. "She's welcome to stay, don't get me wrong. But she's got a medical condition"—she tapped her temple—"all her pills're out on the ash plain, and I believe she's been having withdrawal reactions. Pacing back and forth, yammering to herself. Can't light anywhere—she's upstairs, she's downstairs. I'm in the bathroom and I look up and she's out in the hall watching me like I'm a zoo exhibit. Reminds me of the time we had a raccoon up in the attic. Poor thing got in somehow and worked itself into a frenzy trying to figure out how to get back out again."

"We can find another place for her. Shirley has relatives in town, doesn't she?"

"A niece. Emily Shapiro—married to the pediatrician. She's got more money than God. I suggested Emily, you bet I did. Also, this women's counselor—Lucy—she was trying to sell Shirley on a couple of safe houses. Forget that. All Shirley wants to do is go home, and Lucy's telling her *no way,* not until Marcel vacates the premises. So I ended up dragging her here."

"All right. Let's see if I can get this relief order to pay off. I'll call you in a couple hours." I tucked the papers into my breast pocket. "Good luck with your restless charges."

She clucked and showed me her crossed fingers.

# 4

Hundreds of years before the first white man found his way into this time-worn landscape, the broad bowl around the south tip of Arrow Lake was a seasonal Abenaki settlement. They harvested salmon from the river, gathered nuts and berries in the hills, and later raised corn and squash and beans in the fertile, open bottomland, which they named Passumpsic, Place of Clear Water. Since my great-great-grandfather's day, it's been known as the ash plain, after the potash the French settlers produced there. The plain was a marsh now, but the river ran as clear as ever, and near the mouth of the river a shallow cove embraced a beach of natural white sand. No better spot in Vermont to swim, if you didn't mind cold water. The state maintained a park there and a fishing access a mile or so from the village, west of Black Willow Falls, but beyond that, except for half a dozen old summer places hidden down among the cedars at Westlook, the eight-mile stretch from Tipton village along the lake to the border was empty, nothing but scenic highway snaking along under the façade of Mount Joseph.

After the fall of Québec City to the British in September of 1759, Sam Boisvert, an Abenaki who'd endured the siege with the French, fled south and joined the Passumpsic band. Here he wed Mary Gill, a St. Francis Abenaki, whose people had occupied the land since the time before memory. The Boisverts and the Gills and two or three other families wrung a living from the land any way they could. When the deer and beaver disappeared from the mountain and the bog beyond it, they cut the slopeside timber and burned it for the potash. When that was gone, they raised sheep on the rocky hillsides, and when the sheep had eaten all the grass the soil could produce, they took up tanning and quarrying and mining, none of them profitable for long. By the time my grandfather Norman bought his farm south of the village, Tipton's heyday was behind it, and most of the denizens of the ash plain had left to seek better prospects to the west. The favored—or the ill-equipped—clung to the home place, dairying and logging. Marcel was the last of them.

His father, Philo Boisvert, had worked as a supervisor at the Ethan Allen furniture mill in Allenburg for thirty years. He was an austere, proud man, a town father, and, like Marcel after him, a consummate outdoorsman. Marcel left school at sixteen, having completed the ninth grade. "He wouldn't be taught," my mother once said. From then on he played town baseball and hunted and fished and worked in the woods, cutting pulp and saw logs and trapping. Later on he took a job with the town road crew. The people of Tipton elected him road commissioner at the age of twenty-five, mostly as a means of giving a worthy but difficult son of the town some responsible employment. He'd been in the position ever since.

My grandfather's farm, now Spud and Brenda's, was at the end of the town road. All the once-settled land above us had returned to woods, so any vehicle that came up across the single-lane

Ricker Brook bridge and on out to the farm would turn around in our dooryard. There weren't many—the co-op's silver milk truck, the vet's old Chevy pickup, and the big town plow. Marcel Boisvert roaring up and over the rise after an all-night snowstorm, high in the cab of the red town rig with his window rolled down no matter what the temperature, throwing up great wings of snow, was a joy to see. He was a grinning hero to me, breaking the drifts open so Mom could drive out to school and Duane Boyd's milk truck could get through to the barn. My father would often drop whatever he was doing and step into the barn doorway to wave. Now and then Marcel would stop, too, and the two of them would sip coffee or hot sweet cider, standing on the porch or underneath the great sugar maple across the road, trading stories. "Nothing else could get Reg to leave his chores like that," my mother told me years later. "Marcel brought out the boy in him." At my father's funeral, mourners filed past his open grave with their fingers knit together while my mother and I stood by and watched. Each one stooped down for a handful of loose earth to rattle on the domed casket. Last in line, Marcel pulled a scuffed baseball out of his coat pocket and tossed that in. As we followed him and the others out of the little graveyard, Agnes told me that in a small town the friends a man makes in his youth are often the only friends he ever makes. "I think Marcel is feeling much the way you are," she said. "He's lost someone he can't replace."

Reg and Marcel had grown up together on opposite sides of Tipton village in the years when town team baseball had a following in the north country. They'd played on school teams and then with the Tipton Catamounts for many summers. Marcel pitched and played third base, and his arm was good enough to get him scouted for a year or two by the Red Sox, though in the end he was judged too slight a man to last in the big leagues.

Reg's death forced Agnes to sell the farm and move us in with my father's mother, Beryl, who was living alone in the long, low family house on the southeast corner of the common. It was two years after the Lake House Hotel burned to the ground. That next summer the new town equipment garage—a Quonset hut—went up on the site of the hotel, just half a mile down from Sullivan's store, and as a result I saw Marcel often after we moved off the farm, usually at the wheel of one town vehicle or another, and I'd run into him occasionally at the store or at the town dump, where he volunteered, but he would never give me a nod or even meet my eyes. He'd banter with other kids sometimes, not with me.

The one time he did speak directly to me was by accident. Christmas week in downtown Allenburg when I was around fifteen I'd reached the army-navy store door before him, so I opened it and stepped back to let him go ahead. I wished him a Merry Christmas as he brushed by. "Merry Christmas to you," he said, then glanced at me, and the anger that suffused his face stopped me in my tracks. It was as if I'd tricked him somehow. I didn't follow him into the store.

That night at supper I asked Agnes why Marcel was so mean to me, although *mean* wasn't the word I wanted. She thought for a moment and said, "You know, the same spring I had you, Marcel and Shirley had their first child. They named him Philo, after Marcel's dad. He was a sweet, placid little baby, but by the time he was two they knew he wasn't right. He had no words, and he wouldn't look at people. That was awfully hard on Marcel, he's so proud, you know. As Philo got older, he got so neither one of them could care for him. It was heartbreaking. And there was nothing the doctors could do for the boy, so they sent him away. Two or three years after that we learned he'd died. So, you see, I think it must pain Marcel to set eyes on you. He sees you riding your bike or playing catch out on the green, and he sees his own long-gone son. And that's not all. You look just like Reg when Reg was your age. So that makes two people Marcel has loved and lost that you remind him of."

I wasn't sure what to make of my mother's analysis, but at fifteen I suspected it sprang more from her forgiving nature than anything else. She didn't really understand Marcel. I didn't think anyone could.

At dusk I turned into the willow-canopied lane that led to the Boisvert place. The old farm had declined a lot with the years. I hadn't been down here since I was selling lightbulbs door-to-door for a French Club fund drive in high school. Big whorls of juniper and thorny wild apple and white spruce trees twenty feet tall crowded the old hayfields surrounding the swale where the house stood. For a string of summers after Philo sold his herd and went to work at the furniture mill in Allenburg, my father had hayed these fields. In fact, he was the last man to cut them. I could remember haying here—I must have been eight or nine years old. I still had a vision of Shirley crossing the mowed portion in overalls and barn boots with her stiff stride, wavering, bringing us cold spring water and molasses in a white enamel pail, with a speckled ladle to drink from. After Reg died, there was no one farming nearby who could make use of the hay, and now the fields were past recovering.

The house was brick, a two-story, Federal-style structure, noble but grim, with a mansard roof shingled in gray-green slate. Marcel's side yard, bordered along the river by black willows and cattails, was flooded. The formal front entry and the six tall windows on this side of the house had been sealed with plastic sheeting against the northerlies that blew down the Arrow Lake gap. I had to wonder how Marcel and Shirley could sleep in there with the wind rattling that plastic all night long. The granite block foundation of the house had been banked with a wood-chip mulch for insulation. It had been effective—by the three-foot berm of snow that remained on the north side. Beyond the house was the unused hay barn, its metal roof and most of its windows still sound, a haven now for bats and pigeons.

I saw Marcel's black Ford 250 pickup parked in a pole shed. No lights were burning inside the house, though woodsmoke was seeping out of the kitchen chimney. It was almost dark. I pulled around to the side of the main house and got out.

A bow hunter's plastic deer target and a splitting maul leaned against the back porch stair rail. I loosened my shoulders and knocked hard on the door frame.

"Son of a bitch must be *paying* you to dog my ass."

He was behind me, holding some cordwood in a red Hood milk crate. He looked drawn in the half-light, cheeks unshaven and cupped in, eyes shining.

"We need to talk, Marcel."

"Nothing to talk about."

"The town would like to stake you to a week's vacation. Ella says you've got the time coming, and we thought that if you wanted to do some turkey-hunting in the Dakotas or, say, mountain lion in Wyoming, we'd spring for the airfare." I didn't expect Marcel to bite, though if he did go for it, I'd have myself a job hustling donations.

"What kind of joke is this?"

"It's no joke. It's a reward in recognition of your service. It's a chance for you to cut loose after a long winter. How about it, Marcel? You could use the break."

"Get out of here."

"All right. Here's what's behind the offer. Judge Larrabee has issued a court order requiring you to leave this property for a few days. Ella and I were thinking you might as well enjoy yourself while you're away."

"What order?"

"It's a relief-from-abuse order, Marcel. Shirley has filed a statement with the court. I'm here to serve the papers."

"She has? God, well, that's meaningless. That woman goes off her pills, you can't tell what's gonna come out of her mouth next."

"Would you like to read her statement?"

"I don't read bullshit."

"There'll be a hearing in town in a few days. If you want to postpone your trip till then, you can present your side of the matter at that time. But meanwhile I'm afraid you'll have to find somewhere else to stay."

"It was goddamn Ella put her up to this, wasn't it?"

"You go pack up what clothes and personal items you think you—"

"*Wasn't* it?"

"Marcel—"

"Make way." He shoved by me with his crate of wood.

I followed him through his empty, bark-littered woodroom to the threshold of a dim kitchen. I hesitated there in my mud-caked boots—although Marcel hadn't stopped to remove his. The wide-board pine floor hadn't seen a mop in months. Unwashed plates and cookware stood in stacks on the counter, covered by the husks of dead cluster flies. The knickknack shelves beside the sink held a collection of salt-and-pepper sets—wheelbarrows, gnomes, bunnies, seashells—all furred with dust. A more or less orderly accumulation of newspapers and mail, sorted by size, sat on the table. Under the pleated shade of a low-watt table lamp, a bright red cap inside an open gift box stood out. UTAH, it said, in big white letters sewn in above the bill.

I smelled cat shit, stale coffee, creosote, and grease. A television's soundtrack laughter rose and fell in another room.

Through a pillared pass-through I could see their Christmas tree. Its ornaments were glimmering in the light from the television.

"Listen, Marcel, the reasonable thing to do here is to take the damn vacation. Come on, you *deserve* it. There's no need to make this any more difficult or unpleasant than it is now."

He banged down the firewood box and turned on me. "You're on tribal territory where you stand. Neither you nor any judge has the authority to order me off of it."

"Don't be a jackass. You're obliged to leave this house. Tonight I'm asking for your voluntary cooperation—no big deal. But you need to unbend a little here."

"Unbend how?"

"I've just told you. The judge has ordered you to leave the house."

"Well, I won't do it. This is my house that I lived in all my life and my father and grandfather before me. You come in here telling me a crazywoman writes down a bunch of bullshit for some judge that doesn't have a clue what a crackpot she is, and based on *that* they can throw me off of my family estate?"

"Yes, but it's temporary."

"Hell if it is! I'm not leaving, and that's the end of it."

"You refuse this order and you'll find yourself under arrest, Marcel. You don't want that to happen."

Shaking his head in disgust, he grabbed a lid-lifter from the seat of a backless kitchen chair and opened the top of the cookstove. He laid in a couple of chunks and replaced the plates. "Now you listen to me, Bellevance. That woman's got a split personality. One half's a robot zombie on tranquilizer pills and the other half's her plain, everyday, bat-crazy self. OK? See this?" He stretched his throat to one side, exposing two red welts under his whiskery jaw. "Who do you think give me that?"

"Shirley's getting help, Marcel. You can get help, too."

"She's getting help, is she? From who?"

"From the state."

"The state? No shit. I've been trying to get help from the state for years, and all I got is dog water. If a medically certified nutcase can spout off a bunch of crap, which the state believes is reason enough to order me off of my own land, then the damn state's crazier than she is. Where is she at right now?"

"She's with friends."

"Friends, shit! Who's she got for friends? Goddamn Ella can't keep her nose out of *nothing*." He fingered a Styrofoam cup out of a stack of cups on the cookstove warming shelf and poured himself some coffee from an insulated jug. "You go tell that socially conscious judge if she wants me out of here she's gonna have to *burn* me out like they did them people down in Waco. I won't be run out of my family home by a piece of paper that's half lies in the first place."

"This is not the position you want to take, Marcel."

"It's no *position*. It's *facts*. You tell her, you hear? *Get out!*"

His breath was audible in his nose, and the skin under his eyes was twitching. Another nudge and he'd be diving into me all knees and fists, and then I'd have to hurt him.

"All right, Marcel. I'm going to give you the night to reflect on this situation."

"Don't matter to me what you do."

"I won't be back. Tomorrow it'll be the sheriff or the state police."

"That don't matter, either. I won't be run out of here by nobody."

"I'll pass that message along." I walked to the door. "You and Shirley need time apart, Marcel."

"Then have her stay where she is, goddamn it. Let somebody else deal with her. See how good they manage."

I encouraged him again to sleep on it. When he turned his back on me, I turned, too, and walked out into the cold. Spring peepers were trilling nearby along the edge of the marsh, the first of the season.

"You hear what I'm telling you?" he called after me through the woodroom door. "That's your answer! Let her stay wherever the hell she is!"


The last of the light had gone off Mount Joe's dome, and a biting wind was streaming south off the lake ice as I let myself into the town hall basement. I stamped my cold feet and flipped on the overhead lights. I shivered. This room always felt damp when it wasn't full of people. How did Ella do it? I couldn't stand it a week, working down here every day, and she'd been at it for thirty years.

I left the faxed documents on her desk blotter under her bronze Grand Army of the Republic paperweight, then called her home.

Stephanie answered on the first ring. By her tone of voice, mine wasn't the call she'd been waiting for, but she was good enough to explain that Ella had driven Shirley in to Brooks Pharmacy before it closed so she could pick up her prescriptions. I asked her to pass along an important message, which she agreed to do, although she was annoyed when I told her I'd like her to write it down. She had me wait while she went to find a pencil.

Fire away, she said. I told her that because Marcel Boisvert had refused to accept the court order, Mrs. Boisvert should not return home. Would she repeat that for me?

She did, and I thanked her.

After that, I jotted my own note for Ella on a piece of pink scrap paper.

*Sunday, 7 pm.*

*Ella—*

  *I'm very sorry, but this is a job for the sheriff or the state police. Please make sure they know that the subject has vowed not to leave voluntarily.*
  *I tried.*

*—Hector*

# 5

When the Allenburg Dental offices were closed, the only way up to the mother superior's suite on the third floor of One Ursuline Terrace was by six flights of open stairs inside a cinderblock tower that had been grafted onto the back of the building in the sixties, when the convent had seen use as a convalescent home. Next to the stairs there was a tubular spiral slide for the bedridden, whose entry was bolted closed at the top. Wilma had happened on the place through the kindness of her boss. Clifton Ordway, publisher of the *Allenburg Eagle,* owned the building. When Wilma gave me a key to the windowless door at the base of the tower, she mentioned that Cliff would be tearing it down over the summer so he could apply for historic preservation status, but until that happened it was her private entrance.

I trudged up, sore in the back and knees from the day's walking, and paused outside her door to tuck in my shirt and finger-comb my hair, for what little improvement it made. Over an hour late, I'd had no time to detour by the cabin for a shower and clean clothes. My larger concern was the cold frames, but Spud would be happy to swing by my place to close them for me. I'd just have to give him a call.

I knocked.

"Come in!" she sang out. She was in the kitchen at the far end of the apartment.

I draped my wet jacket in its usual place, over the two-foot stack of newspapers that rested on a cane chair in the hall. Her entryway was her repository for footwear, outdoor clothing, and sports gear. Though I didn't really mind the level of disarray she was comfortable with, it had been six months and she was still lighting the apartment with the awful overhead fixtures, forty-watt bulbs in frosted glass tulip shades. Whenever she wanted a softer atmosphere, she lit candles. The rooms were high-ceilinged and large and had a feeling of grandness, but the floors needed refinishing, the diamond-paned casements hadn't been washed for many years, the plaster walls had cracks everywhere, and the woodwork's paint was peeling. The two Ansel Adams posters—birches and El Capitan—tacked up over the couch were the extent of her decoration. Her few items of furniture had all been donated by friends at the paper and by her mother-in-law, who still harbored the hope that Wilma would move back to the tree farm. I took her lack of interest in the apartment as evidence that she saw it as a bridge, and that once the divorce went through she'd be ready to move out to the cabin. But it was nothing we had discussed.

She wasn't in the kitchen. In the center of the table stood a fountain-shaped blue glass vase with two giant yellow irises leaning out of it. A pork roast sizzled in the oven: thyme, garlic, apple. Two layers of a chocolate cake had been left on wire racks to cool.

I found a beer in the fridge. She had a bottle of Mumm's in there, chilling in a pan of ice.

When she came out of the bedroom, she was wearing the red silk camisole, a long, loose black skirt, and heavy gray wool socks rolled to the ankles.

"Happy day," she said, melting into me.

We kissed and she pressed against my thigh, her heavy cloud of hair smelling like the oven.

"If you don't mind," I said, "I'm going to take a quick shower."

"Go right ahead. I'm going to frost a quick cake. I'll meet you in the boudoir in fifteen minutes."

We kissed again, until she pulled back to catch her breath. She looked at me closely for the first time, bright-eyed and flushed. "Boy. You are one tired truck farmer, aren't you? So how did it go with Marcel Boisvert?"

"Not well. It's a long story."

"OK. Sure, you shower. But—"

She followed me into the bathroom. "Let me just ask you one thing."

I turned to her.

"I've been wondering. Say you were able to backtrack Rowell's rabbit dog to where she found that hand, what do you think the odds are that you'd find the head?"

"Poor. The killer carried the hands for a distance and flung them off into the woods. Back in November, if that's when the killing took place, as cold as it was, the hands would have frozen solid before they could go bad. The irony is if he hadn't gone to all that trouble, the coyotes and the ravens would have done the job for him."

"Well, what about the head?"

"That would have taken longer to freeze. I suppose some fisher or bobcat could have dragged it into a hole, you never know."

She nodded. "Nature's undertakers."

"Yeah. You know what my mother used to say? 'Just lay me in silk on top of a hill.' That's what we did, too."

"Really? But that's *illegal*."

"We cremated her first."

"Of course. You're perfect, you know," she said. "Come on."

She took my hand and led me into the bedroom, where we made love on Wilma's new queen-size Swedish foam mattress. Her one luxury, that mattress, bought for me. Ever since I broke my back, if I don't have good support at night I get no rest.

Wilma served the loin roast with a light gravy, roasted red potatoes with rosemary, and a platter of chilled asparagus dressed with lemon, shallots, and olive oil. I opened the last of the case of pinot she'd bought in January, and we took our meal slowly, savoring every bit. Wilma was a fine cook when she put her mind to it.

Before the cake, Wilma hauled my gift out of her bedroom closet. The box was the size of an air conditioner and wrapped in gold paper. She sat back with her head tipped to the side while I opened it.

A shiny black steel tube, CELESTRON in orange italics along the length of it: a telescope, an eight-inch compound telescope. I was stunned.

During those last clear nights in January, Wilma and I had begun studying the sky together from the high knoll behind the cabin. The instrument we'd used was a toy, an old Bushnell refractor of my mother's, but it gave Wilma a good look at lunar craters, Jupiter's four largest moons, and the tiny, vivid truth of Saturn's rings. She was smitten. I told her that with a good-quality telescope we would be able to see the bands of Saturn and Cassini's division in the rings, along with all the nearby stars and double stars and hundreds of galaxies.

So she'd bought me one.

"Well?"

"I don't know what to say. It's such an extravagance, Wilma. I mean, forgive me, but I know you don't—"

She put her hand up. "Stop. Be gracious. Anyway, I have an ulterior motive."

"What's that?"

"I want to learn the stars with you."

I laughed. "Pretty ambitious project."

She nodded. "Could take a lifetime."

She sang me "Happy Birthday" in a pure soprano voice. I was transfixed. I'd never heard her sing before.

When she finished, I said, "I'm beginning to think there's no end to the wonder of you."

She gazed at me, standing there holding the cut-glass cake plate in both hands, my forty-one candle flames swaying between us like a school of tropical fish.

"Come on," she whispered. "Blow."

I blew. I felt dizzy with love.

The phone rang.

"I'm not going to answer that," she said.

It rang two more times. "This is me! You know what to do and when to do it."

"Hello. Uh, Sergeant Rob Tierney of the Vermont State Police. I don't know if this is the right number, but I'm trying to reach Hector Bellevance. If he shows up there, would you have him call me at the barracks, please? It's urgent."

Wilma clonked the table with the butt of the cake-server. "You cops. You're as bad as reporters. What's that about?"

"Marcel Boisvert, maybe." I gave her the story in a few sentences, then picked up the phone.

"One second, Hector. If those troopers want you to go back out to the ash plain tonight, you can't do it. All right?"

"They won't want me, don't worry."

"Just don't let them talk you into anything. It's your birthday, and besides, there are two very important things I need to discuss with you."

"What things?"

She shook her head. "Make your call."

The dispatcher told me he'd page the sergeant, and Wilma and I hadn't even tasted our cake before it was ringing again.

I took the phone and my champagne flute into the bedroom.

"Hector. I apologize if this is a bad time, but we have a little problem I hope you can clear up for us. You know that homicide victim in the woods up in Tipton?"

"I was up there this afternoon."

"Right. You wouldn't happen to know what became of the victim's hand, would you?"

"Are you saying it's missing?"

He paused. "The ME says Rowell told him you came by his farm and collected it."

"I don't know why he'd say that. I looked at the hand, but I told Rowell he had to sit on it till Griswold came and picked it up."

"If that's the case, it's missing."

"He had the hand in a sap bucket in his bulk tank room. Is the bucket still there?"

"Why?"

"If the bucket's there, maybe Rowell's dog made off with the hand again. If the bucket's gone, whoever took it has two legs."

"I'll call Griswold and call you back."

He did.

"No bucket. Here's the deal. Griswold says he was supposed to stop at the farm and pick up the hand, only he spaced on it until he was halfway to Burlington. So he calls the sheriff's office and they tell him Pete'll go get it and meet him with it in Allenburg at seven-thirty, but either Pete didn't get the message or I don't know what happened, but Griswold's pissed off because he ended up driving all the way back out to the Rowell farm to find out the thing wasn't there. Rowell told Griswold somebody took it while he was milking cows, and we had the impression it was you."

"What does Pete have to say about this?"

"I'm waiting for a call back."

"Either he has the hand or it's still out at Rowell's."

"Look, if he doesn't have it, will you meet me out at the Rowell farm tomorrow?"

"Sure. What time?"

"Eight?"

"Eight's fine."

"Good. If Pete's got the thing, I'll ring you back tonight. Otherwise, I'll see you in the morning. Have a good one."

Wilma and I finished the champagne, made love again, and went to bed. I was spent, and I had to be out of there by six in time to get my chores in before heading out to the Bailey plateau.

I was half asleep, Wilma curled into my side, her head on my chest.

"Hector?"

"Mm."

"Can we talk?"

"Now?"

"Remember those two things?"

"What two things?"

"The two things I said I wanted to talk about."

"Yeah. All right." I rattled my head.

"First, I am—I am completely crazy about you, Hector. That's not going to change no matter what."

I sat up. The only light in the room came from the sky glow of town in the casements. But I was awake now.

"Second . . ." She propped herself on one elbow, and the quilt slid from her shoulders. "I'm pregnant."

I took her hand. "You are? That's great!"

Her expression didn't change.

"Are you all right?"

Wilma had been pregnant once before, during her first semester at Swarthmore. A bad infection followed the D&C. All three years of her first marriage she was on the pill, and later, seven years off the pill and married to Victor, it never happened. Her ob-gyn thought Wilma was too scarred-up inside to conceive. Just as well, she realized after a while, since the paper took all her time and Vic was away from home every weekend, guiding and fishing. What would they do with kids?

After culinary school, Naomi worked long shifts in a succession of rowdy Provincetown restaurants, six days a week, while I was living in a two-room walkup in the Back Bay and joining her on the Cape on my days off. Most of the marital sex we had those years was by telephone. But we were young and we figured we had time. I'd retire at thirty-five and get a teaching job. We'd buy Naomi's Aunt Miriam's saltbox in Wellfleet—on a busy street but with room enough in back for a swing set and a garden.

I did retire, at thirty-six, and by then Naomi had had her own popular restaurant, The Purple Oar (grilled seafood, twenty-two tables on the water), for six years. She had a lover, too—Armando, a Portuguese fish salesman she'd had longer than she'd had the restaurant, though I didn't learn that until Naomi was three months pregnant. She'd been letting me think it was mine, and it was torturing her. In fact, she wasn't sure who the father was. *Most likely Armando* was the killing way she put it. Not that it mattered much by then, since she'd made up her mind to sell the seafood place and move to the West Coast. Armando and two of his Navy buddies had bought a two-hundred-acre avocado grove north of San Diego.

"Healthwise I'm fine, Hector," Wilma said. "But I didn't think it would ever happen to me—you know. And the way my periods are, I didn't stop to *think* about it until I was nine weeks late."

"How late are you now?"

"Twelve. Twelve weeks."

"And you're sure."

She nodded.

"Do you want it?"

She nodded soberly. "It took me a while to get my head around the idea, but yes. Only it's gotten complicated."

"Don't tell me that."

"I want the baby. And I want you. But . . ." She started crying.

"Is that the second thing?"

"What?"

"First, you're pregnant. Second, it's gotten complicated."

She nodded, drying her eyes with the sheet. "Last Friday afternoon I got a call from Gabe Prescott. He's offering me a job, Hector. In Boston." Prescott was editor of the Sunday *Boston Globe Magazine.* The fall before, he'd run Wilma's three-part series on a local drug-smuggling land-grab scheme, which had gotten her a Pulitzer Prize nomination. And now a job offer.

I reached for her. "But that's great! I'm *proud* of you, Wilma. Writing for the *Globe*! People wait their whole lives for a break like this. *Take* the job. Have the baby. I don't see your problem."

"I was thinking of it as *our* problem."

"I meant the baby."

"So did I."

"You *know* I want this baby. And the job's the opportunity of a lifetime."

"So are we," she said in a quiet voice.

"It's not the *Miami Herald*. It's a four-hour drive. I've done it in my sleep. We can manage. You can do it." I stroked her arm.

"So you'll come with me?" she said.

"To Boston?"

She said nothing.

"You want me to live with you in Boston?"

She nodded.

Come on, Bellevance. Did you really expect her to do it all on her own, move to the city, start a new job, and have a baby? She needs you. She wants you with her. How can you blame her for that? I couldn't. She was asking me to leave my serene country life and livelihood for marriage and a family.

"I'm sorry, Hector. I didn't mean to unload all this on your birthday, but I had to take a little time to think things through on my own. I've decided to accept the job. I wanted you to hear that before I tell anybody else."

"Thanks."

"I know it's a lot to take in. A kid, a marriage . . ." She laughed. "A future in the city with wild and crazy me. But we already have our weekend place in the country. Right? You could look at it that way."

"I could," I said softly. But I couldn't move back there. If I knew anything, I knew that.

She kissed my shoulder. "You really are perfect, you know."

# MONDAY

# 6

Many a town has grown up under the gaze of a solitary mountain, a presence the locals look upon as a sort of brooding deity, emblem of time and creation. Ours was Mount Joseph, an ice-scoured monadnock four miles northeast of Tipton village on the other side of the lake. Logged three times over, its flanks to the north and east were dark again with fir and spruce and, lower down, with birch, beech, and ash. There were a dozen ski trails on the south side. On the west the mountain fell into Arrow Lake, two thousand feet down. The cliffs, a sinewy façade of shifting colors, were bearded this morning with columns of pale blue ice.

I was surveying this postcard scene from the sunny east porch of Sullivan's General Store, a cardboard cup of hazelnut coffee in one hand, Sunday's slim edition of the *Allenburg Eagle* in the other. A dog yapped. A single-engine plane droned overhead. There was the hard, ringing whine of a machine somewhere off toward the ash plain—like a saw, or someone revving an outboard motor in a steel drum. A pair of phoebes sat on a power line nearby, buzzing and bobbing their tails.

Although I was running late for my rendezvous with Rob Tierney at the Rowell farm, I'd stopped by the village store and post office to pick up my mail and the paper. Then I bought the coffee and took it out into the sun. My head had been churning since before dawn, and I told myself that if I could slow down and focus on the wonders of the moment, I could recover my calm. It was almost working.

Across the common, kids shouted, chasing a kickball around the academy's asphalt schoolyard. In the center of the green, the village skating rink had become an oblong pond with a hockey goal at either end. Chirping robins patrolled its perimeter, finding their fill of worms.

Traffic on Lake Street was sparse: a few school kids had gotten out their bikes for the pleasure of pedaling to school on a sunny day, the Pepperidge Farm delivery van was pulling away from the dock beside me, and that was it. With the highway flooded at Perry Crossing, the familiar Canadians who drove down the eight miles from Iceville for the savings in American gas wouldn't be making that trip for a while.

This place had seen far busier times. I could recall, before the interstate went through to the west, when we had a high-toned girls' summer camp, a hunting lodge, and a grand hotel on the edge of the village overlooking the lake with its own restaurant and barber shop. There was a Ford dealership, a bank, and an IGA with carts. Today, Sullivan's store, with its dry-cleaning pickup and its single gas pump, was the last vestige of day-to-day merchandising in the village. The customers were largely locals and the occasional bicycle tour or foliage bus.

The body up at Space Research had merited a banner (HUMAN REMAINS FOUND IN NORTH TIPTON), though Wilma's story was short and inconclusive. Half of the front page had been given over to color photos celebrating the break in the weather—a gushing brook, kite-fliers, beds of snowdrops.

Stuffing my empty cup in the plastic trashcan, I looked up and caught sight of a Montcalm County Sheriff's Department cruiser coming fast from the direction of the ash plain. It slowed, swerved between the Road Closed sawhorses, then went fishtailing down the gravel drive to the town hall and disappeared behind the building.

Pete Mueller, stopping by for Shirley's paperwork? Pete wouldn't drive like that, not in a school zone. Probably it was his reckless young buck of a deputy, Delmore Osgood. Either way, it was too late to serve Boisvert with that court order. He got up at five. He'd left the ash plain hours ago—though Ella would know where the crew would be working. Maybe that's what this was about. Or maybe there'd been trouble at Boisvert's.

I tossed the newspaper and mail into the open cab of the Power Wagon, got in, and started down Lake Street toward the town hall. The green was on my right. Ahead of me, across School Street, was the Presbyterian church. Next door on the steamy schoolyard blacktop the kids were still darting around as they waited for the bell, their jackets and bookbags in a multicolored drift against the side of the building.

At the end of the green I paused to let Ken Lloyd's school van make his left turn in front of me onto School Street with the Mayer and Blalock kids he brought down each day from Canada Ridge. Ken and I exchanged salutes.

The van's exhaust tailed into my open cab, and I was holding my breath against it when I heard—

*Ka-POOFF.*

A gunshot. Heavy, muffled. Nearby.

I looked toward the academy. The kids hadn't noticed, but across the the common on the memorial library's pillared side porch, Mercy Petrow, who'd been out emptying the book drop, was peering in my direction, toward the lake, shading her eyes with a book.

I turned that way as the Mercury cruiser came roaring up the short driveway, spraying gravel. It jounced up onto the sandy pavement, rear tires digging for traction, rack lights off.

What *was* this?

The academy's first bell jangled, an irritating noise that always made me think of the sweet bronze handbell Mr. Croaker used to step out and wag back and forth every schoolday morning all the years I was in the grades. The kids lining up at the double doors now were looking in the direction of the red-and-white car squealing toward me up Lake Street.

I flashed my headlights and motioned hard with my left arm to flag him down. No reaction. He went whipping by me with three or four feet to spare.

Whoever that was, it wasn't Pete. Someone smaller was slouched behind the wheel, in dark glasses and a bright red cap . . .

Marcel.

*He'd lost it.* Christ, what was he doing in the cruiser? Where was Pete? Where was Shirley?

I jumped out and watched him as he braked hard for the swing left onto High Street past Sullivan's, skidding, and then sped off toward the state highway.

I ran out past the bandstand to see which way the cruiser would turn at the fork. Either he'd go left onto the state highway, which would take him south toward Allenburg and the interstate, or straight to the northwest, in the direction of my place and Spud's and the Bailey Plateau beyond.

He stayed straight. Heading north toward the flats. Unless he meant to make his way to Greenwood Hollow by the old Stagecoach Road. But it would be a long hike in to Higbee's from there. Anyway, Vaughn would be at the college at this hour. Wouldn't he? Or was the college on spring break?

The second bell jangled: eight o'clock.

Tipton's town hall was a plain frame meetinghouse sided in white clapboard, steel double doors in front, squat belfry on top with a copper arrow weathervane. I drove down around to the gravel parking lot in back, which was bounded by a row of huge white pines between the lot and the village cemetery. Ella's muddy gold Voyager was in its usual spot in the shade of the trees. The snowbanks were thickly embedded with branches and clumps of needles brought down by the ice storms.

The door into the basement offices was open.

I walked into the low-ceilinged common room.

"Ella?" The tang of cordite in the air made me sweat.

There. On her stomach in the doorway of the records office, her silver curls fanned out in the pool of blood surrounding her.

Shot from the front at close range. Slumped to her knees, fell forward, the slug exiting her back. Her Polarfleece and corduroys were blood-soaked. That rich, awful smell. Spatter all up the door, the doorframe, and across the Tipton Community Notices corkboard.

I felt for a pulse, knowing there was none. Her eyes were half-closed and dull as the powder she'd applied to her cheekbones a short while ago. Ella, Ella. Why did this have to happen? She was a friend to everyone. Even Marcel.

I rose and reached for the wall to steady myself.

Where was he headed? Was he settling scores or was he running?

He wouldn't get far in the sheriff's rig. He'd be looking to hide it somewhere. Then he'd take to the woods.

Ella's body filled the doorway. I had to set the sole of my boot in her blood, stepping around her to get to the telephone on her desk. I dialed her place and got Ella's recording. "Shirley," I said, "this is Hector Bellevance. Pick up if you can hear me." I waited a few seconds. "Shirley. Listen to me. Marcel is on his way there in the sheriff's vehicle. I want you to leave that house now. Leave that house and hide somewhere. All right?" Did this make sense? What if Marcel played the message?

I called the Rowell farm. Jan, Thad's wife, answered. I asked her if Sergeant Tierney might be there. He was out back, she said, one second.

On Ella's desk I found the note I'd written for her the night before, but the faxed court documents were gone—

"You're off the hook, Constable," Rob said cheerfully. "Turns out Rowell never told Griswold *you* were the one that picked up that hand. He just—"

"*Rob*. Rob, listen now. I'm in Tipton at the town offices, and I've got a homicide here. Our town clerk, Ella McPhetres, was shot dead just about five minutes ago. I believe the shooter is Marcel Boisvert, and I don't think he's finished."

"Boisvert? The deer hunter? He shot the clerk?"

"Yes."

"Jesus H. Christ . . . You call this in?"

"No, not yet. He's loose, Rob, and he's headed your way. He'll be on the Bailey Road driving a Montcalm County sheriff's cruiser."

"Oh, jeez. He alone?"

"I think so. Well armed, too, I expect."

"What's he doing in a patrol vehicle?"

"I can't say. But he may be on his way to Ella McPhetres's house. His wife is staying there—Shirley. And she's a target. Judge Larrabee granted her a relief-from-abuse order yesterday morning."

"Oh, jeez. Where is this house now?"

"About four miles northeast of the Rowell farm. Take the Bailey Road north past Prentiss Point. Your second right is Ella's road. At the end you'll find a big rambling cottage with cedar siding and a stone chimney."

"Second right. Got it. I'm moving."

"Don't—" He'd hung up. Don't get yourself killed, Rob.

Who else would Marcel want to take out? Besides Higbee. Dwight Osgood. Me. Others. Ella would know.

Marc.

I found Ella's local directory in a side drawer and looked up Rita Brasseur's day care west of the Bailey Plateau.

Rita answered with a bright "*Good* morning!" In the background I could hear kids' piping voices. One was wailing.

"Rita. It's Hector Bellevance. I know you're busy, but tell me, did Vaughn Higbee drop off his little boy with you for the day?"

"He sure did. Half hour ago. Nothing wrong, is there?"

"Are the children all inside?"

"Right now they are. What's this about?"

"Listen, Rita, I need you to trust me on this. If Marcel Boisvert shows up there and asks for Marc, tell him the boy has the flu and he didn't show up this morning."

"What? Why? Marcel's his *grampa*."

"I know that. But right now Marcel is a fugitive from the police."

"He *is*? What did he do?"

"Just keep the boy with you, all right? If he comes for him."

"Hold on a second."

The one kid was still crying. She muffled her mouthpiece. I waited. This wasn't going to work.

"I'm sorry, Mr. Bellevance, but you're gonna have to have the parent call. I can't be taking child-care instructions from any jake that calls me on the phone. Sorry." She hung up.

I counted to ten and hit Redial.

"Rita, Hector Bellevance. I'm at the town hall. Ella McPhetres has just been shot dead. Marcel Boisvert may be her killer, and I'm afraid that he may come after Marc."

She gasped. "Good Lord! *Why*?"

"I don't know why, Rita. But you can't let him take that boy. Do you understand?"

"Yes, oh my—Good *Lord*."

"Don't let any of the children go outdoors for any reason. If you have shades or curtains, pull them."

She was gone.

I called it in. The dispatcher had already heard from Tierney. Two units were on the way to the McPhetres place, ten minutes away at this point. Would I mind waiting where I was until an officer arrived to secure the scene?

I apologized, telling him the best I could do was lock the door behind me.

# 7

Pete must have been really wrought up. He'd reached the Boisvert farm in plenty of time to present Marcel with his choices—Ella would have made sure of that—but to confront the man in his own dooryard without a deputy or two beside him, that wasn't Pete at all.

He lay in a twisted heap in the muddy gumbo of the lawn, about ten yards from where he'd parked the cruiser. His shirt and the ground around him were stained with his blood. His gray campaign hat lay crown-down beside him. His auto was still in its holster. Like Ella, he'd taken a slug though the chest, from the left. He'd been walking backward, hands out, trying to talk the shooter down. *Just put away the gun. You don't want to shoot anybody, Marcel. Put away the gun.*

Marcel's F-250 was still backed into the dilapidated pole shed where I'd seen it the night before. Why hadn't he taken his own rig? And what was it that had got Pete out here alone? He was no cowboy. Besides, I'd warned him. And he knew Marcel as well as I did.

I took my Colt from where I kept it tucked into a leather glove behind the seat of my truck, pushed the magazine home, and chambered a round.

I walked through the woodroom and entered the kitchen.

The window shades were drawn to the sills, sunbeams splintering in around the one over the sink. All I could see clearly were the coffeemaker's orange light and the emerald numerals on the microwave, 8:18. I waited. When my eyes adjusted, I noticed a pile of sliced white bread in the middle of the small breakfast table on top of a layer of mail. The box that the red Utah hat had come in was empty.

On the speckled plaster wall above the lamp I saw a fan of blood. I switched on the table lamp. A sickle-shaped smear a foot wide. I touched it. Dry. If it had been there last night, I wouldn't have missed it.

The curtained living room was crowded with slipcovered chairs and sofas, built-in bookshelves, a TV cart, and a kerosene space heater. The many framed photos on the walls were old: portraits of the ancestors and family gatherings and a few tinted landscapes. A black upright piano blocked the formal entry, its bench heaped with folded laundry—sheets and towels—coated with gray cat hair. The fir tree I'd noticed the night before stood in the uncarpeted hallway, needles rusty, no lights, no garlands, no tinsel, just colored balls winking in the dimness.

Somebody's heavy shoes had left geometric nuggets of mud on the braided rag rug.

The washer and dryer in the laundry room were out of commission, lids hidden under canning jars in stacked wooden apple crates. I found the source of the stink permeating the house inside the galvanized laundry sink: an overflowing litter box.

I followed the mud clots up the bare stairs, listening, holding the .45 up alongside my right ear. Kathy's room stood open at the head of the hallway. It was empty, though her rabbitry ribbons were still pinned to the draperies on either side of the window, two cascades of red and blue.

At the other end of the hall, the bathroom was sunlit. The small window over the toilet was screenless and propped open with a stick of wood. It looked to the east, out toward Canada Ridge. I smelled soap and bleach. The toilet bowl was mossy, the low pedestal sink and clawfoot tub trout-colored with grunge. The oval shower curtain rod sagged, broken out of most of its overhead brackets. The nickel spigots dripped. Lush fronds of mildew climbed the plaster. The tub and the crumbly linoleum floor were wet.

A basinette stood in the middle of the next bedroom, and along the wall a changing table, an antique steamer chest, and an unmade double bed pushed into the corner. Dusty, marble-topped chest of drawers. Hairbrush, a saucer of safety pins, keys, buttons, and change, an empty Lavoris bottle, a pair of steel-framed eyeglasses, a large basket full of loose snapshots. The top drawer hung ajar. Inside lay Shirley's smoky gray Persian longhair, teeth bared, eyes open, blood matted in the ear.

I unlatched the door to the master bedroom, counted to five, and shoved it with my foot. It crashed against something and came shuddering back at me. I heard nothing.

"Shirley? It's Hector!"

I sidled in. No one. No body. Stale odors in the air.

Marcel's gun cabinet stood behind the door, a fine piece of furniture—cherrywood with chromed pulls and hinges. It had a stack of shallow drawers down one side and a tall, open space on the other with felted notches for the long guns. Underneath were ten chamois-lined compartments for the handguns. All gone. Nothing left but cleaning kits, boxes of cartridges and shells, and some holsters.

There were two ornate bureaus, a matching dressing table with a chiffon ruffle, and a scarred oak sleigh bed, its sheets and pillows filthy.

He'd met Pete in the kitchen. Maybe the dooryard. After an exchange of words, Marcel had backed Pete out toward the cruiser and shot him. Then he'd come inside to pack, equipping himself for a battle. Or a siege.

The kitchen phone was a grimy black wall model with a rotary dial. The dispatcher at the barracks—Willis—sounded clipped now that he was recording his second homicide within the hour, his radio jabbering in the background.

"Sheriff's cruiser turn up?" I asked.

"Sergeant Tierney thinks he has it bottled up at the end of the McPhetres' driveway in North Tipton."

"Any more shooting, do you know?"

"No, sir—nothing reported."

"I could head out there now myself—"

"No, no, no. We have three units on the scene now. Best thing for you to do is sit tight till I get somebody out there. Won't be long. There's a whole lot of troopers on the move at the moment, I promise you."

I told Willis I'd head back and wait at the Lake Road intersection, where I could keep an eye on the approaches to both crime scenes. The town hall was more vulnerable than the Boisvert farm, I was thinking—half the town had a key to the place.

Outside, just before I got into my truck, I saw a pair of ravens glide into the top of a sunlit cottonwood at the edge of the flooded pasture. A third raven was there already.

"Hey! You!" I waved my arms. "Get out of here!"

They ignored me.

In the bin behind the cab I had a plastic tarp I used as an awning over my produce stall on the green. I thought of spreading it over Pete's body and securing the corners with stovewood, but I'd tracked up the scene enough as it was.

"*Get lost,* you bastards!"

They shifted their shoulders.

I raised the .45 and fired over their raggedy heads. The report echoed off the mountain.

The three birds dropped out of the tree, swooped low to the ground, and flapped off toward the back bay, grawking to one another.

When I bent down to retrieve the spent casing, I realized I was crying.


Looking north from the junction of the High Settlement Road and the Lake Road, I could see the fishing access and the flooded ash plain beyond. No one would be driving down from the direction for days.

I parked in front of Marcel's ROAD CLOSED sawhorses, got out, and sat on the hood, my heels on the bumper, to compose a statement for the investigation. From "Approx. 8 a.m., Tipton village, heard muffled gunshot" to "9:25, returned to village," it came to three pages.

He'd snapped. It was nothing anyone could have predicted. Men who snapped—and it was always men—usually had no history of violence. The one snapper I'd had firsthand experience with was Rodney Felker. Felker owned a plumbing supply business that the mob had been bleeding somehow. Shot his wife and her mother and held his three children hostage in a third-floor condominium in Dorcester for three days. The oldest, ten or eleven, had called a neighbor. "Daddy's killing us!" she'd screamed. Long standoff. Hot—middle of July. Sharpshooters from downtown on the rooftops angling for shots through the windows. Sal Tonelli and I sweating in body armor outside the apartment door with a ram, ready to break in if he started shooting. Felker kept promising he'd let the kids walk out one at a time. He never did. I wasn't there when he finished the job.

If Marcel had made it to Ella's before the police—unless Shirley had heard my message—he'd already killed her. Then he'd hunch down in the cruiser and try to bust out of there or he'd head down to the lakeshore and slip away in the shelter of the bluffs. He'd make for familiar ground—his hunting camp, most likely. Only this time of the year that camp, up on the rugged, roadless east shoulder of the mountain, was all but inaccessible without a snow machine.

Two state police Impalas swung into the village at the far end of the common a couple of lengths ahead of the state's mobile crime lab. They nosed up to my truck. Steam threaded out of their grilles.

I hopped down.

The Allenburg troopers in the first car—Goomer Ainsley and Darryl Munsinger—I knew. The others had come up from Waterbury, escorting Lieutenant Brian Cahoon and the crime lab. From inside the van, talking on a radio, Cahoon gave me a nod.

I handed Munsinger my statement. He read a few words and relayed it to Cahoon, who rolled down his window.

"So you got two gun deaths out here, Mr. Bellevance?"

"Afraid so, Lieutenant. First one's in the town hall basement." I pointed. "Door's locked. I'll give you my key." I began working it off my ring. "She's Ella McPhetres, our town clerk. Second victim's the country sheriff, Pete Mueller. He's a mile east of us, in the dooryard at the Boisvert farm. He went out there this morning to serve a relief-from-abuse order on Marcel Boisvert. Boisvert's our road foreman."

"So Pete's dead."

"Pete's dead, Lieutenant."

He shook his head. "And Boisvert is the shooter. You saw him."

"Yes, he drove past me in Pete's cruiser. Wearing a red cap. I hear you've got him boxed in at the McPhetres place. What's the latest?"

"Hang on," Cahoon said. He went to the second car and told the driver to go seal off the head of Boisvert's lane, then told Munsinger to do the same with the driveway into the town hall lot.

Turning back to me, he squinted. "You sure you're OK, Bellevance? You look all teary to me."

"Yeah, well, I just lost two friends to a crazy son of a bitch I've known all my life. It kind of gets to you." Cahoon was a small man in too many respects, and I didn't care for him, though I had some respect for his skills and experience. After a few years with the state police over in Addison County and a career with the FBI in New Jersey and Virginia, where he ended up teaching at the academy, Cahoon had returned to Vermont a couple of years ago to retire to his wife's family's place on Lake Bomoseen. He wasn't in the state two months before the Public Safety Commissioner, an old buddy of his, coaxed him out of his leisure to run the state's crime lab. It was a coup for the understaffed force, no question, although Cahoon was about as unpersonable a cop as I'd ever come across. Sloppy dresser, too (very rare in the Bureau), and yet he had enough vanity to cultivate a comb-over.

Cahoon laughed and said, "That's right, somehow I keep thinking of you as a Beantown product, but you're a Vermonter born and raised, just like me." He glanced up toward the van's driver, someone I couldn't see through the glazed windshield. "Bellevance was on the force down in the metropolis. Homicide dick—before he flamed out." To me he said, "I'm acquainted with a lot of boys at Sheridan Square. You ever work with Sam Woolsey?"

I shook my head. "I was off the job before they moved into the new building. You know, if it's all the same to you, Lieutenant, I think I'm going to head on home now."

He raised an eyebrow but said only, "Don't see why not."

I asked him if anybody else had been shot.

He shrugged. "The wife's OK, if that's who you're thinking. Shirley. Hubby's still on the loose, though, so we moved her to a secure location. The BOL just went out."

"Marcel's *loose*? I thought Tierney had him buttoned up at the McPhetres place."

"So did he," Cahoon said. "He got that from you, didn't he?"

"He got what from me?"

"You told him Boisvert was gunning for his wife and she was at the McPhetres house."

"Right. She was. I saw her there last night."

"OK. So that's what he was going on."

"Are you saying Shirley wasn't there?"

"No, no. Shirley was there. The shooter wasn't."

A trooper's giggle echoed up from behind the town hall.

"What is he doing down there?" Cahoon kicked his scuffed shoe against a tire. "I *told* him, close off the the driveway and make sure nobody goes down there. Didn't I say *nobody*?"

"You'd better go," I said.

"We'll be in touch." He climbed back into the BCI van. "Stick around home today, all right? I'll be up after we get this under control. Can you do that for me?"

I told him I had no special plans.

# 8

The office clerk at McPhetres Concrete and Gravel informed me that Tom was away from his desk for the day, but she could get word to him as long as it was urgent. I asked her to have him phone the state police within the hour. After that I tried Higbee's college extension and got a voice-mail message saying his mailbox was full. I decided against leaving a message on his home machine.

Out in the greenhouse a short while later, I caught the sound of Spud's wreck of a Cutlass—he'd lost his muffler weeks ago—over the roar of the brook. The car pulled into the turnout at the foot of my hill.

I rinsed my hands and waited in the doorway, watching as his head and shoulders came over the hill. By his hunched-over stride, he was in a hurry. Though when wasn't he? The farm was just about all Spud and Brenda could manage. Ever since he'd bought the place he'd been struggling to keep up with his costs and never breaking even. Some of the loss in milk he'd managed to make up in the traditional ways—sugaring, raising Christmas trees—but he was working from five in the morning till ten at night every single day, all year long. Over the winter he'd said something about how he couldn't wait to put his boy Lyle in the traces, and Lyle wasn't yet two.

The sugaring had been pretty poor—too much rain and wind and no sun at all. Yet Spud had three thousand taps and the sap hadn't gone off, so he was still boiling, I was thinking. Something must have come up, and he was after me to watch the pan for him.

"Spud!" I yelled, waving.

He veered right around and came trotting down across the matted grass, kicking beaded arcs of water into the sun. We were built alike, lean and long-armed, but Spud was almost a foot shorter. He had Felice LaClair's dark French complexion and our mother's delicate features.

"Hector!" He was breathless. "You hear about Petey and Ella? *Jesus,* Heck, they been murdered! Both of 'em! Shot dead this morning! And you know who did it? Marcel Boisvert! He just blew 'em away!"

We sat on the plank doorsill in the sun. Spud dug out his inhaler, took a puff, and listened, staring at his shoes, while I gave him the rest of the story. His clothes held the sweet smell of maple.

"Hard to believe Marcel would up and do a thing like this, Heck, but I guess that's what people always say, isn't it?"

"That's true, they do. How did you hear? Somebody call you?"

"No, somebody called Brenda. They don't know where he is, either. That's what scares me."

"They'll find him."

"Sure they will, except it could take quite a little while. Marcel knows this country like the inside of his own mouth." He lifted his cap and ran his fingers through his hair. "You shoulda seen Brenda. I'm up at the sugarhouse and she runs in, and she can barely *talk*—" He stopped. "How about that?"

"Can't blame her, Spud."

"No, I mean she came up to the sugarhouse. First time she's been up there since last fall. I just realized that."

Last fall Spud's wife found out he'd been using the sugarhouse as a trysting place for an affair with a married neighbor, and they'd been taking things a day at a time since then. Spud was desperate to keep his family together. If Brenda left him, he'd have to sell the farm. But it was more than that—he loved her.

"You didn't leave Brenda up in the sugarhouse, did you?"

He looked blank for a moment. "What? No. No, actually I quit boiling yesterday. No, I'm cleaning up, but I'm just sayin' you shoulda seen her. She was *hysterical*."

"I'm surprised she let you leave the farm."

"Well, I kinda just slipped away." He rubbed his chin. "Why do you think he did it, Hector?"

"People snap."

"OK, they snap. But what's that mean? They throw a rod through the brain pan?"

"That's not a bad image."

He stood up and gazed down the length of the greenhouse. "You know what I been thinking? What if he has a hit list and you're on it?"

"I doubt he has a hit list."

"Yeah, well, he never thought too highly of you, I know that."

"He never thought too highly of anybody."

"Sure, but you especially. Remember how he used to stare at you?"

"Marcel's all done, Spud. They'll catch up with him before to-morrow. Wait and see. He's probably bushwhacking his way out to his camp up in the east bowl."

"Yeah? I don't know, Heck. I'd worry if I was you. You want to stay at the farm, you're welcome. She'll fix up the spare bedroom."

"Thanks, Spud. I'm fine here."

He nodded. "Something else I been meaning to ask you. You know about computers, right?"

"Why, are you thinking about getting a computer?"

"Yeah. I don't guess you know Bruce Yandow's cousin, but he won this software CD in a raffle at the co-op, and he gave to me. It's all about setting up a corn maze, all the instructions and designs, you know? I've been thinking about it, and goddamn it, I'm gonna do it."

"You're going to set up a corn maze?"

"Sure! I got this real leafy hybrid on order, and you know that ten-acre piece up behind the house? You can't beat that for a location. Nice and breezy, incredible view of the lake, and level parking right across the road."

"That would be the spot, all right."

"See, what you do, you plant your corn same as always. Then in June you walk along and pull up your sprouted plants according to a predetermined pattern. Could be all spirals, could be anything. That's what the software's about."

"Sounds all right, but are you really sure you want to commit yourself to running a tourist attraction?"

"Why? It's no big deal. Takes a couple days to put in a maze, and then you run some ads in the newspaper, put up a few posters at the campgrounds. Build it and they will come, right? And you charge the people five bucks a head for the amazing experience! Plus you sell 'em sodas and T-shirts and postcards and all this when they come out. Think about it. If you're a tourist, what else is there to do around here besides hike and fish?"

"I'm just wondering who's going to run this sideshow while you're milking cows and cutting hay."

"Brenda! She loves the idea. She can sell tickets and refreshments and look after the kid at the same time. All I need to get us rolling is a halfway decent computer."

"That's the easy part."

"And you can teach me how to use it, right?"

"Can you type?"

"I used to. In high school."

"Well, there's not much more to it than typing. This maze is going to be a lot more work than you think, though, Spud."

"Nah. Hey, if I have to hire a couple kids, I will. By September I figure I ought to be clearing a thousand a week."

We heard a car approaching from the village side of the hill, and we paused to listen as it slowed at the sawmill and began the climb up Long Hill.

"Think that's him?" Spud said.

The car stopped at the turnout. Three door slams.

"It's the police," I said. We stepped back inside the greenhouse and watched as Rob Tierney and two uniformed troopers appeared over the rise, marching straight ahead up the path toward the cabin. They didn't look our way. The uniforms carried shotguns. "I'd better go see what I can do for those fellas."

"Sure," Spud said, "but—"

"I'll take care, Spud. You don't have to worry about me."

"It's not that. It's something I been wanting to tell you for a while now." He hesitated, then said, "I know you went through hell down in Mass with your marriage busting up and all that bullshit around you leaving the police force, and then Mom passing like she did, and I know you didn't have to come back here. You coulda gone anyplace, but you came home, and I'm glad you did. Ella was, too. I just thought you ought to hear that."

I could only nod and give his shoulder a squeeze.


Rob Tierney paced in front of my fireplace in his running shoes, hands jammed into the back pockets of his cords. His skin looked waxy, and his hair was tousled. He had on a green state police windbreaker over a blue dress shirt and a gray Kevlar vest, unfastened. Last fall, when Rob was posted up to Allenburg from Brattleboro, his wife and his two boys stayed behind down in Keene, where Marilyn was working in a candy factory and studying for her degree in elementary education. Their families lived down there, which meant Marilyn had plenty of help, but the separation was hard on Rob. He kept a two-room apartment out in Tewkesville and got down to see them once a month, if he was lucky.

I was the only one sitting. Ainsley and Corporal Duquette kept to the tiled kitchen out of concern for my carpets, since they didn't intend to take their shoes off. Ainsley was watching Tierney, while Duquette stood in the doorway, looking out through the sun porch windows. They were tense, their radios sputtering nonstop.

"What gets me is I *saw* him," Tierney was saying. "He had less than a mile on me, and I could've caught him if I didn't just assume he was up in there at the McPhetres'. There were fresh skid marks in the road where the driveway veers off, and I just concluded that was him."

"Well, I'd told you that's where he was headed."

"Yeah, I know. I drove in till I could see the house, which as you know is way back on this rise, and the sheriff's car is nowhere in sight—so I figure he's around back. Only there's no cover between me and the house—it's one big field except for a few skinny birch trees—so I stop and quick grab my vest, and then when I finally get around back, come to find out the son of a bitch *juked* me. How the fuck did he get away in a *patrol* vehicle, that's what I want to know. We had every highway blocked off inside of twenty minutes."

"He didn't get away. He's hiding."

"Yeah, all right. Where?" Tierney turned to face me. "His hunting camp is snowbound and untracked. We had a chopper all over it."

"Where else are you looking?"

"Where aren't we? Four northern counties of Vermont and New Hampshire, the Eastern Townships of Quebec, and all the airports and train and bus stations from here to Hartford."

"I'll bet he's close by, Rob."

He nodded. "That's why I'm here. You want me to leave Corporal Duquette to watch your back?"

"No, no, thanks. You need him. I'll be all right."

"Well, at least let me leave you one of these." He tapped his vest. "Latest generation—Ultima threat level three. I'll stick one in your truck before we take off."

"Sure, thanks," I said, though I didn't see myself walking around here in body armor. "How's Kim Gentler doing?" Kim was Pete Mueller's wife.

"Not great, I guess. But she's got her sister with her." He shook his head. "I never knew Pete had kids."

"From his first marriage, that's right. They live with their mom over in Saratoga. How's Shirley Boisvert doing?"

"Not too bad." He made a snort. "She's in the shower when we go in there, right? So she can't hear us. I knock on the door, nobody answers, so I go in, and we hear the shower running. So we try the bathroom door. It's locked. 'Anybody in there?' The water stops. 'Who is that?' 'Vermont State Police.' Minute later the door opens and out she comes all red from the heat, I mean the room's like a steambath in there, and here are four cops in her hallway and this woman is naked except for a bath towel, and she doesn't seem a bit fazed. 'Was Marcel here?' I ask her, and she says, 'Marcel's working.' Turns out that shower she took was her first shower since the day she got married that she didn't have to get out of in three minutes. Boisvert *timed* her in there. With one of those little egg timers. She tells us this, but it gives you an idea what kind of whiphand we're dealing with."

"Where is Shirley now?"

"Deputy took her and the grandson to her niece's place in Allenburg."

"Did you say the *grandson*?"

"Yeah. Marc. You scared the bejesus out of his day-care provider, Hector. She was all over us to get that kid out of there."

"So you mean you couldn't find Vaughn Higbee?"

"Professor Higbee never showed up at the college this morning."

"That doesn't sound good."

"There's none of this sounds good."

On the way out of the house, I asked if they'd found the hand.

Rob shook his head. "Some officer picked the thing up—but Rowell was milking, and nobody got a good look at who it was. His wife's the one thought it was you. Back burner for now, obviously."

From the lip of the knoll I watched them pick their way in single file down my footpath. To the south the sky had turned milky with mare's tails.

Wilma must have pulled in to the turnout as the police drove off, because she announced herself by quietly clearing her throat in the open greenhouse door. I started, looking up from my trays. She had a big box balanced on her shoulder—the Celestron.

"OK if I set this baby down in here?"

"Sure."

"The tripod and the mount are back in my trunk. I didn't wrap them. This damn thing took enough paper." She set the box down and smiled, and burst into tears.

I held her.

"Everybody *loved* Ella!"

"I know."

"And Petey! He was a blowhard, but he was a *decent* blowhard."

"That's true."

"I keep thinking what if you'd gone back there? He could have killed you, too!"

"If I'd been there, Pete would be alive. Ella, too."

"Don't go there, Hector."

"You brought it up."

"The man hates you! He could still kill you, too, and don't try telling me that's not on your mind."

I shook my head. "Too many people out there hunting for him. It may take a couple of days, but they'll find him."

"God, they should. The county's swarming with state troopers. We've got 'em here from Maine, New Hampshire, and Mass. Plus Customs and Border Patrol. It's a real circus."

"Let's go zap a couple of chicken burritos, how about it?"

"I have to get back to the newsroom. Jules is holding page one."

"Call it in."

"Can't. I have the pictures." She patted her carryall. "But here's another proposal. You remember Penelope Fletcher?"

"What about her?" Penny Fletcher was a biologist who lived up in the woods east of Middlebury. Her organization, Room for All, was devoted to preserving wildlife habitats throughout northern New England. Wilma had written a piece about her for *Smithsonian* magazine.

"I had the woman all lined up to meet me at the Rowell farm at two. But she just left me a message at the newsroom. She can't make it."

"What were you going to do out there with Penny Fletcher?"

"I want to backtrack the beagle, see if we can locate the murder victim's head. Penny was up for it, too. Or so she seemed this morning. She probably heard we have a killer running around the woods up here and she bailed."

"You don't need Penny Fletcher to follow dog prints in the snow."

"Oh no? Maybe you don't. I couldn't tell a beagle print from a fox print. Could you?"

"Sure."

"That's what I figured. So you want to join me on a little snow-shoeing excursion?"

"I'll be amazed if we find anything."

"Well, head or no head, a hike'll do us good."

We walked out to the knoll and kissed.

"Tell me," she said. "Aren't you just a little nervous?"

"Not really. You'll see. They'll have him by tomorrow, if he's alive."

"If he's the guy."

"He's the guy."

"*I* think he's the guy, too, but Nezzie Holmes isn't convinced." Holmes was the Montcalm County state's attorney.

"No? What's Holmes saying?"

"One second . . ." She pulled her stenographer's notebook from her tote bag and flipped it open. "Get this. The guy keeps maybe twenty of us milling around in the snow and mud on the side of the road from ten until noon, and all he has for us is, 'Both deaths are being treated as homicides. We believe they are related. The killer or killers remain at large.' I asked him, what's the story on Marcel Boisvert? 'Nothing to add at this time.' I said, 'Isn't it true that Sheriff Mueller was attempting to serve a relief-from-abuse order that Marcel Boisvert had refused the night before? Didn't his wife, Shirley, file a statement with the court alleging physical abuse? Isn't it true that Ella McPhetres had taken Shirley into her home to protect her from her *husband*?' 'No comment at this time.' Then he turns it over to Detective Sergeant Mason Sammis, who says . . ." She turned the page—" 'When all the evidence has been processed and the offender's motivation established, we will have more to say about the thrust of our investigation.' "

"That's standard, Wilma. Cahoon knows who he's after."

" 'Cahoon knows who he's after.' OK if I quote you?"

"Go ahead."

"Can you give me a little more on your encounter last night with Boisvert?"

"Not until he's been formally named."

"Fair enough. OK, I'll swing into town and drop off the camera, go pick up my gear, and you can meet me out along Rowell Road in an hour and a half. How's that?"

"You've got more energy than any two people I've ever met."

"Yes," she said. "I've been told it's the essence of my charm."

# 9

We walked across a rolling cornfield in the direction Thad Rowell had pointed the day before. The stubbly ground was softening, and snow lay in the furrows like wads of newspaper. The sun was a putty-white stain in a scrim of gray in the west.

Topping a little rise, we spotted a dozen turkeys on the far side of the field. Alarmed, they pranced a few strides, then clattered up into the air and glided into the cover of hemlock along the margin.

"What goofballs," Wilma said. "There's a season on them up in these parts now, isn't there?"

"In May. They're harder to bag than they look, though."

"Poor birds." She gobbled at them. "Did you ever hunt?"

"When I was a kid."

"What? Deer?"

"Everything. Deer, woodchuck, skunk, hedgehog, squirrel, partridge, coyote, rabbit, fox—whatever I could draw a bead on." I stopped. "Look here." On the edge of the field there were lobed craters in the snow.

"Moose!" she said. "*Big* galoot."

"Heading for that grove where the turkeys took cover. Probably a lot of striped maple down there."

"They like striped maple?"

"They crave it."

"For the buds?"

"The bark. They do this." I stuck my jaw out and raked the air with my lower teeth. "*Mooswah.* Old Algonquian word for 'the animal that strips the bark off trees.' "

"No kidding. What's the big attraction in striped maple?"

"The minerals, probably. Moose put a lot of stress on their systems growing that big rack every year."

She pulled me down and kissed my cheek. "I love the gazillion things you have in your head. You're gonna be a *great* dad."

"I'd like to believe that."

"You are. You know what's the greatest aphrodisiac?"

"I'm sure you're about to tell me."

"Knowledge! Command of the world!"

"I'll take your word for it."

"You'd better."

Tracking conditions were poor but good enough for our purposes. With this warmth, the individual prints in the snowpack were fairly degraded. But the patterns were plain enough—hare, red squirrel, porcupine. The plan was simple: walk along the boundary of the field until we cut the beagle's path out of the woods, then put on our snowshoes and backtrack her in. We followed a coyote along the margin. Unlike most domestic dogs, coyotes are economical walkers, their hind feet registering in the prints of the forefeet.

We intersected the beagle's track at the far end of the field. She had a shorter stride than a coyote and a wider straddle than a fox, and once she was out of the woods she'd trotted straight across the middle of the field toward the Rowells' cedar windbreak.

"Here's a tired dog who knows where her chow's waiting," I said.

In the woods the going was slow. I led, every step sinking a foot into the rotten snow. I had on my mother's old ash-and-rawhide bearpaws, and they were too small for me. We followed the beagle's fairly straight course up and up into the hills on the eastern side of the old Space Research compound, where the snow had been firm enough yesterday morning for the little dog to trot right along pretty much on the crust, her paws denting it no more than an inch. Her course was steady. She'd sensed she'd found something important, and she was eager to get home with it.

In time, pushing through a thick stand of young hemlocks, we found ourselves at the border cut, a cleared space twenty yards wide, running straight across the hills as far as we could see. Exposed to the sun and wind, the ground here was bare of snow.

"Now what?" Wilma said.

"We can keep hunting if you want," I said. "The Border Patrol's off looking for Marcel."

"I know, but don't they have hidden video cameras and motion sensors and all that high-tech jazz?"

"Well, yes, but this isn't exactly a hot zone. Even where they have sensors, they can't respond to every hit. They watch for unusual patterns as much as anything else."

Wilma shaded her eyes and peered to the west along the swath. "You think they're watching us?"

I laughed. "Who knows?"

"Hector, would you be annoyed with me if I said maybe we should bag this?"

"Not at all. We've lost her, anyway. She was out here in the open because the walking's easier. Could be a while before we cut her track again."

"Well," she said, "that settles it. Good thing I didn't drag Penny Fletcher up here."

"It was a long shot," I said. "But you knew that going in." I knelt and pointed to a greenish patch of snow the size of a bottle cap. "See this?"

She crouched to inspect it. "What is it? Scat?"

"Snow algae."

"Algae? So it's alive?"

"It's alive, all right. It's a whole colony of animals. They sleep through the winter. This is the time of the year they swim to the surface and reproduce."

"Wow. That's . . ." She blushed. "You know, that's actually kind of sexy. A snow algae orgy. What do they live on?"

"Nothing but light."

She kissed me and started unbuckling her bindings. "How about it, Hector?"

"What?"

"You want to give those Border Patrol guys a little erotic video?"

Wilma sped ahead of me, hurrying to catch up with events. If we did make a life together, I was going to have to slow her down somehow. And that junker Mazda she was barreling along in needed CV joints, shocks, and brake work. With the money she'd be pulling down at the *Globe*, at least she'd be able to buy a car with ABS and airbags. That's something, I thought. We'd agreed to meet for supper at the cabin. "Seven o'clock. Just thaw out some pesto and keep the pasta water boiling," she'd told me. "If I'm running late I'll call."

By the time I reached the Bailey Road intersection she was out of sight. Glancing in the other direction, I happened to see the tip of a crane gantry sticking above the pines out at Prentiss Point. My first thought was that a vehicle had gone into the lake. One summer years ago, while I was home visiting my mother and Spud, some wild kids had stolen somebody's Buick Skylark and pushed it off the overlook into the water. Back then it had taken the state weeks to send a crane up here.

The road into the overlook was a gravel jog off the highway that curved down to a parking area in a stand of red pines. That's where I found Rob Tierney's unmarked Chevy along with a state transportation department flatbed, two cruisers, and Kyle Morrison's sixteen-wheeler. Morrison ran a crane service out of Allenburg.

Tierney waved to me from the bluff. Duquette and a shaggy-bearded Kyle Morrison were there next to him, gazing down into the lake. I joined them just as the crane operator, Kyle junior, lowered a suited-up scuba diver over the edge like a frog on a hook.

Duquette cackled at something Morrison was saying under his breath. They were keyed up, and no wonder: The manhunt of the century was ending right at their feet, and out of all the officers in the chase they were the ones reeling in the prize.

Around noontime, Tierney told me, a UPS driver who had pulled in to relieve himself noticed where a car had slipped between the tarred posts and slid down among the pines right over the edge of the bluff. His dispatcher called the barracks.

From the south side of the overlook, you could hook your arm around a birch tree, lean out, and see a black hole in the ice fifty feet down. In the middle of the hole, under a few feet of clear water on the sloping lake floor, were the Merc's wavery taillights and the word SHERIFF in bold red letters across the face of the trunk lid.

"When we were kids," I said, "we used to jump in from here."

Tierney shook his head. "I bet you were one hairy-ass little urchin, Bellevance."

"Well, it was a thrill. We didn't do it often, though. Pretty rugged climb back to the top."

"I guess." Rob was watching the diver. "Ten to one he's in there. What do you think?"

"I doubt it, Rob."

He glanced at me, surprised. "Nah, he's in there. We fish him out and a whole lot of law-enforcement personnel are going to be mighty relieved."

"Huh," Duquette said. "They're gonna be mighty disappointed is what they're gonna be."

"For a minute, maybe," Tierney said. "But this way everybody gets to go home, and nobody else gets hurt."

"They still up on the mountain?" I said.

"Oh, jeez, they're everywhere."

We looked toward the far shore. The cliffs were hidden behind veils of flurries.

"Where's Cahoon?"

"Boisvert farm, bagging and tagging. He loves it."

"How's the water, Curt?" Duquette called down.

"Kinda nippy!"

They laughed.

The diver ducked under and resurfaced half a minute later. "Nobody home!"

"Shit on a shingle," Duquette said.

The crane's hydraulics kicked in and the Grand Marquis rose from the lake, water spilling out the open windows. Kyle junior positioned the vehicle above the flatbed, as his dad guided it down.

Tierney vaulted up beside it. His pants were wet to the knees. He looked in.

"Keys in it?" I said.

"Yep, they are."

"See if you can reach around and grab 'em without touching the steering wheel. You want to pop the trunk."

"You got it."

I clambered up on the flatbed. Tierney tried one key, then another. He lifted the lid and stood back. "Holy jumping catfish . . ."

"What is it?" Duquette said.

"Whole duffel bag full of guns!" Kyle junior shouted from the cab.

Two more green-and-gold cruisers swung into the parking oval. Duquette went to greet them.

Tierney pulled a modified M-16 out of the water. "Rifles. Five of them. Couple of shotguns in cases, boxes of shells . . ."

Also a snow shovel, a set of chains, jumper cables, a box of flares, rubber boots, and a red first-aid kit. "He hung on to his handguns," I said.

"Yeah. If he had this planned out—like if he had another car here waiting for him—" Tierney said, "you know he wouldn't have left all this hardware behind."

"When you saw him go past you on the flats, did you have your flashers on?"

"I sure did."

"So then he saw you, and he knew you'd catch up with him before he got to McPhetres', so he dodged in here. You blew right past him."

"That's where he was headed, then, to cap his wife."

I nodded. "You saved her life, Rob."

"Well, thanks to you, if I did. So that was lucky then. I just wish I didn't let the fucker get away."

Tierney got on the radio while I showed the troopers to the head of the trail down to the lakeshore. There was plenty of sign at the edge of the bluff—he'd gone down fast, sliding, clutching at branches. We didn't try to follow. The shoreline would have been rough going, a jumble of rime-caked boulders and snags, but if the ice was still good enough, he might have walked on the lake all the way back to the village under cover of the bluff, or else up into Quebec, with little chance of being spotted. Wherever he'd gone, he had a six-hour lead. A trooper asked me if I thought he could have crossed over to the back side of Mount Joe. You couldn't dismiss it, I said, but if he'd tried that, he would have been exposed to the village two miles south the whole time, and afterwards he'd have had a lot of rugged terrain to negotiate. I didn't think he'd crossed the lake.

It was almost four. Since I had more than enough daylight left to get things closed up at my place before night, I decided to take the long way home, thus avoiding the commotion in the village. At the West Branch four corners, I came upon Vaughn Higbee's yellow Mercedes diesel parked on the edge of Mayhew Broughton's alfalfa piece. I stopped for a look. Vaughn's footprints and the boy's led off along the side of the road toward Greenwood Hollow. I decided I ought to drop in.

The road descended gradually through spruce woods and cedar, curving north. Originally it had been a stagecoach road that went straight through the hollow past the Greenwood place and a few other farms and over the open highlands to what was then

Tipton Center—a schoolhouse, a mill, a stable, and a tavern, all gone today. Today the road ended in the hollow, and trees had reclaimed the highlands. Little was left of Tipton Center but a small, disused cemetery and a few cellar holes, if you knew where to look.

Where it leveled out, the road had become a stretch of interlaced ruts filled with water, with the snowbanks high as my side mirrors. I ground through in low-range, grooving the middle of the road with my transfer case.

Marcel hadn't engineered this quagmire, it was true, but he'd made no effort to alleviate it. For one thing, the banks were melting back into the road instead of out of it. The road crew used to make a couple of passes with the grader in March, winging the banks back far enough to keep meltwater out of the roadbed. This winter, of course, we'd seen twice the snow as we'd seen in the last twenty.

Then again, Vaughn was wealthy enough to have had the work done privately. He wasn't as inconvenienced as he made himself out to be, but he was as bullheaded as Marcel. If anybody in modern America needed a great big SUV, it was Higbee, but he wouldn't own a vehicle that got less than thirty miles a gallon. He hated SUVs, as well as ATVs, snowmobiles, and Jet Skis. And he cut his lawn with a push mower.

I left the Power Wagon in front of the house and walked around back through the rose arbor, where I found Marc playing in the mud with a garden trowel and pieces of scrap wood. He had on red rubber boots and a midnight-blue Yankees jacket. This was maybe the fourth or fifth time I'd seen the child, and it struck me all over again how beautiful he was. With a perfect facial symmetry like his mother's and those flaxen curls, he could have been a photographer's model.

"Hello there, Marc."

"Hi, Mr. Bellevance!" We'd been first introduced at Kathy's memorial service and again last month, at town meeting. "Great mud!" he said. He was smoothing a long trench with the back of the trowel.

"I like a fella who appreciates his materials. What are you building?"

"Racetrack. When it dries, it'll be rad."

I crouched next to him. "How are you doing, Marc?"

"Pretty good."

"I hear you had to leave day care this morning."

"Yeah, that was crazy. It was because something happened to Grampa. He blew a gasket."

"Who told you that?"

"My gram. It's like when you have a dog and it gets rabies. You don't know how it happened and if the dog bites somebody, it's not really the dog's fault."

"Your gram's right. Did you have a good time today?"

"Oh yeah. They have a trampoline. Me and Gram got to jump on it."

I laughed. "You and Gram? Together?"

"Yeah! It's more fun when there's two."

So much for Shirley's cracked rib. "I guess you get along pretty well with your Gram, don't you?"

"Oh, yeah. She's my best friend."

My knees popped when I straightened up. "Is your dad inside, Marc?"

He nodded. "I think he's online."

I sat on a bench in the mudroom to remove my boots and stepped into the kitchen in my socks. The wide-plank pine floor looked glossy as butter, and the countertops were empty runways of red-and-black-flecked granite.

I passed through a carpeted dining room and a large sitting

room with overfull bookshelves and a green-enameled woodstove on a raised slate pad.

"Vaughn?" I called up the stairwell.

"Hector! Give me a minute to get out of this, and I'll be right down!"

He'd heard my truck for the last half-mile, and a glance out a window would have told him whose it was. Just the same, it seemed a little strange that he'd left Marc outside in the yard alone and the back door unlocked, while he sat up there engrossed in whatever he was engrossed in.

He came slowly down the stairs and halted theatrically on the last step with his arms out wide. He'd grown his sideburns since town meeting. His rumpled dress shirt was half-buttoned and his blue jeans were pressed. He wore a fat band of tooled silver on each wrist. He had his hair pulled back into a graying, straw-colored ponytail, with curls that wisped out at the back of his neck. The perfect image of the witty, irreverent, party-going prof the college kids revered.

I embraced him.

"You know what I just found out?" he said into my shoulder. I smelled his tea-tree bath soap. He pushed away, holding me by the forearms.

"No," I said.

"Our new chancellor has awarded himself a fifty-two-thousand-dollar raise."

"Lot of money."

"Do you know what his degree is in?"

"No."

"Dental hygiene. I kid you not."

"Strange."

"It's a *travesty*." He led me back into the kitchen. "I suppose you're here about the shootings."

"I am. I tried to reach you this morning, Vaughn, soon as I knew what we were dealing with."

"The *senseless death*! It's never going to *end*, is it, Hector?"

"I don't suppose it is."

"Why did he do it?"

"Rage and grief are a volatile mix," I said.

"Poor *Ella*! Those two were always locking horns, but . . . to *kill* her?" He shook his head. "They haven't caught up with him, have they?"

"Not yet."

"You know why, don't you?"

"I have a few ideas."

"He's out in the woods someplace in a bloody heap," Vaughn said.

"That's one of them."

He pulled out a chair and asked me to sit at his honey-colored oak table, which I did, glad to rest my back.

He opened his monster stainless-steel refrigerator. "Join me in a little libation?"

"Whatever you're having. Thanks."

"Shirley says you found the bodies."

I nodded.

"That must have been a horror show. Though I imagine police work hardens you to those things."

"Only to an extent. When you know the victims, all bets are off."

"Of course."

"Ella was the heart of this town. She and my mother . . ." I paused, surprised at the catch in my throat. "Ella's ex-husband was Spud's father, as you probably know. And yet Ella and Agnes were always close. As for Pete Mueller, I've known Pete since high school. We used to play football together."

"And Marcel, too!" Vaughn cried. "By God, if Ella was the heart of this town, Marcel was its hard-bitten *soul*."

"He was that."

"Seems they should have found him by now, don't you think? The radio's saying we have half the cops in New England up here beating the bushes for him."

"They'll find him."

"How come you're not out there, Hector?"

"I'm retired."

"The hell you are. You're town constable. And you knew the victims!"

"Marcel and my father were best friends. If this thing ends the way I suppose it will, I don't want any part of it."

"Ah." He nodded sympathetically. "I still think he's out in the woods with the back of his head blown off."

"Could be. All the same, I'd be concerned if I were you, Vaughn."

"For my life, you mean?" He poured a coppery brew into pilsner glasses from a brown glass jug. "No. He's a dead man. One way or another."

We clinked rims.

"Here's to the dead," he said.

"To the dead."

He smacked his lips. "Blackberry wheat. Picked it up over at the Dusty Dolphin, in Portland. Fabulous, eh?"

"That it is."

"Hector, a moment ago you said, 'Rage and grief are a volatile mix.' Are you suggesting it was Kathy's death that sent him over?"

"The forensic psychologists would call that a 'precipitating stressor.' "

He snorted. "I'll bet they would."

"The loss of a child can crush a parent, you know that. Especially one as tightly wound as Marcel."

"Marcel's been through it before. He and Shirley lost a son before Kathy was born."

"Long time ago," I said. "Did you have any idea that he'd been beating on Shirley?"

"Not till this afternoon, no. He was a tyrant, sure, but it was all psychological. Never physical. Kathy would have told me." He opened a cupboard and brought out a bag of Doritos, which he emptied into a painted wooden bowl. "What floors me, though, is not that he started hitting her, but that she fought back. And then filing for relief? The counselor must've put her up to it, is all I can think. I admire those people for the work they do, but this one did not adequately explain the possible consequences to Shirley. Dragging Marcel out of his home . . . Shit, talk about stressors!"

"The law's a crude instrument sometimes. Shirley has the right to feel safe in her own home."

"Yes, but we're talking *Marcel* here. Right? Hector, when the police have to remove a batterer from the home, don't they usually seize his firearms at the same time?"

"I know what you're getting at."

"Yeah. Might as well try castrating a mountain lion with a butter knife."

Marc came clomping into the mudroom. "I heard that!" he shouted.

"What did you hear, big guy?"

"Chips!"

"You heard *chips*!" Vaughn shot me a dad's grin. "Kid's got the ears of a fox." He went to the doorway. "*Whoa!* Bath time. Let's take everything off right out here. Except the underpants."

He helped Marc undress and herded him toward the stairway with a small plastic bowl of Doritos. "Run yourself a bath," he told him, though it wasn't even five o'clock, "but don't get in till I test it for you. OK?"

"Can I take a shower?"

"Sure, OK, just be careful in there. *Sesame Street*'s on in fifteen minutes! Then supper. Move it!"

"Are we staying here tonight?"

"We're having spaghetti. You don't want to?"

"No, I do! Can I play *The Sims* on your computer?"

"You don't want to watch *Sesame Street*?"

"Nah, we watch it at day care all the time."

"OK, sure. Shower first!"

He ran up the stairs.

"Kid's amazing. Just turned five and he reads *everything*. Not only that, but he can multiply and divide. You see for yourself what a positive spirit he has. This thing today is just horrendous, and look how resilient he is. How does he do it?"

"He's like his mom. He knows how to keep his mind well occupied."

Vaughn shook his head. "Too true."

"How's he doing emotionally? He say anything about Marcel?"

"I don't know. Shirley gave him an earful, but we'll have a heart-to-heart later when I put him to bed. Rita Brasseur kicked him out of her day care. Did you know that?"

"Sorry, I guess I'm to blame for that, Vaughn. I had to make sure the boy wouldn't be harmed."

"Of course. And I'm glad you did. You had Rita peeing in her drawers, though."

"Tell me, has Marc been getting help? Since last summer, I mean?"

"Yes. Psychologist down in Montpelier. Jane Uhlen. She's been terrific."

"That's good. She can help him through this one, too."

"You know something? He talks to Kathy's picture every night. Tells her about his day. It's heartbreaking. I have to leave the room. But he's trying to sustain the relationship, which is fine. She's gone forever, and he accepts that, but, I don't know, last Saturday morning he comes in like he always does, jumps on the bed, and says, 'Daddy? How far away is heaven?' Now I have to say, if there's one thing I regret, it's letting that minister Wallace lay all this harps-and-angels crap on my son. But that first week, I could barely function. Shirley's the one who took him to this guy. Now Marc believes his mom was called to heaven by the angels, and someday, if he's *good,* he'll get to see her again."

"It's a soothing concept, Vaughn."

"Yeah, so's Santa Claus. Before he was born, Kathy and I promised each other we would never lie to our son." Vaughn got up and began opening cupboards, taking down dinner plates, glasses, a package of pasta, a jar of sauce.

"What did you tell him?"

He came back to his chair and gripped the finials. "What did I tell him? I told him heaven's all around us. It's another dimension."

"Very good."

"Then I said, 'Why do you want to know?' and he said, 'Because if heaven isn't that far and she's still got clothes and all, maybe Mommy could come back one time and fix me a heart-shaped pancake. If she wouldn't get in trouble.' "

"And what did you say to that?"

He sighed. "I told him she would come back—but only in his dreams. He asked why. I said, 'Because Mommy isn't *real* anymore, Marc. She is only a dream.' And *he* said, 'But dreams *are* real.' 'They are?' I said. He said, 'Until you wake up they are.' "

I smiled.

"How's that, huh? The kid's a metaphysician. You want to stay for some pasta and mushroom sauce? Help me finish this growler?"

I drained my glass and rose to my feet. "I've got chores, Vaughn. But before I go, let me just say you're welcome to spend the night at my cabin—if you feel at all uneasy."

"Uneasy? Let me show you something." He unlatched a high, narrow cabinet above the range hood and lifted down a 12-gauge pump shotgun with a black stock. He hefted it. "I have another one upstairs—and before you ask, no, Marc can't get at them."

"At least not without standing on a chair."

He replaced the shotgun and latched the cabinet. "He knows better."

"Some amped-up biker gang roars in here, Vaughn, I'd give you and that pump-action the edge. But Marcel's a deer hunter."

"So why would your place be any safer than mine?"

"He'd have to be looking for you at my place to find you."

"Who says he's not looking for *you*?"

"It was just a thought."

"Sorry, Hector, but that old bastard's been trying to drive me out of here ever since Kathy died, and I'm damned if I'm gonna leave now that the game's just about up."

I stepped down into the mudroom to put on my boots.

"That's the silver lining to all this, in case it hasn't occurred to you."

"How do you mean?"

"Marcel's done tyrannizing this poor town. We're going to be getting ourselves a new road foreman, Hector. Which means I won't have to sue you people after all."

I stood there while the impulse to knock him flat subsided. We were nearly at even height, Vaughn a step above me in his kitchen doorway. His direct gaze infuriated me, until I saw the sheen of sorrow behind it.

Vaughn assumed that it was his advantages—money, education, genes—that cost him sympathy in our town, but it wasn't any of that. It was his presumption that his advantages gave him some special standing. He had no need to be condescending, and yet for some reason his soft job, his family money, his luxurious home— all of it together wasn't enough for him. Even when he had Tipton's princess for his bride, it wasn't enough.

I walked out.

My Power Wagon looked like a mud derby winner. Only the wipers' intersecting arcs were clean.

I stared back at the house. Lamplight had turned the stone lintels into gold bars. Above the house and the bare sugar maples flanking it, the cloud cover had separated into magenta strips against a wash of mint blue. To the west, Venus was an inch above the horizon, calm as a pearl.

# 10

It was after six by the time I got back to the cabin. I started a fire in the parlor stove, set a pot of water on to boil, took a long shower, shaved, made a salad of young greens, chives, and a vinaigrette, and opened the wine. At seven-thirty I poured myself a glass and went out on the porch. No better night to try out the new telescope. Quiet air. The stars were crisp, Arcturus prominent,

Aldebaran, Jupiter, and Saturn in conjunction. The waning moon would rise late. I would have taken the time to put the instrument together, but the tripod and the mount for the optical tube were still in the trunk of Wilma's Mazda.

At eight-thirty I tried her cell phone. It was off. I called the convent and left a message on her machine. "Just letting you know I'm not holding supper any longer. Hope you're all right. Call when you can."

I ate the undressed salad from the bowl with my fingers and finished off the wine. After that, unable to sit still, I went out for a walk up to the high, open field behind the cabin. I hadn't gone far before I began to hear a car speeding up the Creamery Road toward the sawmill.

It slowed and turned, its high beams tumbling through the treetops. Wilma.

I jogged back to the cabin, uncorked another Merlot, and fed the woodstove.

But the footfall on the steps said my visitor was a man. Two men. I switched on the porch light and opened the door.

Lieutenant Cahoon bowed slightly. "Sorry to disturb you at this hour, Mr. Bellevance."

He had his flashlight aimed at his feet, which he was wiping carefully on the mat. A second detective, stocky, mid-thirties, was just behind him. He had a square jaw and a wad of scar tissue like a garden slug through half of one eyebrow.

"Not at all," I said. "I've been expecting you."

Cahoon nodded toward his partner. "You two haven't met. This is Detective Sergeant Mason Sammis. He's new up here."

Sammis's handshake was soft.

"Hector Bellevance," I said.

"Heard a lot about you," Sammis said.

I invited them in. Cahoon seemed more bedraggled than

usual. He'd been kneeling in the dirt somewhere. Sammis had a hyper-alertness about him. He stood balanced on the balls of his feet, shoulders loose, like a wrestler. Military haircut, sharp creases to his twill trousers, slip-on rubbers over his oxfords.

"It's dark in here," Cahoon said. "You didn't pay your electric, or what?"

"Since when are my debts a concern of the state?" The lights were off because I'd been out looking at the stars, but I didn't feel that I owed them an explanation.

"I'm only saying here it's eight-forty-five and I see you got all the lights off." He took in the candles in the dining alcove, the unused china, the linen napkins, the glazed pot of tulips. "We interrupting something?"

"It's OK," I said. "Would either of you like something to drink? Glass of water?"

They looked at each other and shook their heads.

I switched on a couple of floor lamps in the living room and then excused myself to go to the kitchen for a glass of tap water, hoping to chase some of the alcohol from my system. It tasted good. Cold, sweet spring water. You could bottle this stuff and sell it. Arrow Lake Elixir, Pure and Natural Vermont Spring Water. How farfetched was that? I blew out the candles. I was feeling muzzy and scattered. What was going on with Wilma? She said she'd call. She'd never stood me up before.

The detectives took seats on either side of my mother's low oak kindergarten craft table, which she'd salvaged during the academy's refurbishment. The surface was bare except for her leatherbound copy of *Leaves of Grass* and a basket of smooth, gray stones she and I had gathered one fall day in a sea cove in Ogunquit. It was hard to believe that was thirty years ago.

I touched a match to the kindling in the fireplace.

Sammis noticed he had cat hair clinging to his trousers—from the Boisverts' place, no doubt—and he swatted at his cuffs.

"Kindly do that outside, Sergeant, won't you?"

"What?"

"The cat hair. If you don't mind." I lowered myself to the hearthstone.

"Sorry." He sat back.

The lieutenant propped his elbows on the arms of Agnes's birch rocker, steepled his fingers, and pressed his lips to them. "First let me say we appreciated your written statement. Now what I would like you to do is reiterate that verbally by going through everything you did today from the time you got up in the morning until the time I met you down in the village. Will you do that for me?"

Cahoon placed his tape recorder on the craft table and clicked it on. The flames climbed through the split ash logs.

When I'd finished my account, he thanked me and said, "Now, if you will, please tell us about Marcel Boisvert."

"What would you like to know?"

He smiled faintly. "Where he is, number one."

"My guess is he's hiding somewhere within a few miles of where he ditched that cruiser."

"He have any connections up across the line, as far as you know?"

"Why? Did he head north?"

Cahoon didn't answer.

"Marcel has friends all over—the Townships, Maine, New Hampshire . . . He also knows the backside of Mount Joe better than any man alive. This is his people's land. He'd sooner die on it than be run off it."

Cahoon sighed. "So why do you think he shot these people?"

"His only child was killed in June. He's been lost to grief ever since. Hitting his wife, too, apparently, which he'd never done before. You've spoken to Mrs. Boisvert about this, haven't you?"

"Earlier today. Mrs. Boisvert is not that helpful. She's got a few shingles rattlin' in the breeze."

"She told you Marcel was abusing her."

"Yup. Judge granted her a relief-from-abuse order. Which you attempted to serve on Boisvert last night. Where's that paperwork, by the way? You still have it?"

"I left it at the town offices. They were faxes, not originals."

"We found the note you left on the clerk's desk. No documents, though."

"Pete would have picked them up there this morning."

"OK. Backing up here, what I been wondering is how come you let him off last night."

"Marcel?"

"Yeah. What's the deal on that?"

"As I said in my statement, he refused to leave the house, and I wasn't prepared to arrest him."

"Why did you go out there if you weren't prepared to arrest him?"

"I was doing Ella a favor. She thought that if I could put it to him the right way and sort of ease him into the idea, he might see reason and leave voluntarily."

"But you know this guy, and you still weren't prepared to go any further?"

"Right. I've known him all my life. I wasn't about to drag him in to jail. Of course, now I wish I had."

"Judge says the man has to vacate. But you say he can stay."

"Lieutenant, his wife was safe. And I didn't want to hurt the old man. He and my father were like brothers."

"You didn't want to hurt the guy, so you tossed the job to Sheriff Mueller, who went out there the next day and got himself killed."

"Considering the circumstances, I think I made a good decision last night. And Pete made a bad decision this morning when he tried to serve those papers by himself."

"See, that's the thing. We don't believe he did that."

"Did what?"

"Went by himself. We have preserved two or three sets of contemporaneous shoe impressions out there besides the sheriff's. We think somebody else went there with him for backup. Somebody with size-thirteen feet. We also believe whoever it was went into that house."

"You think he had backup, and the backup went into the house."

"Him and the sheriff both, yeah. I think the both of them went upstairs and carried the firearms out of the house. You know why? Because the sheriff's wife told us he had his backup lined up before he left his house this morning. You know who she says it was?"

"Who?"

"You."

I shook my head. "I spent the night in Allenburg. Pete and I never spoke. If he tried to reach me here at home, he didn't leave a message."

Cahoon studied me for a moment. The logs settled in the grate. "Sheriff's wife heard him make the call. He talked to you. She says you were going to meet him someplace this morning."

"She's mistaken. He never spoke with me." I stood up. "If there's nothing more, Lieutenant, you're welcome to leave. And I mean now."

Sammis rose, wiping the corners of his mouth with his fingers.

"Pull your shorts out of your crack, Bellevance." He unbuttoned his blazer, exposing his handguns, one under each arm. "This is routine and you know it. Nobody's offending you here. Nobody's working you. We have certain questions only you can answer. OK?" His voice was raspy.

Cahoon patted the air in Sammis's direction. "Sit down, the both of you," he said. "Sit down. Sit down, all right? Bellevance?"

"Five more minutes," I said. In the porch windows I'd caught the sweep of headlights below—someone turning in at the foot of my path. I sat down.

Sammis lowered himself to the edge of the couch.

"Back to this morning," Cahoon said, sighing. "You say you got out to Boisvert's place about eight-fifteen. You found the sheriff dead in the yard, and you proceeded to go into the house to call the barracks. Let me ask you, did you stand around out there in the yard, or did you go right in the house?"

"I went right in."

"Phone you used was the one in the kitchen?"

"That's right."

"Dispatcher didn't log your call till eight-fifty-two. That's over half an hour later."

"I did a walk-through first."

"OK. How come you didn't mention that in your statement?"

"No good reason. I overlooked it."

"I'm gonna have to ask you for the boots you were wearing."

"Take 'em. They're on the mat by the door."

"Just out of curiosity, what made you do a walk-through?"

"The blood on the kitchen wall. I was afraid there might be another victim."

"Yeah? Like who?"

"Like Mrs. Boisvert. I went upstairs and had a look around,

and I decided the blood must have come from the cat. In the bedroom. Am I wrong on that?"

He sat back. "Nope, actually you're right on that. How come you were looking for Mrs. Boisvert when you knew she was out at the McPhetres place? Which you had already communicated to Sergeant Tierney."

"I wasn't sure where she was. The McPhetres place was the place I'd last seen her. Lieutenant, I believe Marcel shot Ella McPhetres because she was protecting his wife. As it happened, I knew that Sergeant Tierney was only three miles from Ella's house at the time, and so I called him. And if I hadn't called him, I believe you'd have yourselves a third victim."

Footsteps on the porch . . . One person.

"We already have ourselves a third victim," Cahoon said.

I pushed up. "If you'll excuse me—" Then I turned on him. "What third victim?"

"We just haven't found the body."

"Whose body?"

Two sharp raps. The door opened and a trooper stepped inside, his eyes finding us across the room. Nut-faced, buzzcut Darryl Munsinger, a gray envelope in his black-gloved hand. "Lieutenant? You got your search warrant."

I rocked my head around. "What the hell is this?"

Cahoon opened the envelope and pulled out some paper. "I apologize again for the intrusion, Mr. Bellevance, but we're going to make a close inspection around the premises. With your kind cooperation."

"Shit, Lieutenant, all you had to do was *ask.*" My ears burned.

"That's nice to hear, but with a . . . *sensitive* guy like you, we didn't want to be too presumptuous."

"What's your rationale for this? Besides making me look bad?"

"Rationale?" He gazed up at me. "My rationale begins with you tracking up two crime scenes like a yokel who has never been on a homicide before. Additionally, you filed a report that omits the fact that you rambled around in that house for half an hour before you called in the crime. What can I say? You're a person of interest, Mr. Bellevance."

He handed me the envelope and added, "Look, I don't know what went down at the Boisvert farm this morning, and I don't know what went down at the Tipton Town Hall. But I do know that what you *say* went down is not the truth. There's omissions and distortions. This troubles me—which I don't think I have to explain to you. So why don't you sit back and read a book while we look around some? We'll be out of your hair before midnight, I promise."

The envelope contained the search warrant and results from the forensics lab in the form of an affidavit. I read them while Munsinger and Sammis poked through my mother's pine secretary.

Cahoon's techs had pulled a lot of bloody gunk out of the trap under the Boisverts' bathtub, and an application of luminol had turned up blood traces clinging to the tub's accumulated residue. "RFLP DNA analysis findings are pending," it said. "Until this data is obtained, standard ABO serological analysis supports a strong probability that the blood samples belong to Marcel Boisvert."

The blood in the trap was AB positive. According to his medical records, Marcel was AB positive, a blood group he shared with less than four percent of humanity. That was all Cahoon needed to conclude that Marcel Boisvert hadn't gotten away as I had been maintaining. He was dead.

According to the warrant, they were looking for "pertinent

court documents," along with "any physical evidence that might support or contradict the Subject's signed Statement of Discovery." Three hours later when they left, besides my new Chippewa work boots, they took my nickel-plated Colt .45 semiautomatic and the brass casing they'd found on the hooked rug out on the glassed-in sleeping porch. It had fallen out of my pocket while I'd changed clothes before dinner.

# TUESDAY

## 11

I woke at six-thirty to another brilliant morning. She wasn't here. I'd gone to bed telling myself she'd tiptoe in cold and tired in the wee hours saying she'd explain everything in the morning. But she wasn't here. I'd been dreaming about her. We'd been flying, or, rather, floating together through the air, drifting above some city park, banking around large trees, barely eluding a few pursuers on the ground below.

I lay in bed trying to reconstruct the dream's particulars, as the sky brightened over the mountain.

The phone rang.

I ran into the kitchen.

"Wilma?"

"It's me."

"Are you all right?"

"Sort of. Are you mad at me?"

"Mad? No, I was worried about you."

"I was hoping you were mad at me."

"Where are you?"

"The greenhouse. I just delivered the rest of your telescope."

"*My* greenhouse?" I went to the window over the sink and looked out that way, even though the greenhouse was out of sight underneath the curve of the hill. "What's going on? How are you?"

"I'm scared. Also pissed off, miserable, and emotionally fried. Not in that order."

"Come on up the hill. I'll make you a waffle."

"A waffle sounds wonderful. But I can't. I thought I could, or I

wouldn't have come all the way out here. But I *can't*. I'm too con-
fused right now. I know I love you, but I don't know if that's
enough."

"Enough for what?"

She didn't answer.

"Do you mean enough to have the baby?"

"Yes."

"That's all right, Wilma. You're just tired. Let's—"

"It's *not* all right! How can you say it's all right?"

"Wilma. Walk up the hill. Please."

"Ordway canned me yesterday."

"He fired you?"

"He fired me, yes."

"How did that happen?"

"Sixty hours a week I put in for that dickwad and his fascist
rag, for seven stultifying years. In exchange for twenty-nine K and
a paid vacation. All I did was give him my two weeks' notice. Common courtesy, and what does he say? *We're gonna miss ya, Wil?*
No. *Good luck in Boston?* No. I would have happily settled for a
simple *Thanks*."

"It's a hard business you're in."

" '*Leave,*' he says. 'Leave today. You're done.' His actual words.
I—I was *speech*less." Her voice broke. "He used to *adore* me!"

"Wilma. Walk up here."

"I can't. I told you, I need time. Maybe it's just hormones, but
when I'm like this I'm no good to anyone. I need time to myself.
Can you respect that?"

"Come up the hill now or I'm coming down there."

"You do and I'm gone."

"Wilma—"

"I'm sorry." She was quiet for a moment. "I'm sorry, Hector.
It's been a real rollercoaster, these last few days."

"Just walk up the hill, Wilma."

"I'll call you when I land someplace. I'll be leaving my cell at the newsroom, just so you know. Sorry, Hector. 'Bye."

I pulled on some jeans and a sweater and jogged down there, but of course she was gone. She'd left the chain-link tread of her Bean boots on the doorsill and, inside, the tripod carton, emblazoned down the sides with red Chinese characters. A copy of yesterday's *Eagle* lay on top.

## Shooting Deaths Rock County

Montcalm County Sheriff Pete Mueller was shot and killed early today at the home of Marcel and Shirley Boisvert in Tipton. Tipton Town Clerk Ella McPhetres was also shot to death this morning in the Tipton Town Hall, according to state police investigators. "We are regarding the two deaths as homicides, and we believe they are related," said Montcalm County State's Attorney Nezzie Holmes.

Marcel Boisvert, a Tipton selectman for 42 years and lifelong resident of the small town, is being sought for questioning in connection with the killings. An intensive manhunt for Boisvert is under way. He is believed to be armed. State troopers from the barracks in Allenburg, Bradford, Middlesex, and Derby are being aided in the statewide search by the New Hampshire State Police, the Vermont National Guard, the Border Patrol, and sheriffs' deputies from five counties.

Minutes after the shootings, an unidentified man was seen speeding north through Tipton village at the wheel of the Montcalm County Sheriff's patrol vehicle, according to Tipton Town Constable Hector Bellevance. That patrol vehicle was recovered by the state police several hours later from the depths of Arrow Lake at the Prentiss Point overlook in Tipton. It has been trucked to the crime lab in Waterbury for detailed analysis. The unidentified driver is missing.

Detective Sergeant Mason Sammis, of the Allenburg Barracks, would not comment on possible motives for either homicide. "This case is just beginning to come into focus. We're not jumping to any conclusions until we have a more complete idea of what happened here."

Lieutenant Brian Cahoon, of the state's Bureau of Criminal Investigation, added, "We obviously want to talk to Mr. Boisvert, but we're still gathering information and processing the evidence from two crime scenes. We don't want to get too far out in front of this."

Town Constable Bellevance, a friend of the two victims, discovered both homicides. He reported them in 911 calls to Allenburg State Police Dispatcher Kevin Willis. Asked if Marcel Boisvert is the chief suspect in the two shootings, Bellevance said, "Definitely. Cahoon knows who he's after."

Residents of this small lakeside community expressed shock and disbelief at the explosion of violence. In conversations this morning . . .

*Cahoon knows who he's after.* Did I say that? Hell. No wonder he was annoyed with me.

A minute later, walking back up from the greenhouse, I happened to notice what looked like woodsmoke far up the ridge north of the mountain, just a wisp against the blue. It might have been in Canada.

I fixed the telescope to its mount and carried it up the knoll, where I sighted in the spotting scope on a tall fir on the ridge, attached the eyepieces, and slowly scanned the ridgeline, north to south. The image trembled in the air currents, but there was definitely a fire out there, a small one, a strand of pale smoke on the boundary of Gaylord Bog. Twelve miles from here. Or more. Wild country. Just a few hunting camps along the west edge of the bog, none of them occupied this time of the year. Couldn't be Marcel. Even if he'd managed to walk across the lake and bushwhack through six miles of softwoods to shelter in some remote cabin, he wouldn't be sending up smoke. Not on a clear, quiet morning.

Some trapper, probably.

Hugh Gebbie had been my mother's partner for twenty-two years, up until the afternoon two summers ago when he found her dead of an aneurysm in her flower garden. A couple of lefty activists, they'd taken on all the good causes, fund-raised for Amnesty International, pushed petitions for hormone-free milk, protested the Gulf War in vigils at the federal building. They traveled all over, snorkeling in the Bahamas each winter, ballooning in Switzerland in the summer. They were also into yoga, birding, mushrooming, wine-making, and dowsing. Agnes was sixty-three when she died. Hugh's remembrance of her at the funeral service had us all laughing for a full half hour.

Hugh Gebbie had been an English teacher at Mount Joseph Academy, the ski school up on the mountain, for most of his life. In the eighties, when the school fell upon hard times, he quit teaching and took up hot-air ballooning. In a few years he found himself the proprietor of Adventures Aloft, a lively business booking aerial tours out of a sheet-metal shed at the turf airstrip in East Allenburg. He decided to sell Adventures after Agnes died, but I knew (because he'd told me) that he still welcomed any excuse to leave the ground—all I had to do was ring him up. So I did.

Hugh called back after checking with the airport. He said the day promised to be ideal for the outing I had in mind, winds light and variable up to 1,000 feet, where they were blowing a steady ten to fifteen out of the northeast. That would make for a funnel effect down the lake gap, which ought to allow us a low sweep of the snowy ice. We agreed to meet in North Shadboro on the heights past Brassaway Pond—the old International Paper Company landing—at eleven.

By the time I'd reached the landing, Hugh and the young couple he had working for him had the balloon laid out on the ground. They were inflating it with a box fan powered by a diesel generator.

We made introductions. Simon and Maria had come from Arizona after answering an ad Hugh had placed in a balloonists' magazine. In exchange for flying lessons, they were serving as his ground crew.

As I watched them scurry around tugging at the billows of red fabric, I couldn't help admiring Hugh's quickness. He was more spry than I was, and he was well over seventy. The yoga, I thought. He made up for his baldness with great, wiry, batwing eyebrows that reached all the way up past the hem of his black knit cap. He had on tan coveralls and a flannel shirt under a down vest.

The balloon was fashioned of eight broad red crescent sections separated by narrow yellow panels. As it filled it looked like a pasha's lounge cushion.

Hugh fired the burners.

Simon guided the basket upright. Hugh scissored over the leather bolster, beckoning for me to follow.

He released the tethers. Condensation from the burners dripped into my hair.

"We've been flying before, haven't we?" Hugh called over the burn. "You and Naomi, right?"

"That was a good many years ago, Hugh."

"The best kind!" he laughed.

We rose fast. Simon and Maria shrank beside the pond, the bog spreading out around them, Simon sweeping his baseball cap back and forth over his head.

Hugh closed the gas valve. At 100 feet the conifers began to look like so many overlapping circles in several shades of green. At 1,000, the air began to carry us west out over the buff and white mosaic of the bog, and you could see it for the prehistoric lake it once was, now a basin of quaking moss, tamarack, sedges, grasses, fir, and black spruce. The welt of an abandoned railroad bed stretched straight across its middle toward the St. Lawrence. The panorama was magnificent.

"This must be what keeps you young, Hugh."

"Ah! Would that it could!"

A five-second burn every minute or so kept us at about 1,200 feet, bearing west-southwest toward the mountain. The view was broad. To the north the plains of Quebec were speckled with houses and farm buildings and crisscrossed by hedgerows and highways, and to the west the spine of the Green Mountains looked dark and worn along its length, except for the thorny crest of Jay Peak. To the south the wooded north pitch of Mount Joseph hid most of the bent finger of Arrow Lake, which gradually seemed to straighten as we sailed around the mountain.

Hugh pulled his radio out of a red daypack. "Maria, this is Fat Bird. Copy?"

"I got you, Bird. You look gorgeous."

"We look like a sore thumb. I just hope the crazed mountain man doesn't decide to take a potshot."

"Whoa, don't say that! You want to jinx yourself? Don't be talking that way, Bird."

Hugh winked at me. "Check you later, amiga. Over and out."

Bubbly, tea-colored ice and crescents of drifted snow filled the oxbows. Snow crusts hugged the reeds and hummocks. The sunlight shimmered where the flow was open through the bog, and vivid scraps of our reflection flashed by beneath us.

Hugh fired the burner. "Pretty ugly terrain, Hector."

"That's the truth."

"This wind's right out of Labrador, too."

"If anybody could survive down in that bog, it's Marcel."

"Oh, I'm sure you're right."

Hugh ended the burn. Leaning down, he pulled a plastic Y-rod out of his pack and extended it out over the bolster, its legs in his upturned fists.

We cruised over a tract of regenerating softwoods in the lee of the ridge where what few camps there were had been built long ago. No woodsmoke anywhere as far as I could see.

After a time, Hugh put away his Y-rod.

We gained speed traversing the ridge, in the flow of air between the face of the mountain and the bluffs across the lake. Out on the plateau, Thad Rowell's twin Harvestor silos were prominent, and the border cut was an unmistakable scar.

Out ahead of us, the flooded marsh near the village looked like pewter. Rafts of ice had been heaved up on either side of the river. As I scanned the piebald surface of the lake with my birdglasses, I realized that Larry Tetrault had managed to get his fishing shanty off the lake, which made me wonder how trustworthy the ice might still be. The track patterns I could make out didn't look recent, but their age was impossible to estimate from these heights. Dog, coyote, deer, a lone skier, and the ribbed beelines of snowmobiles. In the middle of the lake there was a series of mealy pressure cracks, like stretch marks.

"Whoa! See there, to the west?" Hugh said. "Are those snowshoe tracks?"

They looked like a laurel garland stenciled into the ice. "They sure are. Big long Alaskans, by the drag."

"Trending southeast, aren't they?"

"Right. Can we get closer?"

Hugh released heat through the vent at the top of the envelope, and we began to drop. I retraced the snowshoe garland to a cove where a summer pier had been drawn up on the shingle. I lowered the glasses. McPhetres' cove. The curving drive, the fieldstone chimney, the path down through the softwoods to the lake.

Hugh fired the burners. We veered to the south, gaining height again as we flew.

"Troopers," Hugh said. "Out at Prentiss Point."

Two uniforms had come out of the trees for a look at us.

"That's where he sent the sheriff's car off the bluff."

"Yeah, I see the hole," Hugh said. He pulled out the Y-rod again and held it over the ice. "Seems odd, though."

"What does?"

"If he ditched the car here, you'd think he'd cross here, too, wouldn't you? Instead of a mile farther up?"

"Not if he wanted to kill his wife first. He was sure he had time for the job, too. But the police got to Ella's before he did."

"So you think he walked up there and got scared off, then strapped on his snowshoes and hightailed it across the lake?"

"Something like that."

"Why didn't the police see him out on the ice?"

"They must have been concentrating on the house. I don't know."

Hugh got Maria on the radio and instructed her to head for my cabin. He wanted to set us down on the east slope just above my blueberry plantation. He'd put down there in the past, with Agnes. If we didn't make that, he told her, we'd be a hop and a skip from Spud's high corn piece.

The state beach and the fishing access parking areas were flooded. Where the river had sprawled out of the main channel at the inlet, the flow was choked with ice and deadwood. Beneath the village bluff, where the grand Lake House Hotel once overlooked the water, herring gulls had congregated, a lot of them, swirling like confetti.

"See the gulls?"

Hugh nodded. "Masters of the air. It's perfectly glorious, isn't it, the way they seem to— Hey! There he is again!"

The snowshoe prints, stitching the flow and disappearing under the water at the fishing access boat ramp.

"Well, well. He didn't cross after all, did he now?" Hugh said. "He circled back home, the old fox."

I nodded. Once he'd reached the fishing access, he would have been well out of sight of the village. All he had to do was cross the empty highway, walk up through the defunct Lakeview Cabins motor camp, and wade across the flooded pasture. He'd be home.

"Why would he go back to the farm, though?" Hugh said. "Especially when he already knew the law was on to him."

"Must have been something there that he had to have. I left the farm at around nine, and Cahoon didn't make it out to Tipton until after ten, so he had a decent window of time. Though he couldn't have known that."

"Pretty damn chancey, if you ask me, even for a cagy old woodsman like Marcel."

"Whatever he was after, he would have calculated his risks."

Hugh vented a little heat, watching the tops of the trees as we descended toward the rectangle of rooftops that framed the green, the blushing maples, the granite Civil War Widows horse trough, and the new bandstand. Opposite the library on the west end of the common there were three satellite trucks, but no people, none that I could see except for a white-haired woman pumping gas at

Sullivan's store. Branches and dead leaves, a large wooden spool, and a pink Frisbee lay on the tarred roof of the loading dock. The woman caught sight of us and started banging on the top of the car.

"Patrick! Look at the balloon!" We were just a hundred feet overhead.

A small boy pushed open his door. "Ya-HOO!" he called. He waved.

"Greetings, Earthlings!" Hugh intoned in a deep voice.

"Greetings!" they answered together, laughing.

Once everything was packed up onto the trailer, the four of us toasted our excursion with the traditional champagne, and Hugh presented me with his card:

## HUGH GEBBIE
### Geomancer, Remote Locator

**Treasure, Water, Persons, and Noxious Fields Detected
Harmful Energies Dispersed, Sundry Mysteries Resolved**

*12 Buell Way, North Allenburg, Vermont 802-668-9099*

"You be sure and call me, Hector—or better yet, stop by the Dowsers' Society bookshop sometime tomorrow afternoon. By then I ought to have more for you on Marcel Boisvert."

I promised I would.

I had seven messages: Jill at the food co-op, trying to line up suppliers; two Tipton selectmen wanting to make sure I would come to an emergency meeting Monday night; a reporter from the *Burlington Free Press*; another reporter from Vermont Public Radio; and the AP stringer out of Montpelier. Last was Rob Tierney, asking me to call him at his office right away.

He picked it up on the third ring. "Hey," he said, "I hear Lieutenant Cahoon's been giving you a hard time."

"I'd be doing the same."

"Yeah, well, I'm behind you a hundred percent."

"Thanks, Rob. Find anything in Pete's cruiser?"

"Some latents and some blood traces, and you're gonna love this—we found the missing hand."

"In the sheriff's car?"

"In the glove compartment. Wrapped in a plastic bag."

"Then it was Pete who picked it up out at Rowell's."

"You'd think. Only when Griswold talked to Pete Sunday night, Pete told him he didn't know where the hand was. Why would he say that if it was in his glove compartment?"

"Don't know. What's Cahoon think?"

"He thinks somebody stuck it in there later. You, for instance."

"I never had it, Rob."

"That's what I told him. The problem is Cahoon's convinced Boisvert never left that house alive, and you're not only insisting that he did, but that you actually *saw* him. Cahoon also thinks the killer knows a thing or two about homicide."

"He's basing all this on blood evidence?"

"Yeah. Also, as first responder, you went and tracked up both scenes. And you fired your .45, which was loaded with hollow points. And you admit that you and Boisvert almost got physical the night before. And also there's your take-no-prisoners reputation."

"That's bullshit."

"I know. Personally, I think Cahoon's out to make you look like a fuckup."

"I am a fuckup. Where does that get him as long as there's a killer loose out there?"

"Or two killers."

"You don't think it's Marcel."

"No, I don't."

"You think I killed him?"

"No, Hector, I don't. But whoever did kill him had a cold-blooded attitude about it. Plus, as far as your past? The record shows you made reasonable decisions in every single situation they looked into."

"That's my recollection."

"You're not a fuckup is what I'm saying. I told Cahoon, 'Belle-vance never made a bad shoot.' "

"I appreciate it."

"Yeah, he wasn't impressed."

I telephoned the house in Allenburg where Shirley was staying, hoping she'd feel composed enough to talk to me. She couldn't have found a more comfortable refuge than the Shapiro home. Emily and her husband, Michael, a longtime pediatrician in town, owned one of the majestic Victorian-era mansions that lined South Main. Today most of them had been taken over by law firms, accountants, and undertakers, if they hadn't been subdi-vided into apartments, but the Shapiros' was still the elegant residence it had been built to be in the days when Allenburg was a rail hub and trains drove the nation's commerce.

Emily answered. She knew me, knew who I was, anyway. She'd served with my mother on the board of the Montcalm County Arts Council. She said Shirley was upstairs resting. The state police in-vestigators had been at her for three hours that morning.

"Is she holding up all right?"

"She's subdued. How much of that is the medication she's tak-ing I wouldn't want to guess. Michael and I have our concerns on that score, I don't mind telling you. The woman is downing a *lot* of Ativan, and she's not being monitored at all. Her primary care—naming no names—is an octogenarian she won't hear of kissing off, and she hasn't been to see her shrink since last summer, which *I* think—"

"I'm sorry, Emily, but I'm pressed for time. Would you put Shirley on the line, please?"

"Oh, certainly. Forgive me. You hold on." I heard her set the phone down.

Shirley picked up an extension. "Mr. Bellevance?"

"How are you doing, Shirley?"

"Pretty good, I guess. Marcel has gone and done it now, hasn't he?"

"It looks that way."

"The papers are saying it's my fault for going to the judge about a court order. But I took about as much as I could of him beating on me. And Lucy Pratt, the social worker that come down to the hospital, she backed me up on it. You can ask her."

"It wasn't your fault, Shirley."

"I know it! He coulda killed me, too. He knew where I was stayin'. Ella let that slip—unless it was you."

"You're safe now at Emily's. There ought to be an officer watching the house."

"It's just Lew Pfister. He's out there pickin' his nose right now." Her voice drifted from the mouthpiece. "Who's looking after Marc? They're not leaving that up to his dad, I hope."

"Marc's all right, Shirley. No need to worry."

"No? I hear Rita Brasseur kicked him out of her money-grubbing operation. Where's he supposed to stay all day while Vaughn's up at the college teaching his classes?"

"Wherever he is, I'm sure he's fine."

"But how do you *know*? That's what I'm saying."

"Vaughn's a caring, responsible father. He'll make sure—"

"Not when he's keeping him cooped up in his office like he was last fall. That was just a *terrible* situation. People walking in and out, trying to get their work done. Those fat-ass secretaries, all they did was stick him in a corner with a box of crayons and tell him to keep himself busy."

"All right. I'll look into the arrangement, Shirley, if it'll make you feel better."

"I'll tell you one thing. He just had the best time when he was here Monday. Emily's kids are away in college, you know, and there's all these books and games and toys downstairs like you wouldn't believe. Marc was in seventh heaven."

"I'll talk to Vaughn."

"Good. If I just knew where he was, I'd feel better. And could you check on Celeste for me while you're at it?"

It took me a second to realize she was asking about her cat. "Did the police tell you anything about Celeste?"

"They said they ain't seen her. I told 'em, look under the house. Anything scares her, she goes under the house where it's broke away there under the porch. You got to crawl in under there and grab her."

"Shirley, with all the commotion out at your place the last two days, it's no wonder Celeste has disappeared."

"I'm telling you, you got to get down on your knees and *look*."

"OK."

"And if you don't see her, it could be she went all the way up to the salvage yard. She'll do that. That's the only thing about Celeste I don't like—how she'll cavort with them Osgoods."

"Shirley, while I have you, let me ask you something. Does Marcel wear a bright red cap?"

"What you can do, just leave a dish of tuna out under the step—oil tuna—even if you don't see her."

"Shirley. Does Marcel ever wear a red cap?"

"Huntin', he does. Or else orange. For everyday, he's got a black cap. He's got two. Both of 'em are Ford, with the Ford insignia."

"He doesn't have a red cap that says 'Utah'?"

"Oh, *that* cap? He don't wear that one. Kathy sent him that cap when she went out west last spring. Come in the mail the day after we heard. Marcel never even touched that cap. Just left it setting there on the breakfast table. He wouldn't let me clear it away, either. Just left it there to torture himself with."

"Thanks. Do you and Marcel own a canoe?"

"Nope. Used to, but he traded it for something. You probably think that's strange, couple old Indians living down on the river and they don't even got a canoe."

"I was just wondering. Suppose Marcel wanted to cross the ash plain and the river. How do you think he would do it?"

"How would he do it? I don't know how he'd do it. Maybe take that kayak."

"What kayak?"

"Kathy's kayak. Been out in the shed right where she left it since the last time she used it. Her and Vaughn."

"What color is it?"

"What color? No color. Brown, I guess you'd call it."

I told her I'd call back when I had some word about Marc.

"You'll be talking to Vaughn, then?"

"I'll try, Shirley. Sometime tomorrow."

"Well, when you do, you tell him the boy's good with me. Just like it was before. Nothing's changed. Tell him I won't charge him a nickel."

"I'll tell him."

"And don't forget about Celeste, either. Put some food out like I said, a little oil tuna, if you see her or not. It's on the east side there, where the slats is broke away, down behind the hydrangeas."

"I'll do what I can, Shirley."

# 12

I tossed my waders into the bed of the Power Wagon and drove down to the village, stopping at Sullivan's for gas, mail, milk, and eggs. It was good to see Peg Gonyaw back at her post again behind the register after another round of treatments for breast cancer. Peg had been a fixture at Sullivan's, day in day out, six days a week, since I was in grade school. I asked how she was feeling.

"Hoo! I am *whipped*." She lifted her eyeglasses and rubbed the bridge of her nose. "When did all this *start*? Two days ago? I have fixed more pots of coffee in the last two days than I make in a *month*. And I hope I never *see* another doughnut. Doughnuts and sticky buns. That's about all these jokers recognize as *food*."

"Quieting down out there, by the looks of things."

"Yeah, they been cutting out for some reason. I don't know why—it's not like the case is solved. Quite the scene while it lasted, though. Jesus, we had CBS-TV here, NBC, CNN, Fox News, couple Canadian stations . . . and oh, yeah!" She reached for my arm across the belt. "*People* was here. This little shitass from *People*—kid, basically, suit and tie. He comes in here—" She glanced behind her toward the meat case to be sure the new owner, Jerry Eubank, was not in sight. "Get this—" She jabbed her thumb over her shoulder toward the wall behind her, where a patchwork of Cy Sullivan's look-what-I-killed photos still covered the corkboard divider. Cy used to run a game-reporting station out on the loading dock. Peg whispered, "I sold this city kid *three* of them snapshots. Fifty bucks apiece!"

"Of Marcel?"

"No, *Madonna*." She frowned at me. "Of *course* Marcel!"

"Nice goin', Peg."

"Then I go home and tell Frankie and he goes, 'Dummy, you shoulda said a hundred.' " She rang up my purchases. "He's dead, ain't he, Hector?"

"I wouldn't venture to say, Peg."

"You know Misty Hoyt? Her son works Customs? Misty says either he slipped across into Canada while the Border Patrol was looking for him over on the other side of the mountain, or he went off in the bog somewhere and blew his brains out."

"Anything's possible."

"I guess! First Kathy kills herself sky-diving, and now Marcel goes berserk and shoots Petey and Ella." She clucked. "No telling what's around the next bend, is there, Hector?"

"That's for sure. What's Del Osgood smoke, Peg?"

"Deputy D?" She bunched her lips. "Dorals—if he can't get Camels."

"I'll have a carton of the Camels, then."

She took the box from the rack beside the lottery machine. "What do you think, Hector? You think Marcel's still alive?"

"I think we'll find out before too much longer."

"You know what I think? I think he went out on the lake, and *ploop*—offed himself. He won't be bobbing up again till the ice goes out."

"You could be right."

"Everybody that comes in the store, they ask me, 'Can you *believe* it? *Marcel*?' " She hooted. "You kiddin' me? Damn straight I believe it! Ever since Kathy got killed, the guy's been a walking time bomb. All you had to do was look at him. Only thing that surprises me is he didn't take out Vaughn Higbee while he was at it." She glanced around for Jerry again. "Instead of Ella, who was a perfect angel. Comes to seventy-two twenty-five, Hector."

I made the change for her.

Del Osgood had his cruiser parked across the lake road where it joined School Street, same spot I'd first met Cahoon the day before. Someone had moved the town's orange sawhorses to one side.

I pulled up next to Del. His window slid down. On the passenger side sat some blonde. By the way he was sitting, I gathered he didn't want me to get a good look at her.

"I'm going to drive around you, Del, if you don't mind."

"Can't let you do that, Mr. Bellevance. Authorized law enforcement personnel only."

"Add me to the list. I'm not going out to Boisvert's. I'm headed for the fishing access."

"Sorry, can't be done. All flooded anyhow. Why you want to go down there?"

"My regular patrol, Del."

"What regular patrol?"

"The Lakeview Cabins are an attraction for vagrants. I cruise by there every evening."

"Bullshit. There's no vagrants out there."

"That's because I cruise by every evening."

"Yeah, right. Well, tonight you're cutting the vagrants a break. State police got a grid search in progress out on the High Settlement Road, and nobody that isn't connected to the investigation goes beyond this point."

"Del, let me ask you something. You're the officer who picked up that hand out at Rowell's on Sunday afternoon, am I right?"

His eyes narrowed. "Wait. What's this about?"

"Pete sent you to Rowell's to pick up that hand. And you did, but then you got off track somehow. Because instead of turning the hand over to the ME as you were supposed to, you ended up taking it home. Didn't you?"

He turned in amazement to the blonde beside him, then back to me. "Who the hell's feeding you this stuff? Maureen?"

Maureen Osgood was his father's third wife. In recent months she'd been managing the family scrap metal business, D.O.A. Recycling & Salvage, a mile or so beyond the Boisverts', since Dwight Osgood had declined enough to need portable oxygen.

"Monday morning you and Pete went out to Boisvert's together to serve that court order. That's when you gave Pete the hand, isn't it?"

"No! I gave him the hand, all right, but I didn't go out to Boisvert's with him. He didn't want me to. He was pissed at me— and that's what he was pissed about, was that fucking *hand*."

"Don't give me that, Del. We both know he wouldn't take on Marcel by himself. He couldn't locate me that morning, so he recruited *you*."

"Yeah? You think you're a fucking genius. You don't know what happened. We got into it that morning, all right? Me and Pete. He threatened to get *rid* of me. He called me an *electorial liability*."

"And what did he mean by that?"

"He told me he didn't approve of some of my associations— so-called. Like I need his approval who I hang out with. Ask

Maureen. She heard what he said. Hey, I'm sorry he got himself killed, but after the way he reamed me out in front of my parents? I wouldn't have watched his back for him if he *asked* me to."

"You gave him the hand."

"Sure I gave it to him. I wasn't gonna keep it. Thing was starting to smell bad enough."

I extended my arm into the space between our vehicles, offering Del the carton of Camels.

"What's this?" He took it.

"Token of appreciation. You do your job well, Delmore. I'm counting on you to let me do mine."

I rolled up my window and drove straight ahead onto the Presbyterian church lawn and around onto the Lake Road, spraying clots of turf, dragging my tailpipe through the ditch. In my sideview, I could see Del. He'd gotten out of his car and stood watching me over the roof until I rounded the long bend down toward the ash plain.

The light was off the lake surface. The willows along the shore were like a fringe of black lace against the sunlit face of the mountain. Where the High Settlement Road met the Lake Road it was blocked by two cruisers parked nose to nose. Beyond them there were half a dozen more cruisers along the roadside. I slowed for a look. Two unmarked cars and the mobile crime lab occupied the short, tree-canopied lane down to the Boisverts'.

I left my truck at the line of ice and flood debris where the water lapped at the pavement and walked into the field along the margin of the flood, waders over my shoulder. After about five minutes I cut some clearly recent scrapes in the duff and, after that, about ten feet up the slope, the plain curve of a boot heel in a pad of club moss.

On the rise, under a stand of venerable white pines, stood two rows of decrepit clapboard huts with tattered screens and small, rotten porches. The Lakeview Cabins hadn't seen lodgers since the interstate went through east of the mountain. The grounds were buried deep in pine needles and branches.

The prints lacked detail, but it was obvious that someone had passed between the last two cabins, over the crest, and down the other side into a long-neglected hayfield, making straight for Marcel's flooded pasture, which was marked on this side by a tumbled stone wall. Ahead, across twenty acres of shallow water, Marcel's derelict outbuildings were lit up like a movie set.

As I sloshed up under the willows that bounded the yard, a couple of million-candlepower spotlights picked me out, obliterating the twilight.

"Halt right where you are!"

I shaded my eyes with my arm.

A generator was chugging somewhere out front.

"Is that who I think it is?" a deep voice said.

"Shit, do you believe this guy?" It was Cahoon.

I said, "Redirect those spots, will you, please?"

The glare left my face.

Cahoon and Sammis met me at the edge of the water. Floodlights stood on tripods behind them. I couldn't make out anyone else in the glare—though most of the activity seemed to be inside the house.

"You truly astound me, Bellevance," Cahoon said. "What in the *hell* are you doing out here?"

"I found some footprints back across the way, in among the old cabins along the highway. I think it's possible they're Boisvert's."

"You do? What makes you think that?"

"Someone on snowshoes came off the ice at the estuary within the last day or two. I followed the waterline up from the fishing access, and I found a string of partial impressions heading straight for this farm."

He considered this. "OK. You're suggesting Boisvert fled from the scene in the patrol vehicle, then he ditched the vehicle at the overlook, put on his snowshoes, and walked back to where he had just fled from. On the frozen ice. That it?"

"Somebody came walking back here, yes."

"In broad daylight. What would he want to come back here for?"

"There's a good chance he was planning to walk across the lake, but then thought better of it. Tell me this. Did you happen to come across a kayak out here anywhere?"

"A kayak." Cahoon turned to Sammis. "I get it. Boisvert came back for his kayak. So he could paddle across the flooded river and then vanish into the puckerbrush like Eric Rudolph. You like that theory?"

"Shirley Boisvert told me there was a kayak here," I said. "In a shed. It belonged to her daughter. Did you come across a kayak, or didn't you?"

"Did we or didn't we?" Cahoon asked Sammis.

Sammis shook his head. "Didn't."

"Right," Cahoon said. "I gotta tell you, Constable, we've been all up and down that side of the river. It's super muddy along through there, as you know. We turned up no scuffs, no depressions, no footprints, no nothing—no sign of human traffic whatsoever."

"The boot prints I found are easy to miss. He came off the lake on snowshoes and hiked over the rise from the county road. If you can tear yourself away for a moment here, I'll be happy to show you."

"Boisvert wasn't wearing his boots when he bought it, Mr. Bellevance," Sammis said.

"What's that mean? You found him?"

Sammis blinked.

I turned to Cahoon. "Did you find him or not?"

"Did you kill him or not?" Sammis said behind me.

I spun around. "I didn't kill him, for Christ's sake. That makes no sense! Tierney and I both saw him go by in the sheriff's car. If that wasn't Boisvert, who was it?"

Cahoon said, "I am of the opinion that Boisvert is dead. And I know for a fact that you're a killer. My apologies if you're offended by the implications."

"I'm not offended. I'm disgusted."

"You know what I don't get, Bellevance?"

"Where do you want me to start?"

"A man with all your experience, how come it's so hard for you to grasp the position you're in?"

"I grasp it. If I didn't grasp it, I wouldn't be here."

He took a step closer. "Listen to me. The only connection you have to this homicide investigation is that you are a subject *of* it. You understand me? You stay out of my face from here on out. If you can't restrain yourself, I will jail your ass for obstruction. Is that clear to you?"

I said that it was.

He nodded. "Fine, then. You're free to go. Have a nice evening."

"You check out those footwear impressions, will you? Before the weather intervenes."

They were already headed back toward the lights.


After I got a fire going in the greenhouse, I went up to check my messages. It was about thirty degrees. Snow was sifting down as I climbed the hill.

Three hang-ups and three reporters. Nothing from Wilma.

I called the farm. "Am I too late for supper?"

Spud was delighted. "Hell no, we barely sat down. Hope you're hungry—it's Brenda's pork-chop-and-noodle casserole with onions and mushrooms and sour cream. She fixed blueberry-cinnamon cobbler for dessert, too—made with *your* blueberries."

"Sounds terrific. Want me to bring the beer?"

"I never turned down a beer in my life. But don't dilly-dally, all right? It's ready. Heck's comin' up right off," I heard him say as he hung up the phone.

I found them on opposite sides of the trestle table with a Corningware casserole between them on a trivet, watching *Wheel of Fortune*. For atmosphere in their dining nook they liked to keep an antique oil lamp burning, both of them unfazed by the stink of kerosene.

"Lyle sacked out already?" The baby's high chair was empty.

Brenda zapped the TV. "Yeah, he's got a bug. Poor little guy's not sleepin' too good. You have to keep suctioning the mucus out of him."

Spud half rose and patted the bench next to him, "Sit down, sit down."

Brenda dished out the egg noodles and pork chops and passed around a bowl of pickled corn and a jar of her applesauce. I opened three ales.

"You seen the paper?" Spud asked.

I shook my head. "Worth reading?"

"Hell, yes! The manhunt's national news, Heck."

"So what's the latest?"

"Marcel friggin' juked 'em. If he got up into that bog, shit, that's his own preserve up there."

"Hugh flew me out over the bog this afternoon. I don't see how he could have gotten that far. North of the ridge the snow's still waist-deep—tough going, even on snowshoes."

"You flew out there? You and Hugh?" He laughed. "What did he do, dangle a crystal over the ground?"

"He had a Y-rod."

"I love it!" Brenda said. "Old Hugh. He is a piece of work, isn't he?"

Spud held his rough hands over the table. "He detects earthly emanations."

"Don't be mocking him," Brenda scolded. "You were pretty impressed by the whole Fred Urie thing."

"I'm not mocking him. I wish I was smart as old Hugh."

"Tell Hector about the Urie farm."

Spud sat back. "Guy I know, Fred Urie, farms with his dad over in Morrisville. Four-five years ago he calls up Hugh because he's just desperate and somebody told him to call Hugh Gebbie. Seems Fred's herd is having all kinds of problems—lot of mastitis, low appetite, production's way down—and his kids are cranky doing chores, and basically nothin's going right. Anyway, old Hugh goes over there, and in one day he solves the problem. Turns out Fred's barn is situated right over a vein of bad energy. There's all this energy running underground like water, right? And Urie's bad vein was screwing up their immune systems—the cows' *and* the kids'. Hugh scopes it out with a crystal, and then he takes a hammer and he pounds a bunch of rebar in the ground in the right places, and the farm gets cured! Swear to God. Urie doubles his production and his kids and cows mellow right out. It's true. Ask Wilma. There was a whole article on it in the *Times-Argus*."

"Hugh's got some kind of paranormal ability," Brenda said. "I really do believe that. We don't know half what there is to know about how this world works. We think we do, but we don't."

Spud said, "How come Wilma isn't doing the murder story? This guy Baxter, whatever his name is, I never heard of him before. All he puts in is what somebody tells him to put in. There's no *analysis*."

"Wilma's left the paper," I said.

"What do you mean? She quit?"

"She got hired away by the *Boston Globe*."

"The *Globe*? No shit. So does that mean she's moving down to the big city?"

"I expect so."

Spud nodded, not sure what to say. He cut out the heart of a chop and piled so many noodles onto it with his knife that he had to lift it to his mouth with the tines pointing down.

"Hear that?" Brenda said.

She meant the noise I'd been thinking was a tree branch screeching against the clapboards.

"The kid," Spud said.

Brenda excused herself. "One sec."

Spud served me more applesauce. "Man. Don't ever have kids, Hector. You start in having kids and it's always something."

"Like cows."

"Oh God. Worse. Cows pay you back."

"Wilma was pregnant when she left," I said.

He tapped his bread knife on the table. "Yours?"

I nodded.

"Damn. She gonna keep it or what's she gonna do?"

"She hasn't decided."

"Well, hell. Be a damn shame if she bails on you. You'd make a great dad, Heck."

"Wilma said the same thing."

"Because it's obvious. No better place for a kid to grow up, either."

"She's moving to Boston, Spud."

"No, that's what I'm saying." He pushed his plate away with

his thumb. "Boston. Shit, you just barely got your ass *out* of Boston."

"I can't go back, either."

"That's a tough one, Heck. These professional women, you can't keep 'em in the pasture. Weak spot in the fence, they're gonna find it."

I nodded.

"Anyhow, I got something I want to show you."

He motioned for me to slide off the end of the bench so he could leave the table. When he came back he was carrying a thick, four-foot slab of sanded pine that he'd cut with a jigsaw into the shape of a half-shucked ear of corn.

"Not finished, obviously, but . . ." He handed it to me.

"This is a very fine piece of work, Spud. Your sign, right?"

" 'The Amazing Maze,' you got it. I'm gonna paint it yellow and green and stick it up down at the end of the Creamery Road."

"Well, I wouldn't put it where I couldn't keep an eye on it."

"How come?"

"This is just the kind of ready-made folk art some city person'll make off with first chance." I gave it back to him.

"I didn't think of that."

"Spud, here's a question for you. You remember who those kids were, ten-twelve years ago, the ones who pushed a car off the overlook out at Prentiss Point?"

"Yeah. That was Jeremy Hinton and them. Summer before junior year."

"Delmore Osgood was in on that prank, too, wasn't he?"

He chuckled, nodding. "It was Jeremy Hinton, mainly. He was the badass. But Delmore, yeah, him and Russ Wheatley. I almost think a couple of summer camp girls went along for the giggles."

"They were hell-raisers, weren't they—Del and Jeremy?"

"Oh God. Wicked. It was them shot four of Dan Felton's

heifers next Halloween night. They even bragged around about it, but nobody could prove they did it. They torched Crooked Bridge over in Tewkesville, too. Same deal. They finally got nailed trying to steal a brand-new snow machine off a trailer down at the truck stop. Turned Delmore right around, though, getting busted like that."

"What's Jeremy Hinton up to these days?"

"Hell, he's in jail, Hector. For selling *heroin*, if you can believe that. Shithead was dealing bags out of a motel room down in White River."

"No kidding. How long ago was this?"

"Oh, must be three years now. He had this Colombian drug connection in Springfield, Mass. Shit, I never thought there was any kind of market for heroin up here in Vermont."

"It's everywhere."

"Well, I guess so. Whole damn *world's* goin' to hell."

"Strange to think of Jeremy doing a stretch for trafficking while Delmore's an officer of the law."

"Yes, didn't them two turn out different?" He shook his head, then brightened. "You know what I just thought of? That time that car was in the lake, you remember Marcel telling everybody he could just winch the wreck out of the water? Remember that?"

"Didn't the state send a crane up from Montpelier?"

"Yeah, but they took so damn long getting around to it that Marcel was gonna get it done himself. Took the grader out to the point. State engineer talked him out of it. He woulda tore the bank all to hell if he'd tried that, but goddamn, that was Marcel. He said it was polluting our lake and he was sick of setting back and letting that happen. But you know what? *That* is what it took to get the state's ass in gear. Marcel. I'm gonna miss him."

Brenda never did return to the table. We cleared the dishes to the sideboard. Spud offered me a bag of Lorna Doones and a cup of instant decaf. I wondered about the blueberry cobbler, but all I asked him was whether he'd mind looking in on my operation now and then over the next few days—just to make sure my tender things stayed warm and watered.

He nodded. "Glad to. How come? You headin' to Boston?"

"I might."

"Women. They sure do complicate things, don't they?"

"They do. We ask for it, though."

He laughed. "Yes, I guess we do."

# WEDNESDAY

# 13

G old capital letters glued to the door of a chest freezer read:

**D.O.A. RECYCLING & SALVAGE**
**DWIGHT OSGOOD, PROP.**

A long, potholed drive led through twenty acres of junk interspersed with popple and white spruce. Dwight Osgood collected and processed metals and sold them by the container load to a recycler across the line in Sherbrooke. Gutted car and truck bodies made up the bulk of it—wheels, engine blocks, frames, and body parts all in their own hills. Home appliances, steel desks, paint cans in rusty mounds, snowmobile cowlings, ductwork, sinks and toilets and bathtubs set out in rows, sheets of roofing and siding, lengths of pipe and used culvert and girders, and a palisade of fifty-five-gallon drums.

The drive ended in a gravel clearing on the riverbank. Two mobile homes—office space and residence—stood side by side, connected by a crushed-stone patio. The covered patio had a big gas grill and a picnic table and two motorcycles under shrouds.

Dwight was dying. Because of that, the local outdoorsmen and environmentalists who had mobilized last year to force him to move off the water had backed down. Marcel, a lifelong fisherman with a family farm two miles downriver from D.O.A., had been one of the main agitators. He and the others were sure that heavy metals, motor oil, battery acid, and who knew how many other pollutants had to be leaching into the water table and the river.

When a few trout and bass were caught last summer with spongey growths on their gills, and the kids began finding two-legged frogs in the back bay, the concerned residents of Tipton persuaded the state's Agency of Natural Resources to send up a team of inspectors for a site visit, but for some reason the team was unable to find proof that Dwight's business amounted to more than a visual blight on the landscape.

Of course, that didn't end it. After town meeting, four of Tipton's selectmen—Marcel among them—petitioned Paxton Massingill, our state senator, to sponsor a bill that would have allocated state funds to seize the Osgood property by eminent domain. Massingill never offered the bill, but the ploy infuriated Dwight Osgood, since he'd already been cleared by the state's own experts. It also angered Ella. Ella wanted Dwight's eyesore off the river as much as the next person, but for Marcel and the others to threaten a sick man that way looked to her like an attempt to drive him to his grave.

"It's Hector Bellevance!" Maureen called out. She pushed the porch door open for me. "What do we owe the pleasure?"

"Few questions, Maureen"—I held up my spiral-bound notebook—"if I may."

"What about?"

"The sheriff and Delmore."

"Oh God. All right, come on in," she sighed. "Don't mind the clutter."

A dirty white dog, part pit bull by the muzzle, was crouched in the seat of a glider, growling.

"Dee-dee," Maureen scolded, "act nice. Her back legs don't function," she told me. "She's nothing but a pitiful cripple. Aren't you, Dee-dee?"

The dog kept growling.

Maureen ushered me into an overheated kitchen space and

lifted a stack of newspapers from a wooden chair to make me a place to sit.

"How's Dwight been doing lately?" I asked her. "I missed him at town meeting."

"He's doing good. 'Course, since Monday we both been spooked by the murders. But I feel a little better now that they're figuring Marcel ain't the one behind this carnage."

"What makes you think he isn't?"

"Well, the blood. You know."

"No, I don't. Tell me."

"They found blood in Marcel's septic, which they know is his. And from the *quantity* of it, they figure he probably got killed, too."

"Did Delmore tell you this?"

She nodded and colored. "I thought you knew."

"The police don't have a body yet, Maureen. Or a DNA result. Until they do, we can't be sure of anything."

"I know that, but it could be quite a little while before they find it. If they find it."

"Maureen, on Monday morning before he was killed, the sheriff stopped by here to see Delmore. Right?"

"Well, he called first. Dummy wasn't answering his pager. Sheriff apologized and all, and I gave him Tildy's number, this piece of trash Del's been seeing, and then half an hour later sheriff shows up all in a lather, and he's like, 'Where is Del?' How the hell do I know? We're still in bed, right? I mean, it's barely light out. Then, two minutes later, Del drives in. OK, fine. I go inside and I'm in here making French toast, and the window's open so I can hear 'em out in the yard, Pete's ragging on Delmore, calling him a poon-hound and all these names, right? Calling him an undependable, lying piece of crap, this kind of thing. And Del's yelling for him to frig off, he won't let no button-dick lard ball insult his fiancée. And here I'm thinking, *fiancée?*"

From another room Dwight called, "It was 'cause of that *hand,* Maureen. He left it in the bathroom—the office bathroom. Remember?"

"I was getting to that. Yeah, see, Del had custody of this mummified hand. Some dog found it out in the woods someplace, and Pete and Del went out there, and Del found the dead body it came from, and so he brought the hand by the yard so me and Dwight could look at it."

"You say he left the hand here?"

"Dwight?" she called over her shoulder. "You sure he left it here? Actually," she said to me, "I think he took it with him. He wanted to show it to Tildy. His *fiancée.*"

"It was in the office!" Dwight said.

"No wonder Pete was angry," I said. "He's got his deputy treating forensic evidence like a trophy."

"Yeah, well, Del never was that big on rules and regulations. You know, Pete only hired him as a favor to Dwight. Myself, I never thought he'd last six months."

Dwight came toward us trailing one arm along the wall for balance and wheeling a tank of oxygen, the tubes yoked to his nose. He wore moccasins flattened at the heels and a baggy sweater over a T-shirt. Dwight had been a hard, robust man all his life, with glinting eyes, sharp cheekbones, dark wavy hair that stood high in his head, and a menacing thinness to his nose and lips. Now his face was liverish and slack, all the menace gone, and he kept his long, oily hair hooked behind his ears in crescents. Maureen helped him lower himself into a plaid recliner in the living room.

I squatted beside him and patted his knee. "You gonna make it, Dwight?"

"Doc says I got a couple years. I don't believe him, but I ain't cryin'." His breath was foul. His rootlike fingers wagged on their own.

"This contraption must be a nuisance," I said.

"Shit, you kiddin' me? This here's a goddamn lifesaver."

I laughed and stood. "Do either of you remember hearing gunshots early Monday morning? Cars speeding by?"

"No shots," Maureen said. "Cars, definitely. Troopers were tearing up and down the Settlement Road the whole damn day."

Dwight shook his head and coughed. "I'm dry, Mo."

Maureen found an open can of Dr Pepper beside the recliner and set it between his legs.

Dwight took a long swallow, sucked his teeth, and said, "It don't surprise me one bit Marcel Boisvert's in the middle of all this."

"Why's that?"

"You know why. Bastard's been persecuting the people of this town too long. It was bound to come back around and bite him in the ass." He looked at Maureen. "I told him, too. Didn't I, Mo?"

"You told him, all right. That day he was up here tromping around with these geeks from Natural Resources—Dwight told him right to his face."

The gas furnace kicked in with a whoosh. "Let me ask you, Maureen. When Pete left the scrap yard that morning, did Del leave with him?"

She shook her head. "Sheriff drove off separate. Del left a few minutes later."

"How many's a few minutes? Three? Ten?"

"Less than ten. I remember, I yelled out to him, 'You want some French toast?' He never answered me. I think he was too wrought up to eat."

"Where did he go when he left?"

"Hell if I know. Back to his girlfriend's."

"Tildy?"

"Tildy, right." She shook her head. "It'll kill Dwight if he marries that slut."

"Where does Tildy live, do you know?"

"Some apartment in town. She waitresses out to R&J's, if you want to talk to her. Skinny blonde with a boob job."

R&J's Diner, just opposite the North Allenburg interstate exit, was famous for its Green Mountain fries and huge glazed doughnuts. The truck stop behind it—showers, lockers, video games, twenty-four-hour diesel—made it a popular spot. I pulled in at the height of the breakfast rush, all the booths and stools jammed with college kids, log-haulers, deliverymen, along with a fair number of state troopers and other uniforms, and half a dozen people waiting for a table.

I watched the waitresses' station for a minute or two. No skinny blondes, so I walked over to the manager—gold wristwatch, starched white shirt, red bow tie—who was talking sports with a couple of salesmen. He broke away and offered to seat me at the counter if I was alone. I thanked him and said I just wondering if he would tell me when Tildy might be working.

"Would I?" He lowered his glasses and studied me. "Tildy won't be in till three. What are you, her parole officer?"

I explained who I was. "I need some information from her, that's all. Where does she live?"

"What am I, her pimp?" He glanced at the salesmen beside me. "A comedian we got here."

I jabbed a hard finger into the middle of his chest. "Listen. This is as unfunny as it gets. Monday morning two people I have known all my life were murdered a few miles from here. Whatever I have to do to nail their killer I'm going to do. My advice to you is don't stand in my way."

His cheek was trembling. "Tildy and Crissy. Yellow tenement house on Mexican Street. Gallery porches along the front. Right across from the new Cumberland Farms. Can't miss it."

I thanked him for his cooperation.

Mexican Street was a steep little jut off the truck route just east of Allenburg. Three buildings on the right—Ribidoux Welding, a boarded-up duplex with NO TRESPASSING signs all over it, and a three-story clapboard monstrosity on the shoulder of the railroad embankment. Pigeons roosted under the flaking eaves. Matted paper trash lay under the sumac along the embankment. Burger King bags and supermarket sales flyers. Three sagging galleries in front, the one on the ground floor hung with laundry, men's underwear and socks.

Three scabby mailboxes were nailed to the newel post one above the other. A card taped to the second box read, in round, childish print:

APT. 2 M. Hinton C. Cook.

Matilda and Crissy.

I climbed a narrow flight of open, roofed stairs and knocked hard on the wood-framed door. The panels rattled. They wouldn't be morning people. I waited and knocked again.

"Take it easy!" A shrill voice. The door opened against a chain, and I glimpsed a cheek and a sheaf of bleached hair before it banged shut again. "We don't want any!"

"I'm an investigator, Tildy. I need to ask you a couple of questions."

"Blow it out your ass."

"I'm working with Delmore on the Tipton murders. Please, just a few minutes of your time."

The door opened again. "You can tell that *scum*bag if I see either one of them again, *I will kill them!*"

She tried slamming the door again, but this time my foot was in the way. I grabbed the knob and shouldered the chain out of the doorframe.

Tildy reeled backward on her toes with her fists bunched at her collarbone. She was wearing a long-sleeved, plaid flannel nightgown and silver rings on all her fingers. The sunlight in the kitchen behind her made a halo out of her uncombed white-blond hair. The carpeted room had nothing in it but a Naugahyde armchair, scattered pillows and blankets, a CD tower, and a huge TV on a plastic pedestal with a chunky purple candle on top of that.

"Sorry, Tildy, but you just said the wrong thing. Your name is Tildy, isn't it?"

"Why? What did I say?"

"Killing people's getting to be a trend around here lately, and I'm trying to put a stop to it."

"Oh, and that gives you the right to bust into my apartment?"

"Tildy, this is a police matter, and I need your help."

"I think I seen you before. Haven't I?" She was early twenties, with a pretty, heart-shaped face, slender shoulders, huge breasts, and a brittle, angry glint in her eye. She fluffed her hair with her fingers. Her breasts wobbled inside the flannel nightshirt. "Who are you again?"

"Hector Bellevance. I'm an investigator for the town of Tipton. Did Delmore stay here with you Sunday night?"

"No. Why?"

"When did you last see Delmore?"

"Monday morning."

"And he didn't stay with you the night before?"

She looked away. "I was workin'. Crissy weren't."

"Your roommate."

"My fucking *sister*!"

"Your sister. So is one of you married?"

She snorted. "Yeah, me."

"Your husband's not in the area?"

"My husband's incarcerated, so there's not too much he can do about it."

"I'm sorry. What's he in for?"

"Different shit."

Right—Hinton. Del's buddy. With the Colombian dope connection. "Jeremy Hinton? Got sent up for dealing smack?"

"He was in the room, that's all."

"So you were working Sunday night, and Del was here with your sister. Crissy."

She started to make a reply, then threw up her hands. "I don't even know why I'm talking to you."

The phone rang.

She skipped back on her toes to the caller-ID display on the other side of the kitchen. "*Shit.* That's him right there."

Another ring.

"That's Del?"

"It ain't his friggin' parents. I'm *not* picking that up."

It rang again and stopped.

"What happened Monday morning?"

"That's when I found out."

"Found out what?"

"About him and my sister."

"He told you?"

"He didn't tell me shit. I found his used condom in the fucking bathroom."

"Did you fight about that?"

"How could I? He already left."

"What time did he leave?"

"Early. Sun wasn't even up."

"Did he say where he was going?"

"Tipton. Sheriff was all pissed at him."

"He got a wake-up call from the sheriff."

"Yeah."

"What was the sheriff angry about?"

"I don't know, it was so stupid. You know that body they found Sunday up in the abandoned space facility?"

I nodded.

"Del had the hand from it. He was all bent out of shape because he was the one that found the body, but that wasn't what it said in the newspaper. His *name* wasn't even in the story until the end. But Del still had the *hand* from it. That was the proof right there."

"He show you the hand?"

"No." She shuddered. "I didn't want to see it. He was going to take it down to the barracks and pull up the FBI file of fingerprints on the Internet and identify who the hand was from. Jerk."

"Where would I find your sister?"

"Why would I want you to find my sister?"

"Where does she work?"

"Crissy?"

"Crissy, right."

"I have no clue. You know, you are one very tall dude. You ever play basketball?"

"For many years."

"Duh. You're probably famous. Are you?"

"I'm far from famous."

"I know I seen you before. I ever wait on you?"

"At R&J's? I don't think so."

She scrabbled around in the mess on the counter until she

found a book of matches and a half-smoked cigarette in a pottery saucer. "I guess I'm awake now, whatever time it is." She lit the butt and shivered.

"Tildy. Where does Crissy work?"

"Shit if I know. She cleans houses."

"Yeah? She doesn't clean this one."

"Huh." She laughed, surprising herself, smoke tumbling down her chin.

"Who does she work for?"

"Some girl, drives a Mustang. Jessica." Tildy lifted her foot— red toenails—and set it down in place. "Can I go *pee*?"

"I'm sorry, Tildy. Of course."

I watched her dance down the hallway, her white calves bunched under the scalloped hem of her nightshirt.

With its high ceiling and four sun-filled, double-hung windows looking south over the tracks to the trees along the river and the red-brick Allenburg skyline on the other side, this kitchen might have been pleasant, if it hadn't been trashed. The wallpaper's pattern of thatched cottages, grassy orchards, and split-rail fences had its charm, despite the bib-like water stains under the windowsills. The tap dripped into a dull steel sink. Pizza boxes and KFC chicken tubs were piled next to the harvest-gold electric range. A plastic trash barrel near the back door brimmed with deposit beer and soda bottles. The table was a mess of smeared plates, lottery tickets, pizza rinds, pistachio shells, crumpled bags, ashes, bottle caps, and puddles of candle wax.

Tacked to a corkboard under the wall phone in the hallway I found a list of phone numbers. They'd been written on the back of a large envelope in the same hand that had lettered the mailbox card downstairs, half of them crossed out or scribbled over.

I untacked the list and took it into the light to scan the names: *Steven, Lizzie, Ray's Sunoco, Jeremy, Manny G, Fremeau's, Placy,*

*Linda Stack* . . . No Jessica jumped out at me. I tucked it into my notebook.

A roll of toilet paper rattled on its cylinder. The toilet flushed.

I went to the window and watched the pigeons outside. Sacks of spider eggs like felt beads were suspended in the upper corners of the windowpanes. Dust hung from the moldings in tendrils.

Tildy came out into the hall with her face shining, her blond hair brushed back and pulled into a knot, pink flip-flops on her feet. She cleared her throat. "Here's the thing I want to know. If it's true you're a town officer and you're investigating the shootings, how come you're here talking to me?"

She opened the fridge and took out a two-liter jug of Orange Crush.

"I'm trying to get the clearest possible picture of what happened that morning."

"OK, that's great, but why me? I mean, this is about that old guy that went postal up in Tipton, right?" She rinsed out a cup and poured herself some soda.

"Right. When did you last talk to Del?"

"Couple days. They don't have the guts to come back here, either one of 'em. Not while *I'm* here, at least."

I turned to a window to look at the freight passing below. The house was shaking and the empties tinkling in the trash barrel. "Tildy, the sheriff and Del had an argument the morning of the murders. Do you know what it was about?"

"Yeah. It was about him being an asshole."

"Who being an asshole?"

"The sheriff! He wanted Del to *charge* me, but Del wouldn't do it. Del was *protecting* me—he said. Huh, right, he was *using* me, the shit. He was trolling for my little sister ever since he moved in here."

"The sheriff wanted Del to charge you with what?"

"Didn't matter. Solicitation, drugs, shoplifting . . . The thing about deputies is they're supposed to *fight* crime, they're not supposed to live with it." She snuffled. "Now the fatso's dead, and I know Delmore's gonna run for sheriff. Plus, him and Crissy'll probably move *in* together, the bitch." She was looking for another butt. "I will fucking *hurt* somebody if that happens."

"How old are you, Tildy?"

"Why?"

"Come on, Tildy . . ." I waited until she raised her eyes.

"What? I just turned twenty-three."

"Did you finish high school?"

"Barely."

"Here? Allenburg High?"

She nodded. She'd found another smoke and was pinching it into shape.

"Is there anybody in these parts you're still close to? Parents? Grandparents?"

"Not hardly."

"Have you ever thought of leaving? Starting over?"

"Why?"

"I think you can do it."

"Do what?"

"Leave this place. Change your life."

"Oh, right. I don't even got a car."

"If you're using, Tildy, you need to get yourself into detox. That shit'll kill you."

She rolled her eyes. "Mother Teresa."

"I'm serious. If you want to go someplace where nobody knows you, I can help with that. You can get clean and find a job. You can save some money, take a few college courses, meet some new people . . . Who knows?"

"Right. I'm gonna go live in some strange place where I got no friends and no money?"

"What I'm trying to say is you can get help. Just ask."

She blew smoke. "See, it's not like I haven't *been* places. Shit, I been to New York, Washington, D.C., Montreal . . . I been to Philadelphia, I been to fucking Buffalo. They all suck. Del took me to Florida last fall. We spent a week at Pompano Beach. Climate's decent, but the *people*? The *traffic* and the *garbage* all over? You can have it. I need a little fresh air. I need real trees—"

The phone rang again.

She ran over. "I am not answering that," she said.

"Tildy, if that's Del, I really would like to talk to him."

She picked up the phone and yelled into it, "You *fucked* her in *my* bedroom!" She slammed the phone down.

"Where was he calling from?"

She hugged herself.

"Tildy?"

"The scrap yard."

"Thanks. I'll be going, but remember what I said, all right? Call me. I'm in the phone book. Call anytime."

"Wait one second." She was poking around in a drawer. "Here." She handed me a screwdriver and gestured at the door. "I'd like you to fix that door chain."

It had been ripped out more than once. The molding was split, and the holes in the frame were stripped all the way into the stud. "You need longer screws," I told her. The best I could do was push them in and tap them home with the butt of the screwdriver.

"Is that my problem?" She leaned against the wall with her arms folded under her chest. "Something tells me you got the answer to that one, too."

It took me a second. "I wish I did," I said, my scalp tingling. I tossed her back the screwdriver. "At the moment I've got more problems than I can shake a stick at."

She smiled. "Any chance I'll see you again?"

"I hope so. Keep my offer in mind, will you?"

"You're a boy scout. Hey, when you see Delmore, if you find him, tell him from me he's a sneaky weasel-face bastard."

Even with the drugstore magnifiers I kept in the glove box of my Power Wagon, I wasn't able to find a Jessica on Tildy's crowded phone list, but at the bottom, written sideways, there was a *Cris/JJ's* and a *Cris cell.* From a hard-used pay phone next to the air compressor outside Cumberland Farms, I tried the cell.

"Who is this?"

"Cris?"

"It's me. Who's this?"

"The name's Heck. I'm a friend of Del's."

"How did you get this number?"

"From your sister. You got a minute?"

"I don't know—I'm working."

"It's about the killings in Tipton. Crissy, think back to Sunday night. Remember that severed hand Del had?"

"Yeah . . ."

"After Del left the apartment to take that hand back to Tipton Monday morning, when did you see him next?"

"Who'd you say you were again?"

"I'm an investigator for the town of Tipton. Here's our problem. Some of us believe that Del went with Sheriff Mueller when the sheriff drove out to Boisvert's to serve those papers that morning, but Del maintains that he didn't. I'd like to hear what you know about it."

"All I know is what he told me, which is he went up to

Boisvert's *after* the sheriff went up there. What happened, the sheriff forgot the hand at Del's parents', so Del had to go chasing after him."

"I see. Del followed the sheriff to Boisvert's to give him the hand. What happened after that?"

"Mueller *suspended* him. So what could he do? He left."

"It wasn't just the hand the sheriff was mad about, was it? The friction between them had more history than that."

"What do you mean, friction?"

"Trouble. Between Del and the sheriff."

"I know you. You're the guy that gave Del them Camels."

"Crissy, listen to me. Withholding information about a felony is a felony in itself. You don't want to go down that road with him."

"What road? I'm not going down any *road.*"

"What time did you see Del again Monday morning?"

"I never saw Del that whole day. I was *working*. Like I am now!" She dumped the call.

I bought a cup of coffee at Cumberland Farms, stepped outside with it, and gazed back toward the dilapidated apartment house across the street, where Tildy had launched her day with sugar and nicotine. And junk, I was betting. Would she call me? I told myself she might, but I didn't really believe it. Would Del shoot Pete? In a heated moment, he probably would. But not Ella. Not just to set up Marcel. That was beyond Del. And anyway, no one could have killed Marcel and also disposed of him between seven and eight that morning. It just wasn't possible.

Unless he'd had a partner. Two people working separately. That, I allowed, was possible.

# 14

I drove back across the river into the commercial heart of Allenburg, one long block of nineteenth-century brickfronts lining the river above the old railyard, up the length of Main Street to the fork, then right on Everett toward the high school. Petey Mueller had lived for years in a little house at the end of Everett on a slope across from the Allenburg Crusaders' track and football field. It was a sky-blue ranch, the front yard paved for parking. His wife, Kim Gentler, ran Kim's Shear Sensations inside the glassed-in breezeway between the living room and garage.

The Gentlers were a local family. I remembered Kim's father, Arthur Gentler, a clerk for decades in Grassley's Shoes and Sportswear. The Gentler girls, Kim and Pam, were close to fifty now. They were twins—not identical, both fleshy. Their brother Maury was another one of Pete's deputies. I didn't know Maury Gentler, but I remembered Kim and Pam. They used to drive a white convertible and sun themselves on the grass at the state beach with a bunch of other older girls.

Three cars were parked out front, Petey and Kim's black Le Sabre, a new red Beetle, and a sorry-looking Eagle with rusted-out rocker panels and no wheel covers.

A note taped inside the door glass read, CLOSED "TILL" EASTER MONDAY.

Pam answered the doorbell. She had a bleached mustache on her rabbity upper lip. Her perm, coal-black and smooth, like an ornamental helmet, made me wonder if Kim had created it.

"I know you," Pam said. "Hector Bellevance, right? I read a

long article about you a few years ago. In the *Globe*. What was that about again?"

"If you don't mind, Pam," I said, "I've come to pay my respects to your sister."

"OK, but I don't think she's much in the mood for socializing. Pete's having his autopsy done today over to Burlington."

"I'm sorry, but I really do need to have a word with her. Will you let her know I'm here?"

She glanced over her shoulder into the darkened beauty parlor. Three chairs, three hulking dryers, a number of glossy styling posters, Redken stickers on the mirrors, bottles and beautifying implements crowding the sinks, hairdo chemicals in the air.

"Kimmy? It's another officer out here to see you. Hector Bellevance, remember him?"

Kim was a larger, softer-looking version of her sister, with golden, feathered hair. She came into the room sideways down a two-step stair. Her face looked puffy, her nostrils and eyelids inflamed. Close behind was a younger woman, maybe thirty, square-faced and serious-looking. No makeup, dark hair cropped short and moussed into spikes. She had a box of tissues under one arm. Corduroy jeans and a green cotton-knit sweater.

"So I'll be going then," Pam said.

"OK, hon. Drive safe."

"I'll be back tomorrow."

"Well, you call first," she said.

I took Kim's soft, hot hand in both of mine. "I can't tell you how sorry I am about Pete. He was a dedicated sheriff, and he was an exceptional man."

Tears brimmed and spilled down her cheeks. "Thank you."

"We're going to find his killer. You can count on that, Kim."

"What good'll that do if he's dead?" She plucked a tissue from the box the younger woman held out for her.

"Would you mind if we sat down?"

The spiky-haired woman guided Kim out to the waiting area. Kim lowered herself into one pink vinyl-covered loveseat and heaved a sigh. "Gal from the clinic give me this Paxil. I believe it's beginning to have the desired effect."

"I think you'll be able to sleep now," the woman said.

"Are you a paramedic?" I asked her.

She straightened her shoulders. "No, I'm an advocate with Women Helping Women." She offered her hand. "Sorry—Lucy Pratt."

"Hector Bellevance, Tipton town constable. You must be the Lucy Pratt who wrote Shirley Boisvert's request for relief."

"I did no such thing," she said. "I explained the protections available to her. That's it. We never put words in someone else's mouth, Mr. Bellevance."

"Excuse me. Somehow I had the wrong impression."

She softened a little. "I'm just grateful she's alive, that's all."

"Of course," I said. "Kim, I have a question for you. Did Petey make or receive any phone calls on Sunday night?"

"Any calls?"

"That's right. Can you remember anyone he might have spoken to that night or the next morning?"

"Well . . ." She closed her eyes. "Sunday suppertime the state medical examiner called. Griswold. Seems like a month ago now, Jesus. But there was this human hand that they lost track of somehow. Pete was trying to hunt it down, and he phoned *you*. 'The overqualified constable.' That's what he called you."

"He never reached me, Kim. I wish he had."

"I heard him cursing out Delmore to somebody. If it wasn't you, I don't know who it was. Then early next morning he got a call from Ella McPhetres—I remember it was still dark out—and Ella was cranked up about something. I could hear her yelling from the other bed." She blew her nose. "So he got up, fixed coffee, made a couple short calls, to who I don't know, and he told me, 'I'll see ya later,' and he left." She was whimpering, her head to one side. "I never saw him again after that."

Lucy Pratt knelt and took Kim gently by the cheeks. Lucy turned her head so she could look into her eyes. "Pete gave his life doing his sworn duty. Protecting his community. You can be *proud* of him."

"Thank you. I know that. It's just I—I just keep realizing I'm never gonna *see* him again."

"I know."

Kim turned to me, sniffling. "There was somebody else called after he left. I can't remember who, but I must've wrote it down. Give me a minute."

Lucy steadied the woman as she wobbled up, compressing her lips with the effort, and watched as she left the room.

"She going to be all right?" I said.

Lucy Pratt nodded. "She's a lot better than she was yesterday. That sister of hers, though, she's something else."

"They were close, growing up."

"All I know is the whole morning she was pestering Kim to go down to the bank and open up their safe deposit box. What's she thinking? Kim can't be out in public looking the way she looks. She's a *beautician*."

"Pam's anxious. She wants to be sure Kim's taken care of."

She smiled. "You have more faith in people than I do."

"Until I have reason to think otherwise," I said.

"Higbee!" Kim called out. She stood braced in the doorway. "Vaughn Higbee! Teaches up to the college."

"What did Higbee want?" I asked.

"Who the hell knows?" She sidled down into the beauty parlor. "Last week it was some snowmobilers had broke his pasture fence. Week before that, it was some other damn thing. Higbee's a one-man complaint factory."

"Did Petey say where he was going when he left that morning?"

"Yeah, Tipton. He said he had to go meet 'that miserable excuse for a lawman.' Who I—" She blushed and lowered her eyes. "I thought he meant you."

"But he meant Delmore."

"I guess."


I swung in behind the Allenburg Federal Building, a brick cube on the south end of Main Street where the postal service and the armed forces recruiters and the IRS were ensconced, on the chance that I'd find Rob Tierney at his desk upstairs.

The state's attorney's staff occupied a large open room on the second floor, down the hall from the Department of Agriculture. The receptionist, a slit-eyed woman stationed behind a thick pane of Plexiglas, had me pass my driver's license to her through a little grid before buzzing me into a sunny warren of cubicles.

On the far side of the room, Rob was signaling me with his hand in the air.

"How'd you know I was here?"

"Just guessing. I figured you'd have paper to deal with."

He looked ragged. "Bane of the job. It'll all be computerized someday, but someday's a long way off."

"You getting any sleep?"

"Is that the thing where you lie down and close your eyes?" He pulled out a chair for me. "What do you need, Hector?"

"Sounding board. I'm trying to sort a few things out."

"I can't give you much under the circumstances. As you know."

"All I want to do is follow up on what you told me the other day."

He sat back.

"I have two questions. First, the hand you found in the sheriff's glove box. Was it inside a bread bag?"

He frowned. "How'd you know that?"

"Somebody entered the Boisvert kitchen that morning looking for a bag. The first bag he found had a loaf of bread in it, so he dumped the bread out on the table. Pete wouldn't have done a thing like that."

"So if it wasn't you, who went in and dumped the bread?"

"Second question. You found a significant quantity of type AB blood in the Boisverts' septic. Is that all that makes you think Marcel's dead?"

"That and the fact that about half the town hated the old guy."

"OK. If he is dead, I see two possibilities."

Tierney nodded.

"Somebody got out to Boisvert's before Pete, cornered Boisvert in his bath, and shot him. Then he killed Pete when Pete showed up unexpected."

Rob looked away for a moment. "OK. Why kill the town clerk?"

"I'm working on that."

"You got a PI's license?"

"I've got a duty to the Town of Tipton."

"Cahoon'll have your ass. Second possibility?"

"Somebody followed the sheriff out to the Boisvert farm in another vehicle. Maybe two people. They killed Pete and Boisvert, then one of them drove in and shot Ella McPhetres and dumped the cruiser in the lake, while the other one took care of Boisvert's body."

"Somebody as in who?"

"Del Osgood."

"Why Osgood?"

I told Tierney what I'd pieced together from Maureen, Tildy, Crissy, and Kim Gentler.

He thought for a moment. "You think Delmore has the smarts?"

"I think Maureen does."

"Delmore and *Maureen* Osgood. They shoot Petey and Marcel Boisvert, and then they decide that if they can make Boisvert's body disappear, Boisvert'll look like the killer."

"What have you got for footwear impressions?"

"Six sets. How definitive that is I don't know."

"How many haven't cleared?"

"Two."

"And one's a large boot—size thirteen or so?"

"Right. Del's got the big hoof, but we got no match to the standards he supplied for us."

"Better check his other shoes. What else?"

"Medium-size work boot, lot of wear, might've belonged to Boisvert."

"Any prints turn up at both scenes?"

"Yeah, yours. You stepped in the woman's blood pool, Hector."

"I had to get to her desk so I could phone *you*, Rob. And if I'd reached you about thirty seconds sooner, you would have caught the bastard."

He just looked at me.

"What about those partials up by the Lakeview Cabins? Anybody cast those?"

"I don't think they even looked for them."

"Right. Ballistics?"

"Griswold autopsied both bodies yesterday. Sheriff Mueller and Ella McPhetres were each killed by a single gunshot to the chest. Sheriff was shot by a jacketed slug frontally from six feet. Probably facing the shooter, walking backwards, trying to extricate himself, talk the guy down. McPhetres was shot by a hollow-point, most of which the techs recovered. Probably forty-five caliber. Contact entry. Muzzle jammed into her left breast."

"So. Two shooters."

Tierney rocked his head. "Or two guns. Or he mixed a loading."

"Delmore was at that scene. He put that hand in the sheriff's glove box. Go tell him you want more shoes and a polygraph session. That'll support a warrant to go through that scrap yard."

"Be a bitch of a place to mount a search."

"Not for human remains. Couple of cadaver dogs will cover it in an hour." I stood up. "Call me when it's over."

"Cahoon's gonna ask if this came from you."

"Tell him I'm behind him a hundred percent. All I want is my quiet life back."

I groaned as I slid in behind my steering wheel. Tension had concentrated low in my spine, like a red-hot rivet. *All I want is my quiet life back.* Was that true? If it was, I wasn't about to get it back until Wilma made up her mind to call me.

Back at the cabin, I phoned Vic Parkhurst. A county forester and a weekend fishing guide, Vic was soft-spoken, a solitary type. Wilma met him after tripping over him one day in an arboretum in Ann Arbor. She married him three days later. Now there was a decision she could have taken more time with.

"I sympathize," Vic told me. "She can turn on a dime, that Wilma."

"Did you talk to her before she left?"

"She came by to pick up the roof carrier. All she said was she was moving to Boston."

"She didn't say what part."

"No. But you know who I would try? Her friend Marcia—lives in Wellesley. Marcia. . . . Can't think of her last name. Her and Wilma were in med school together, big marathon runner, came and visited a couple summers ago. Husband's a big contractor."

"And she's a doctor?"

"Yup. Dermatologist. Some foreign-sounding name, that's all I can remember. If I think of it I'll call you back."

I told him I'd appreciate that.

At dusk I carried the telescope outside to give the elements time to adjust to the cold, and just as I walked back into the cabin the phone began to ring.

It was Tierney.

"You were dead right about the shoes, Hector. Del gave us the wrong pair when we hit him up for standards on Monday."

"Those things happen."

"Yeah. He also admits he was at the farm that morning. The reason he didn't mention it the first time was because he didn't want to get into the embarrassing business about him getting suspended from the department. He was apologetic about it until we started turning his parents' place of business inside out."

"No corpse, I take it."

"No corpse, no murder weapon, no bloody clothing, no traces of note, nothing. Nothing out at Delmore's little summer camp, either."

"How did Delmore react to all this?"

"He was pissed off, especially when we impounded his vehicle, but he was cooperative. I asked him if he'd sit for a polygraph. 'Any fucking time,' he says."

"What about Maureen?"

"Same. According to her, neither her nor Dwight ever set foot on the Boisvert farm in their whole life. State of Vermont couldn't destroy their livelihood, she says, so now we're destroying what's left of their reputation in the community. She says the only reason we're on Delmore's ass is because you're trying to get us off yours."

"She's right. What's Cahoon's take?"

"He's into it. He just got two DNA matches on the blood samples we sent down to the lab—nothing surprising."

"Wow. You get autorads that fast these days?" When I was on the job, the techs got bands to compare by taking a nylon membrane with the DNA material bound to it and exposing it to X-ray film. The process could take a week or more.

"No autorads. Chemiluminescence. Uses enzymes and light instead of radiation. Very speedy."

"Must be."

"The blood in the septic is definitely Boisvert's. We matched it to saliva from his pillow. The samples in the sheriff's vehicle are Ella McPhetres's. Shooter left traces on the steering wheel and shifter. That's it."

"Any latents?"

"Boisvert's and Mueller's on the firearms. Nothing in the sheriff's car. You know what's weird? For all the blood in that septic tank, we found no traces anywhere else in the house. The diluted stains around the bathtub were probably blood in the grout, but somebody cleaned up pretty good in there with bleach, and the luminol reacts to bleach just like blood. But it's just strange, you know? No traces on the rugs, the stairs, the woodroom floor, and nothing on Osgood's shoes. I mean, could you lug a hundred-fifty-pound body out of that house without getting a single drop of blood on the stairs or on your clothing?"

"What if you drained the body in the tub, sawed it up, and wrapped the pieces in plastic?"

"OK. Then what do you do with it? Stick it in a freezer locker?"

"Sink it in the river."

"Right. Or out in the bog somewhere."

"Ever consider dowsing for it?"

Tierney snorted. "Dowsing?"

"I have a gifted friend who'd be happy to have the assignment."

"You believe in that hocus-pocus?"

"I have an open mind."

"I'll run it past Cahoon and let you know."

"Forget it."

"OK, anything turns up on Delmore's car, I'll let you know. Meantime, keep clear of the Osgoods, you hear?"

From memory I punched in the number of Blackie's Tavern—a cops' bar in Dorcester where I'd put in some stool time. I identified myself to the bartender as a detective who used to work in the district and asked him to put a cop on the line.

Officer John McGowan. Nobody I knew, though he knew who I was. Heard all the stories, he said, pronouncing it *stow-reez*. How was I doin'? Still shucking clams out on the Cape? I steered him toward the bar's Yellow Pages, and within a minute he'd found me a physician named Marcia with a dermatology practice in Newton. Marcia Koenig. That was the one. But there was no residential listing. The only Koenigs in the book were up in Ipswich.

A few minutes later the phone rang again.

"Mr. Bellevance?" Shirley Boisvert.

"How are you doing tonight, Shirley?"

"Not that great. I wish I could go home."

"Might be a while before that happens. What's wrong? Are you uncomfortable at Emily's?"

"I'm not saying that. No, she give me a canopy bed and I got my own bathroom. It's just, home is home."

"The farm is a shambles at the moment, Shirley. Also, I'm sorry to have to tell you this, but Celeste is no longer with us."

"What do you mean? She died?"

"Yes. I found her."

I listened to her breathe into the mouthpiece. I thought she was going to ask if I knew what had happened to the cat, but all she said was, "I bet I got a fair amount of spring cleaning to do, I get home."

"I'd say so."

"Anyhow, the reason I called, did you talk to Vaughn?"

"I haven't gotten around to that yet, Shirley, but I'm confident Marc is fine."

"How can you be confident he's fine when you don't even know where he's at?"

"He's at home now, Shirley. Why don't you give him a call?"

"That's a laugh. All you ever get's his answering machine."

"All right. I'll speak with Vaughn tomorrow. I think I can wangle you and Marc a little time together, if nothing else."

"Would you? That would be good. I appreciate you taking the time to do this—with everything else that's going on around here."

"I'll be in touch as soon as I know more."

"Mr. Bellevance?"

"Yes?"

"Something I was wondering about."

"What's that?"

"Remember you asked me about a red cap? How come you wanted to know about that?"

"Because Monday morning I saw a red cap on the head of somebody I would very much like to talk to."

"Well, Vaughn has a cap like that."

"Vaughn Higbee has a red Utah cap?"

"Keeps it up in his office at the college."

"You've been to Vaughn's office?"

"Coupla times. Last fall, when he had Marc up in there."

"In his office?"

"Yup. Vail Hall. I used to go and visit. Until Marcel put a stop to it."

"How did Marcel put a stop to it?"

"Took my car. My baby blue Escort."

"He took your car?"

"My own fault. Since Kathy died, he didn't want us to have nothing to do with the Higbees, either one of us. He got wind of it somehow."

"So you've been housebound since the fall?"

"Well, he'll bring me in the village if I need to go. And if it's ever an emergency, I can take the lawn tractor."

"What did he do with your car?"

"Sold it. Sold it for Kathy's funeral, he said. Only it was Vaughn paid for that funeral, not us. Vaughn wouldn't pay for no decent monument, though. We had to pay for that. Maybe that's what Marcel meant. *Monument.*"

I went back outside. Perfect night: brilliant with stars, the waning moon not yet risen, no wind. I checked the stove in the greenhouse, then hiked up to where I'd left the telescope. I played with the ascension and declination knobs, scanning a patch of sky just south of the Big Dipper until I found the Whirlpool galaxy. But I couldn't quite clear my head of the clutter of disjointed thoughts, and after a few minutes I capped the tube and carried the instrument back to the cabin.

The phone rang while I was brushing my teeth.

"Hector? It's Vic Parkhurst. Listen, if you're still interested, I came up with the woman's phone number, if you want that."

"Sure, Vic, thanks."

"Wellesley, Mass. Got it here in an old phone bill." He read it to me. "Good luck."

It was after ten. I took the phone to bed with me and pressed the keys by starlight.

A man's voice answered.

"Mr. Koenig?"

"This is Jack Petrie. Who's this?"

"I'm sorry. Is this the home of Marcia Koenig?"

"Who is this, please?"

"Sorry. This is Hector Bellevance. I'm trying to reach Wilma Strong. I was told I might try this number."

"Hector. All right. One moment, please."

I waited.

"Hector?"

"Wilma?"

"Hector! I'll be damned. How'd you find me?"

"Telepathy."

"You're such a detective, I love it. So, how's the investigation going?"

"Wilma. I need you to tell me what you're thinking."

"I'm thinking I wish I were in bed with you. This damn house is freezing."

"About us."

"Didn't I just cover that?"

I said nothing.

"I *love* us, you dope."

"Are you coming back?"

"Of *course* I'm coming back."

"When?"

"How about Friday? Friday morning. Meet me at my place at

nine. We'll have smoked-salmon omelets and Bloody Marys, and then we'll ravish each other. Or vice versa. Then we'll talk. How's that sound?"

"It's a start," I said.

"Don't be like that. I was going to call. I *told* you I was going to call, and I was. But I've been busy. So have you, I gather."

"How're things at the *Globe*?"

"Great! Super! I don't start officially till the twenty-third, but everyone has been very welcoming. There's a lot of— There's a lot we have to talk about."

"Are you still pregnant?"

She gasped, then said, "I deserved that, I suppose. Yes, I'm pregnant. Most happily pregnant."

"Well, then, I think we should skip the Bloody Marys."

"What? Oh, right!" She laughed. "God, you're a great dad *already*!" She sighed. "Hector, look, I'm sorry I said what I said yesterday morning. But that only illustrates why I couldn't *see* you, do you get it?"

"Not really."

"I'm *impossible*. I am. Get used to it."

"I can't move back to Boston, Wilma."

"Shh. How about Friday? Friday we'll talk, OK? Friday?"

"Friday."

"We'll work it out. Love triumphs in the end. Right?"

"Right," I said. Unless it doesn't. But that night I slept like a rock on the ocean floor.

# THURSDAY

## 15

The Allenburg State College campus occupied the heights just west of town, a crenellated silhouette against the sky, with a lofty flagpole in the middle. The heights had been sheep pasture until the turn of the century, when the president of the American Telephone and Telegraph Company, Theodore H. Vail, built a summer cottage on the commanding knoll—a sprawling monstrosity with a tower and deep steamboat porches. Twenty-two rooms, eight fireplaces. By the 1930s the cottage had become the home of the Allenburg State Teachers College. Vail Hall was declared a fire hazard in the seventies and razed to make room for the current Vail Hall, a brick pile more in keeping with the brick piles that had by then surrounded it.

Two slack flags, America's and Vermont's, hung at the top of the flagpole in the middle of the crowded main parking lot. The women's track team was out on the concrete patio near the gym, limbering up before a run. I noticed their eyes following me as I walked by.

The Humanities Department secretary was a large-hipped woman about my age, with lots of gold and silver bangles jingling on her chubby wrists. She was busy at her computer, a stack of folders beside her on the floor. Yes, she was Daphne Withers, she said without looking at me, tappity-tapping at her keyboard.

"I'm Hector Bellevance. We spoke on the phone this morning."

She paused to take me in, her eyes widening as they flew up the length of me. "Are you the cop that called about Professor Higbee's office hours?"

"That's right. Where is his office, by the way? Downstairs?"

"Yes, but like I said on the phone, just because they post their office hours, that's no guarantee they'll be in there. I haven't laid eyes on Professor Higbee this entire day."

"What about Monday?"

"Monday?"

"Do you recall seeing Professor Higbee on Monday morning?"

"Uh, no. Well, you know, Professor Higbee canceled his classes Monday morning."

"Did he? And why was that?"

"Field trip. Soon as the weather got decent, he took his Native America seminar to that dig out in Shadboro."

"What dig would that be?"

"Howell Hill—where the FCC wants to pour a pad for a microwave tower? The Abenaki are all up in arms over it, if you read the paper, because it used to be a burial site. Vaughn says the Abenaki buried their dead sitting up and facing toward the east, and that's one of the historical locations where they did it. People of the Dawn."

I thanked Daphne and headed down two flights of bare concrete stairs to a row of small, ground-level rooms opposite the darkened interactive-TV chamber.

Vaughn's announced hours were two to three, Tuesdays and Thursdays. Here it was two-thirty, and as Daphne had predicted, my knock underneath his PROF. V. HIGBEE plaque went unanswered.

The corridor was empty in both directions. I tried the knob. It was unlocked.

I stuck my head inside. "Vaughn?"

Nothing. His green glass desk lamp was on.

I left the door open behind me.

Tight space, though comfortable enough. Two modular bookcases. Brown leather club chair, a pair of large reproductions on the gray wall above it, geometric prints in chrome frames, red, blue, yellow. Early Mirós. Some Indian pot on his table desk, big Dell spinning, monitor dark. Potted jade under the window on a threadbare kilim. The room's single window was a narrow slot set so deep in the wall that you had to stick your head into it to get the view: out toward a cramped 1960s housing development called Spruce Knob and the interstate's twin ribbons snaking north toward Shadboro.

Next to the window was a tall beige steel locker. I lifted the latch. Umbrella, Prince tennis racket, blue and white windbreaker, and, on the top shelf, the red Utah cap, bright as a tomato. I latched it shut again at the sound of someone's light step in the hallway just outside.

A double knock on the open door and it swung in. "One minor problem— Oops. Excuse me. I didn't know—"

A small, fine-featured young woman, mid-twenties, with curly chestnut hair, complicated wire earrings, bulky Irish sweater, painter's pants, clogs, was giving me a disapproving look, as she realized I was here alone. "I'm sorry. And you would be?"

"Constable Hector Bellevance. I'm a friend of Vaughn's."

"I see. And where is Vaughn?"

"Away from his desk. May I ask your name?"

"I'm Janet. Fleury. I work for the department. Are you the constable who found those people shot to death up in Tipton?"

"I am. Are you a student?"

She nodded. "Work-study. I help the faculty with research, copying, stuff like that."

"Anthropology major?"

"I am now," she said, coloring slightly. "I was recreation management, but I couldn't handle the accounting."

"Are you involved with the dig out in Shadboro?"

"What dig?"

"That Abenaki burial ground up on Howell Hill?"

"That's no dig. Better not be."

"I hear there's a dispute over how the site should be treated."

"It's outrageous. The FCC decides they want to stick a humongous structure in the middle of your community, and legally it turns out there's not a whole hell of a lot you can do about it."

"Did you go up to Howell Hill with Vaughn's seminar Monday morning?"

"Why? Is there a problem?"

"I'm not sure. Actually, I've dropped by Vaughn's office to see him about a small matter on behalf of his mother-in-law."

"God, Shirley? Don't tell me she's got you pushing for her."

"If you know Shirley, you know that she's been through a lot in the past year."

"Oh, definitely. I had to deal with her a few times fall semester. She was driving Vaughn up the wall."

"How come you had to deal with her?"

"Well, after Kathy died Vaughn didn't feel good about leaving Marc with Shirley all day, so he was bringing him to the office. She *hated* that."

"So she came here to visit with Marc?"

"Not too often, but yeah. Till her nutcase of a husband found out. Mostly she called him on the phone, and she used to send him stuff in the mail."

"What stuff?"

"Oh, like brownies, modeling clay, colored pencils . . ."

"But when she was able to visit Marc, she came here, to Vail?"

"A couple times. Usually I would meet them at the pool at the field house. The pool was a real big attraction. They hung out in the snack bar, drew pictures, played Chutes and Ladders—you know. Marc loved it. He got along great with her. That's why Vaughn put up with her."

The professor appeared in the doorway. He was carrying a

green day pack and a coffee mug. Rough silk sport jacket over two dress shirts, both open at the collar, the inner one white, the outer one blue with a gray stripe, a fount of chest hair at his throat like a silver ascot.

"Why, it's Hector! And it's Janet Fleury. A double whammy." They exchanged a look. "What's shaking, people?"

"He was here waiting for you when I came in," Janet said.

"So you've met?"

"Just."

Vaughn crossed between us to his locker and opened it, exposing the red Utah cap. He set his pack in on the floor and closed the locker. "Now, Hector," he said, "sorry if I seem abrupt, but I've got a few things to do here before I dash off to a committee meeting at three. Was there a question?"

"More a proposal. Shirley would appreciate some time with Marc. I'd like to arrange an occasion for them."

"An occasion," he said.

"Tomorrow, if it's no trouble."

"Don't you think we ought to wait until things die down a little?" He smiled. "Sorry, poor choice of words. What I mean is, Marc's feeling overwhelmed just now. So am I."

"So is Shirley. It might benefit them both to spend some time together."

"Fine. Let's discuss this later. I really—"

"I'd like to have something to lift Shirley's spirits. Tell you what, Vaughn. Tomorrow at noon I'll stop by and pick up Marc at his day care, and Shirley and I will take him out for lunch. How's that? We'll have him back by four."

"He's not in day care at the moment. We're between situations."

"Wherever he'll be at noon tomorrow, the offer's good."

"Let me see what Marc thinks. Best I can do, I'm sorry."

"Fair enough. Can I call you tonight?"

"Of course. Call." He spread his arms and shooed us toward the hallway. Janet went out ahead of me and stopped. I turned in the doorframe.

"One last question, Vaughn. Monday morning—may I ask where you were?"

His eyes flicked past me to Janet and back. "I took my senior seminar out to Howell Hill for a look at a piece of sacred ground."

"You met them here first?"

"No. We rendezvoused in Shadboro. Then we shuttled to the trailhead."

"What time?"

"Nine."

"You met your students in Shadboro at nine."

"Yes. Now, would you mind?"

I left the room as Vaughn gently closed the door on my back.

Janet Fleury and I walked up the stairs together in silence. Two boys rushed past us trailing the smell of pot. When we reached the top, before she could turn away I stepped around into her path.

She drew back. "What's the deal?"

"One moment, Janet. I hope you won't be offended by my asking whether you and Vaughn are seeing each other."

"Why, what are you, the love police?"

"Not a chance."

"Right." She crossed her arms.

"I'm serious. Consenting adults who're hurting nobody else? I'm all in favor. Tell me, though—it's important. Monday morning, was Vaughn up in Shadboro at nine? Do you remember?"

"Well, we might have been late."

"You went out there together?"

"He picked me up at my parents' condo."

"Where is that?"

"Mount Joe Meadows."

"Vaughn was late picking you up?"

She eased around me. "It's not like they could get started without him."

I followed her into the vestibule. "Were your parents at home at the time?"

She glanced back. "My parents live in Mystic."

The glass doors flashed.

I found Daphne Withers still hunched close to her computer, half-glasses on her nose, transcribing files.

"Daphne? Sorry to bother you again, but I need the class list for Vaughn's seminar. I'll be wanting to chat with a student or two."

She grunted, rolled her chair around to a file drawer, and fingered out a sheet of green paper. "Just grab some scrap and write down what you need. I don't have time to make you a copy. Leave it right on top of that pile."

Janet Fleury's name wasn't on the roster. I jotted down a few others and placed the list where she'd told me to.

"You've been very helpful, Daphne. One last thing. Can you tell me the room where Vaughn's committee meeting is happening right now?"

She had to look that up in her onscreen desk calendar. "Liberal Arts Committee. Founder's Lounge, third floor."

On the sloping campus green, in a fine, sifting snow, kids in soccer shoes were booting a ball around. In the Moore Student Center's glass-brick entry vestibule I found two campus telephones and a dorm directory. Third number I tried was a hit.

"Bruce Capello?"

"Speaking."

"Quick question. Did you go out to Shadboro last Monday morning as part of Professor Higbee's Native America seminar?"

"Sure. First day the sun was out. Was that Monday?"

"Yes, Monday. You met in Shadboro at what time?"

"What time? Ten. Why?"

"Not at nine?"

He paused. "No, Higbee's class starts at ten. If it started at nine, I couldn't take it. I got Senior Life Saving from eight to nine-twenty. Then I have to shower."

"So you all met at ten that morning."

"Yeah. Well, but pretty much everybody was late. We didn't get back to the college until after one."

I gave the Founder's Lounge conference room door a couple of pops and tried the knob. It opened. I took a step inside, one hand on the jamb. The committee, all men in neat beards, sitting in cushy swivel chairs at a long table, turned their eyes on me. Not one smiled.

"Forgive me for interrupting, but I'd like a brief word with Professor Higbee. It's a police matter."

"Christ," Vaughn said, shoving back from the table.

"I do apologize," I said. I nodded around the room.

"You've got a lot of gall," Vaughn said when we were out in the hall.

"Come off it, Vaughn. Where's your civic responsibility?"

"I'll have you know I've been *seething* over these intrusions of yours ever since Marcel went ballistic. Whatever your harebrained agenda is, I assure you I have no part in it."

"I'd try to keep from seething if I were you, Vaughn. It clouds the mind."

He snorted. "You're full of yourself. What do you want from me?"

I led him to a littered alcove overlooking a small, empty atrium on the floor below. We sat on wood-slat benches opposite the snack machines.

"The state's investigation is evolving. There is a strong argument for believing Marcel may be a victim, too."

"Murder victim, you mean?"

"Yes."

"That's unbelievable. Based on what?"

"I can't say."

"Well, I hope it's based on more than the fact that you can't find him."

"It is."

"So who's the suspect?"

"You know anybody who might have been feuding with the road commissioner?"

"Long list, Hector. It starts with the Osgoods."

"Just clear up one thing for me. On Monday morning, when you—"

"Hold it, hold it. You can't really imagine that *I* would be capable of such an act?"

"I can imagine all kinds of things. That's why I need your help."

He smoothed his hair. "This is *nuts*. This is *offensive*."

"Why did you tell me you met your seminar at nine Monday morning when the time was actually ten?"

"What possible difference does it make to you?"

"I'm asking why you misrepresented the time."

"I was seething. My mind must have been clouded."

"Where were you between six and nine on Monday morning?"

"As I told the state police, I left Marc at Brasseur's at about seven-fifteen. Then I stopped by my office and drove out to Shadboro."

"Did you stop anywhere else on the way?"

"Not that I recall."

"You don't recall meeting Janet at her parents' condo?"

He tilted his head back. "Yes, of course. All right. I gave her a ride."

"You tried to reach Sheriff Mueller on the phone that morning, too. What was that about?"

"I wanted to let him know I was conducting an excursion to the contested site on Howell Hill. Lest he read it the wrong way."

"Why would he have done that?"

"There was an incident last fall. Somebody hiked up there and pulled out all the surveyor's stakes. Sheriff Mueller was convinced I knew who that was."

"Did you?"

"Definitely not."

"When did you last see Ella McPhetres before she was killed?"

"Ella?" He cast his eyes upward. "Town meeting, I guess. Is that all, Hector?"

"That red hat in your office locker. Where'd you pick that up?"

"What red hat?"

"The Utah hat."

"The baseball cap?" He seemed amazed. "That was a *gift*. From my sister. What does that have to do with anything?"

"When did she give it to you?"

"Last June. Kathy and I spent a few days in Salt Lake with her and her husband—just a week before Kathy's accident. Inky and Clark are big Utes boosters. She gave each of us a baseball cap."

Inky. I remembered her. A flutist, with thick, prematurely white hair. "Your sister Ingrid," I said. "I believe I met her at Kathy's memorial service."

"Very possibly you did."

"What became of Kathy's hat?"

"She sent it to her father for Father's Day. She was sure he'd love it. I'd like to know how the hat is connected to the murders."

I stood. "So would I, Vaughn. That's all I have for now. I'll be calling you later about the possibility of getting Marc and Shirley together."

All at once it seemed Vaughn was in no hurry to get back to the Liberal Arts Committee, half reclining there in the scuzzy alcove, legs stretched out and crossed at the ankles, fingers laced at the back of his head, shirt untucked. "You're clueless, aren't you, Hector? Boisvert's disappeared and you want to make him a ghost. Jesus, here you are, three and a half days into this thing, a hundred cops on the case, and every one of you is buffaloed." Vaughn pushed himself to his feet. "You're a bunch of blundering lunks, you really are."

"It does seem that way sometimes," I said. "Even to us."


Snack time. Deputy Pfister was still pulling soft duty, parked outside the Shapiro residence on oak-lined Lower Main in his Montcalm County cruiser, windows rolled down, listening to country music, eating what looked like macaroni salad out of a plastic tub.

We exchanged nods as I motored past.

The house stood far back on a landscaped four-acre lot that was fenced along the roadside by wrought-iron spears in graduated lengths, set between rough granite stanchions.

I turned onto Palmer and parked around the corner in the entry to the old service road, which was gated by a swag of heavy black chain. I stepped over and followed the lane toward the back of the house between rows of tall, twiggy mock-orange bushes.

Wet oak leaves covered the lawn. The tennis court's wire backstops sagged, and the clay was mossy and pasted with leaves, but the rose garden's trellises were in good repair. Stained cedar. I climbed a myrtle-quilted slope to a stone patio, crossed that, and knocked gently on the multi-paned sunporch door. The floor inside was quarry tile, the large room funished with wicker pieces upholstered in white canvas with a navy stripe. In one corner Emily maintained a tropical glade in huge glazed pots—palms and citrus and a few octopuslike philodendrons.

Someone was playing a piano somewhere inside.

I knocked again.

The music stopped.

Emily Shapiro appeared in a blue jogging suit, shading her eyes to see who it was. She had her graying blond hair pulled back and gathered above the neck. She took a few steps closer. I waved and smiled my apology for surprising her.

She came to the door. "Hector Bellevance! Is something the matter? Are you all right?" She turned the latch.

"I'm fine," I said. "I didn't mean to alarm you. I was trying not to arouse the deputy."

"Gotcha. You'd think they could do better than him, wouldn't you?"

"The law's stretched pretty thin these days, Emily."

"So I understand. Come in, come in."

"I was hoping to have a word with Shirley, if she's available."

"Oh, she's been waiting for you to call. Why don't I fix us a pot of tea?"

I said I'd love some. I loosened my laces and slipped out of my boots, leaving them outside on the marble doorstep.

We sat in the late-day sun around a low, azure glass table. The tea was excellent, the scones fresh, the jam homemade. Shirley's iron-gray pageboy was damp and her skin pink from a shower.

The swelling in her lip had gone down. The split was a wine-black seam. In a peach turtleneck and a cream-colored fleece vest, she seemed relaxed, rested. Back on her meds, I figured.

"You're looking well, Shirley."

"Well, these ain't my clothes. We saw a red cardinal at Emily's feeder. Up to the farm I have my purple finches, but this was the first *red* bird I ever seen in the wild."

"Must have been swept north by that last storm we had," Emily said. "This is the earliest we've ever seen a cardinal."

Shirley broke a corner from her scone with her fingers and poked it into her mouth. "Marcel's got everybody fooled, hasn't he?"

"Well," I said, "in fact, the focus of the search is changing. Some investigators have begun to think Marcel may be dead."

Shirley finished chewing. "Yeah? Who's thinking that? How come?"

"The details are confidential to the investigation. I wish I could say more, but I can't."

"Don't you sell the old muskrat short. He's out there some-where."

"I hope he is."

"I hope he isn't. I hope they're right. I hope he drowned him-self in the lake."

"So do I," Emily said.

"The thing I want to know," said Shirley, setting down her cup, "is what Vaughn thinks about me looking after Marc."

"I've asked him if he'll let us take Marc out for lunch tomorrow. How would that be?"

"Who's us?"

"You and I. We can go to Burger King."

"Burger King! I don't want him eating at no damn Burger King."

"Why don't you bring him here?" Emily said. "We'll bake another lemon pound cake."

"Oh, but didn't he love that pound cake?" Shirley said. "With the lemon sugar glaze on top?"

I turned to Shirley. "Should I make that suggestion? That I'll bring Marc to visit you here?"

"Fine by me."

"Marc was with us all day Monday," Emily said. "Such a delightful child. Polite and observant, and so chipper, too. He's a wonder, considering everything he's been through."

"Where's he at right now?" Shirley said.

I cleared my throat. "Shirley, first let me ask you something, if I may. Was Marcel having any special trouble recently with Delmore Osgood?"

She tossed her head. "Nothing special about it. Nothing recent about it, either. Delmore and his dad been polluting our river for many a year."

"I have to say," Emily put in with as much edge as she'd allow herself, "it's a disgrace to the town of Tipton that you can't get that scrap metal business off the banks of that lovely river. If you all would make a push for zoning up there, somebody just might be able to step in and *do* something about it."

"We *did* step in," Shirley said. "We *all* stepped in. State environmental agency come up there for an inspection. So-called. Before it was all over and done with, *somebody* got bought off."

"Nobody got bought off, Shirley," Emily said. "It's all about local control. You get involved or you get shafted. It's that simple."

Shirley frowned. "That's what I just said! We *got* involved! Marcel and me, Kathy and Vaughn, Len Gerrity, the Blodgetts, the Robillards. We got Senator Gasbag involved, too, for all the good that did us. Old fart just takes positions so he can cut deals down the road. Who do you think got the environmental board up there? *We* did. They had hearings and viewings and all this non-sense, and they conducted all these sample tests and whatnot, and when it was all over and done with, Dwight Osgood come out spotless. Somebody's palm was bein' greased. Nothing else explains it."

Emily gave up. "More tea, Hector?"

"A drop, thanks." I turned to Shirley. "Was Ella McPhetres a factor in this dispute?"

She laughed sourly. "Hell, no. Ella was all for letting the *system* work out a solution. Ella was nothing but a damn bystander, like most of the town—including your high-toned mother, if you want to know."

"Marcel must have been pretty unhappy over how that one came out."

"He was unhappy, all right. That was right around when he started in cuffing me and all this. Forty years of marriage, and he's got to start in with the rough stuff."

"Knowing Marcel, he wouldn't have been content to leave the Osgoods alone after the board made its decision."

"Oh, he left 'em alone all right. You know where you take the fork to go out past the Osgoods'? Well, this past winter that whole stretch of road sunk to dead last on Marcel's plow list."

"How did the Osgoods take to that?"

"They didn't. They went straight to the sheriff—she did, the wife, Maureen Clancy, used to be a hippie—and you know Delmore is one of his deputies. And he went to Marcel."

"Who went to Marcel?"

"The sheriff. He come by the house. 'Be reasonable, Marcel,' he says, 'you got a sick man living out there, rescue squad has got to be able to get in.' "

"What happened?"

"Nothing happened. He even quit sandin' up there, for all I know."

The sun had slid into trees. I felt a chill at my back through the wicker. With thanks for the tea, I excused myself, saying I'd phone that night to confirm the get-together with Marc.

Emily walked me to the door. "This is good of you, Hector. She really appreciates your advocacy. Nobody's been making things easy for her and that little boy—least of all Vaughn Higbee."

"Well, we're not there yet, Emily, but I'm hopeful. I'll call."

Outside on the step, as I was putting on my muddy shoes, someone inside the house began singing. She had an impressive voice.

I stood and looked back through the windows.

It was Emily. She was clearing the table onto a tray, singing an old summer camp song: "I'm gonna getcha with my big shotgun, I'm gonna getcha if you don't begin to run. Oh, Mister Moon, Moon, bright and silvery Moon, won't you please shine down on me?"

Shirley had left the room.

# 16

Past the interstate ramps and the access road to the regional hospital, the state highway north out of Allenburg followed the river for several rolling, sparsely settled miles. Where it crossed a high marshy section over a mile-long causeway, in recent years there had been a lot of moose collisions, and dusk was the worst time. I was taking it slow.

On the way back to Tipton, my plan was to drop in at McPhetres Concrete and Gravel, where Tom McPhetres lived in the stark, flat-roofed house his father had built in the fifties out of interlocking concrete panels. I'd been inside the place once in high school, for a party. All I remembered was the windows were fixed glass, and the walls of the entry were covered by giant photos of the house that once had been part of a display at the Futurama Pavilion at the New York World's Fair.

As I came off the causeway, a patrol car hiding in the rest stop swung in behind me, rack flashing, headlamps pulsing. I pulled over and rolled down my window, angry at myself for not having foreseen this wrinkle. I could as easily have taken the old highway through Allenburg Center.

I shut off my engine and lights. He kept a car-mounted spot on me and held a four-cell in his cocked fist as he approached my truck.

"Please extend both your hands out the window, sir."

"Delmore, don't be a fool. What's this about now?"

"Sexual assault and home invasion. I want both your hands—stick 'em out the window."

I showed him my hands.

"Now open the door from the outside and exit the vehicle. Don't try getting fancy on me, either."

"You're abusing your office, Delmore."

"I guess you know all about that."

"Damn right."

"Once again. Open the door and exit the vehicle."

I slid out and stood in the gravel at the side of the road, palms open at my sides. The moving air had a damp bite. Del held the light above the brim of his hat so I couldn't see his face. Blue glints flashed off his gunbelt, where his hand rested on the butt of his automatic.

"All right, Bellevance. Turn around and assume the position."

"I'm a law enforcement officer, Del, and you can see I'm unarmed. Lighten up, for Christ's sake."

"Do what I'm telling you!" he yelled. "Turn around, spread your legs, and put your hands on the roof of the vehicle! *Do* it!"

I had a sweaty premonition that this was not going to turn out well for either one of us if it kept on much longer. Del's light left my face. I turned and extended my arms, propping myself on the cab roof. "Del, you don't want to mess with me. Whatever your problem is—"

"Shut up!"

For a moment I contemplated the bluish light caroming over the reeds—until Del brought the haft of his four-cell hard into my crotch, *whump.*

I sank to the wet road, folded into myself, nauseated, furious.

He kicked me in the back. I gritted my teeth.

"You been *fucking with me!*"

"This is not going to fix anything, you dumb shit."

"You been harassing my *parents*! You busted in the *door* to my girlfriend's *apartment*!"

"No, no. Listen—" I tried sitting up, but he kicked me again with the heel of his shoe.

"Enough!" I said.

"Lay still then!"

My back ached. My balls throbbed. The wet from the gravel seeped through my trousers.

"You sent the troopers out to tear up the salvage yard! And my camp! That was all because of *you*!"

"I didn't send anybody anywhere."

"Bullshit! Hey, I talked to Crissy. I talked to Tildy. Yeah, you remember Tildy. Little blonde, tits out to here? She called and told me everything. Fuck, man. Guys get *locked up* for that shit! Or maybe you figure she's a truck-stop whore, she won't say nothing."

"She'll say whatever it takes to rile you, Del. After what you did to her?"

"What *I* did to her?"

"Sunday night—you and Crissy. She's playing with your head." And mine, I thought.

He paused. "You didn't bust into her apartment?"

"The lock was already broken. We talked about you. That was it."

"You didn't ask her to perform oral on you?"

"Hell, no."

"No? If that bitch is yanking my chain, I will find out, don't worry. So forget her. *You're* the whole reason I got the state police crawling all over me and my car and my parents' place of business. *You're* the reason they're trying to put these fucking homicides on me and my family. Instead of *you*!"

"Shit, Del, you gave them the wrong shoes. That's all they needed!"

"That was by accident!"

"You told me you weren't at Boisvert's place that morning."

"I never told you that! Why would I tell you that?"

"They knew Pete had backup. Cahoon thought it was me, because you didn't tell him it was you."

"It *wasn't* me. I went in there *later*. Which is what I told them."

"Come on, if that hand hadn't turned up, nobody would have figured out you were ever there. Isn't that right?"

"Hey, super dick, what he asked me was if I was Pete's backup, and I wasn't. Which is all I said. They didn't ask for the whole story until later."

"Look, I'm going to sit up. You kick me again, and I'll break both your legs first chance I get."

"I believe it. Fucking vigilante."

"You letting me sit up?"

"Sit up, go ahead."

I pushed myself straight and slowly crossed my legs, leaning over my crotch.

"Pete and I both went there, but we went there separate. OK? The reason was I had to give him that stinkin' hand, because he had drove out of the yard without it, the stupid shit. And the guy was accusing *me* of negligence!"

"You mean you followed him up to Boisvert's, gave him the hand, and left."

"Right! Fucker didn't *want* me there. What happened after I left, I never saw it, never heard it, nothing!"

"Did Maureen go with you?"

"*Maureen?* Where do you come up with this?"

"What were you driving?"

"My Grand Am—which they impounded."

"Did you see any other vehicles at Boisvert's?"

"Fuck you! You're *interrogating* me. You got no right to interrogate me."

"Did you see anyone else?"

"I didn't see nobody! No body, no vehicles, no nothing."

"But you went inside the house. Did you see anything there, hear anything?"

"Back off, asshole! I got no more to say to you." Del reached into my pickup and tugged my keys out of the ignition. "I'm disabling your wheels. Maybe you'll take this chance to slow down, get your head clear out in the fresh air."

A car was approaching fast on the causeway. Del glanced that way. It slowed just slightly in spite of Del's flashers, then sped up. Del made a big flagging gesture with his light as it closed on us.

The car's horn blared and dopplered as the vehicle swerved around where we stood. Big Dodge Durango.

Del glared after it. "Fuckin' moron."

I pulled my feet in and launched myself at him, bowling him sideways into the roadway. The light went spinning. I bore down on his right shoulder, cocked my elbow, and sent my fist toward his face.

He got an arm in the way. My knuckles met gravel.

I had him flat on his back, but I had no leverage, and Del was a muscled-up young man. He bucked to heave me off. I grabbed a handful of his shirt and shoved him down, then reared back with my right for another shot at his head.

He blocked it again, grunted, and hacked his forearm up into my throat. I gagged, holding on. It took all I had to slam him back down onto the road. Hard as he hit, his head rebounded and he butted me between the eyes. Then his knee came up into my groin again.

He pushed me off and I rolled away.

He was panting and standing over me with his gun pointed at my head.

"I could *kill* you! I could shoot you right now!"

I had no words.

He knelt down and snugged the gun's muzzle into the base of my skull. "I'm not gonna report this," he breathed into my ear. "We don't need the hassle, either one of us. Just so you're all done sniffing up my asshole. We cool on that?"

"Yes."

He flung something off into the cattails. My keys.

He retrieved his hat and his four-cell, then twisted my sideview around to see himself. "Shit and damn. I am bleeding like a pig."

I pushed up gradually until I was standing, bent over my feet, my wet ass taking support from the panel of the Power Wagon. I spat blood. His rack lights felt like cold gusts of wind.

The cruiser door slammed shut.

Del jacked the car around, heavy tires spraying grit. He stopped next to me. His window slid down.

"Here's the truth, Bellevance, same as what I told the troopers. I get to Boisvert's, right? And Pete's up on the porch cutting the mud off of his shoe with a stick. I come up, and he says—without looking at me he says, 'You're suspended.' I couldn't fucking believe it. What *for*? Here I'm doing the guy a favor! Then he looks at the hand and he goes, 'Don't give me that thing like that. It stinks. Get it wrapped up or I ain't taking it.' So I went in the house and got a bag to put it in. Then he says, 'Go put it in my car,' so I went and put it in his car, and then I left. And that, if you would've just asked me, is all I fucking know."

He screeched off toward Allenburg.

Overhead the sky was blue-black, the brighter stars just emerging, Betelgeuse, Sirius. Saturn and Venus hung in the west just above the orange horizon. It was beautiful. A barred owl called.

I got slowly to my feet and brushed off my hands. Everything hurt. Nothing broken, though. Except my nose. For the fourth or fifth time. Both nostrils were clear at least, and my septum seemed to be in place. Lucky. I was in no shape for fisticuffs. He could have killed me.

The killer would have.

I found a screwdriver in the glove box and hot-wired the truck.

From the highway, the sodium vapor lights over the mounds of sand and crushed stone at McPhetres Concrete and Gravel made them look like so many scoops of orange sherbet. I drove past a row of parked cement mixers up the broad, paved grade to the house.

Unusual home. No landscaping whatsoever—not a tree, shrub, or scrap of grass, nothing but asphalt and concrete. The way the structure disappeared around the hillside, like a train on a curve, it was impossible to get a sense of its dimensions. The courtyard was bounded on one side by a long garage that looked like a warehouse. I pulled into the carriageway and got out, leaving the motor running.

The portico entry in a sculpted concrete alcove was austere but majestic—two ten-foot, center-opening pivot doors in varnished veneer with tubular aluminum levers. I pressed the doorbell button.

I'd cleaned up as best I could with a rag I had in the truck, but here under the milk-glass sconces I could see that my dishevelment was major. I tried brushing the dirt off my wet pants. My knuckles were sore and swollen. My face would earn me some sympathy, however, enough to get me in the door. That was something.

I rang the bell again.

A gargly intercom responded: "Please state your business."

"Tom? It's Hector Bellevance out here."

"What do you want, Hector Bellevance?" He was drunk.

"I've come to pay my respects."

"How civil of you. I'll be right down."

Tom pulled the doors inward. The entry floor was bare green slate. The enlarged photographs that used to cover the vestibule walls were gone. In their place were woven wall hangings. Tom's wife, I recalled hearing, was a fiber artist. A bad one.

"God almighty! You been in an accident!" Tom was not as hefty as his mother, though he had her doughy face and small chin. He was wearing a gold chain with a cross outside a black velour pullover. Bleached blue jeans, loafers, eyes all bloodshot.

"It's nothing serious," I said.

"You sure? You need a ride someplace?"

"I'm fine. I'd have a drink of water, though."

"Of course! You want to go wash up? I'll get you some ice."

"Thanks, Tom. That would be nice."

"I'll get you a drink, too. Come on in."

He led me to a white-tiled half-bath off the hall. The booze wafting from his pores was almost nauseating.

I did what I could with soap and water and a clean hand towel, but both my sockets were coloring up. And the nose ought to get looked at—might need some adjustment. Still, it was a good sign that my sense of smell was functional.

When I came out, Tom handed me a few ice cubes in a Baggie and an inch of whiskey in a leaded crystal glass. "Cures all ills," he promised.

We toasted the advent of spring and sipped. Fine bourbon— some small-batch product that brought back the days when fine bourbon had mattered to me.

"Hector . . ." He touched my wrist. "You know, if you would say a few words at Ella's memorial service, I'd be grateful. I know she would have wanted it."

"Certainly. I'm honored to be asked. When is it?"

"Saturday morning at ten at the Presbyterian church in Tipton." He tinked my glass again with his empty one. "By then the damn cops ought to have a better idea who's responsible for this mayhem, huh?"

"Let's hope. How are the kids doing?"

"How are the kids doing," he echoed. "You tell me. Their

grandmother gets murdered in cold blood—who they have been living with for the past two years—and the killer *gets away,* and they're totally unfazed! The two of them, bopping and grooving around the house like it never happened." He shook his head. "Where are their human feelings? I know I wasn't like that growing up, and neither were you."

"Murder stuns young people," I said. "They cope by ignoring it."

"Maybe. Somehow I don't think that's what's happening here."

"It's fear as well, Tom. They can't face it. Remember, it was just a couple of years ago their mother ran off on them. They're still dealing with that."

But the reminder rankled him. "Oh yeah? Well, having them back *here* again is driving my wife nuts. Burt's a total slob, clothes everywhere, plus he pees on the bathroom floor—how did Mom put up with it? His sister's worse in her own special way. My sweet Stephanie! You should see her picture when she was little. Prettiest little thing . . . This young woman has no respect for *anyone*—least of all herself. And a vicious mouth. Sometimes you want to pop her one. And this rasta thing with the hair? What's that about? Jamaican ganja? All the leather she wears . . . She looks like a dominatrix. You oughta see what she goes to school in!"

"Go easy on her. She'll grow up in a few years."

"Cool, and what do I do in the meantime? Stand back while she turns into a sociopath?"

I set my glass on a small slate table. "I'd like a word with her, Tom, if that's all right with you."

"What, now?" He looked at me. "You mean about Mom?"

"That's right. Burt, too. They may be the last two people to have seen Ella alive."

He nodded. "Steph's in the house. Burt busted out of here yesterday morning. Julie was reading him the riot act about some-thing. Haven't heard from him since."

"You must be worried about him."

He made a wave. "I'd worry if I thought it would help."

I followed Tom's walrusy bulk down the wide corridor and into a sort of den. Recessed perimeter lighting, fans spinning over-head, soiled beige wall-to-wall pile, cone-shaped hood over a cir-cular fireplace, two minimalist couches with swooping chrome arms, octagonal card table with built-in drink wells.

Stephanie, in her headphones, sat in the conversation pit, jerk-ing around on a beanbag chair to hip-hop we could hear as soon as we'd entered the room. She had on a black lace teddy over a white sleeveless undershirt, cut-off army pants, and big, thick-soled leather boots. She didn't shave. Her dreadlocks rattled against the vinyl chair, which was leaking. A thousand floaty white beads were scattered over the pit's parquet floor.

Tom cupped his hands. "Steph!"

She couldn't hear him.

Tom maneuvered himself down into the pit, took Stephanie's bare knee, and waggled it.

She tore off her headphones. "*Jesus,* Dad! Freak me out!"

He indicated me with a nod and raised his voice over the pumping headset, "You remember Mr. Bellevance?"

She punched her Discman. Quiet descended.

"You're going to make yourself deaf, Steph," he said.

"Great. Deaf Steph. That's what they'll call me."

"Mr. Bellevance would like to ask you some questions."

"What happened to him?"

"I'm all right," I said. "I had a little misadventure on the way here."

As she pulled her spaghetti straps up to her shoulders, I no-ticed she had some rash on the back of her neck, probably from the chair. She said, "If this is about putting me in foster care, you can book it, both of you."

"Chill, Steph," Tom said, "it's about Grammy."

" 'Chill.' " She rolled her eyes.

Tom gave me a dry glance and left.

I lowered myself gingerly to the carpeted rim of the pit—my back ached. The reason I was here, I told her, was to learn more about the events leading up to her grandmother's murder. I noticed the knees of my trousers were speckled with blood.

"Why do you wanna do that?"

"Because it may help me figure out who took her life."

"What are you, a cop?"

"Constable."

"Whatever. I don't socialize with you people."

"I understand, Stephanie, but your Gram was a goodhearted, hardworking, well-respected woman, and we owe it to her to find her killer."

"We?"

"I'd like you to answer a few questions."

"Like?"

"Did she drive you and Burt in to school that morning?"

"I don't see why you're asking questions. On TV they said it was the plow guy from up in Tipton, that was married to the lady that was staying with us. You know who I mean, right? The road foreman?"

"Marcel Boisvert. He's a possibility."

"You mean there's other possibilities?"

"That's right. Any ideas?"

"Me? Shit, no. Who are you thinking it could be? Not *me*?"

"No, no, no." I paused. "But you were pretty mad at her Sunday night when she told you you couldn't go to Canada."

"I *guess* I was mad at her. All winter she was suffocating me.

Sunday night I was just—I don't know, I was *through* with that shit."

"How was she suffocating you?"

"You know—controlling me! Like she would go, 'You're not leaving this house with your shoes untied!' So I tie my shoes. 'You're not leaving this house without a hat!' So I go get a fucking hat."

"That comes with the territory, Stephanie. Ella was supporting you. She was trying to look after you the best way she knew how."

"Oh, right! By making all these rules and then she changes them?" She jumped up. "I didn't flunk anything except fucking *typing,* but all of a sudden she's counting typing, so any parties— even if there wasn't beer—I couldn't go. Just because I flunked bullshit fucking *typing.* I was a *prisoner.* Two months, I was grounded. Then Sunday was *so great,* it was this beautiful day, and my two months' groundation was up, and Shawn and them finally invited me out, and she says 'I won't let you go'? Based on *what?*"

"Those guys were going drinking."

"That didn't mean *I* was!"

"Did you?"

"I don't drink, except beer. But she was gonna say I was anyway, so they were all laughing like, 'Girl, what's the difference?' "

"So you went to Canada with those boys?"

"Yeah. I told her I was going, and when they showed, I went."

"She didn't try to stop you?"

"She wasn't there."

"Where was she?"

"Town. They had to get to the drugstore before it closed."

"What did she say when you got home?"

"Three o'clock in the morning? She was in bed!"

"Stephanie, did Ella drive you and Burt to the bus stop the next morning?"

"I was sick that day."

"You didn't go to school? She must have been angry with you."

"Check this out. You know what she called me? Through the bathroom door? She called me a 'stupid little slut.' You know what I said back? '*Die,* you fat bitch!' Then, couple hours later, she's dead."

"That's too bad."

"It's weird. It's like you have satanic powers."

"You must have been at the house when the police took Shirley into protective custody."

"What police?"

"The state troopers. They came into the house. Are you telling me you never heard the police?"

"Dude, I was zonked."

"How did you find out Ella was dead?"

"Burt. He called me from school."

"I need to talk to Burt. You know where he is right now?"

"Burt? Why would I know where he is?"

"Has he been in school?"

"Not since yesterday. Day before, actually."

"He must be staying with a friend."

She shrugged.

"Did your dad call Nick Olson's?"

"They don't give a shit where he is."

"Julie must be pretty hard on him."

"Oh God. She's a bitch. You know Burt's bedroom? His room ever since he was a baby? Well, she stuck her weaving loom in there and these things of wool, and all he did was *ask* her if he could have his room back and she blew a fucking artery. All she had to do was say no."

"If he's in school tomorrow, make sure he calls me, won't you?"

"OK. You know where he might be, though? He might be up at Gram's."

"You think so? That house is empty."

"Yeah, but his stuff's there—his comics, his PlayStation . . . He likes it there. He likes the lake."

"Good enough. Steph, thanks. Take care of yourself, OK? The whole town's feeling for you right now."

"That's such bullshit," she said. Then she softened, adding, "But it's nice of you to say that. Nobody here gives a fuck what I feel."

"Well, I do. Will I see you at the memorial service Saturday morning?"

"Huh, I doubt it. Saturday morning I'm going to visit my cousins in Hartford for spring vacation. Get my ass out of this soap opera."

I nodded. "OK, then. If you ever need a ride anywhere, or a meal, or a place to crash, you be sure to call me."

"I will," she said. "Thanks. You're all right."

It took some effort to concentrate on the road. Grains of snow ticked against the glass. The whiskey buzz I'd ridden out of Tom McPhetres's place had left me sleepy, with a dry mouth and burning eyes. When I got to my turn, all I wanted was a few Tylenol and bed, but I pushed on past the sawmill, through the village, and out along the west bluff to the Bailey Road, beyond the Prentiss Point turnout, and up the winding lane to Ella McPhetres's cottage.

The house looked vacant, windows unlit, no vehicles in the open car shed, but when I pulled around back beside the screened porch, I could see TV light flickering against the ceiling in an upstairs dormer. Good call, Steph.

My knock went unanswered, so I let myself in through the

back door and flipped on the porch light. Its yellow glow spilled across all of Ella's redwood lawn furniture piled inside for the winter, along with a sizable collection of sporting gear: canoe paddles, touring skis, a primitive snowboard, inner tubes, pogo sticks, badminton racquets, fishing poles, golf clubs, plastic sleds, croquet mallets . . .

What would happen to this old camp? Probably get torn down. The land alone—more than twenty acres fronting the most beautiful lake in Vermont—was easily worth a million plus. Who had Ella left it to? Tom? The grandkids?

I found my way to the stairs off the dining room. The house was overheated. I could feel the furnace thrumming under my feet. The air was rank with burned fat and rotten garbage.

I followed the sounds of slashing music, explosions, and tinny hollering up the stairs and stood on the shadowed landing watching through an open door, as Burt engaged the forces of evil in a cramped, under-the-eaves room. He was bouncing around in his chair in nothing but his jockey shorts, utterly oblivious, just the way I'd found his sister an hour earlier.

"Yo! Burt!"

He scrambled around in the chair, losing his joystick. *"Shit! What?"*

I raised a hand. "Sorry, didn't mean to frighten you. I knocked downstairs, but you couldn't hear me."

He shut off the television. The reading lamp clipped onto the bedstead behind him cast a reddish light through the T-shirt he had draped over it. "God! You scared the *crap* out of me."

"My apologies."

"What happened to you?"

"Little mishap. I'm all right." The kid needed a shower. "You know, Burt, you can't be staying out here by yourself."

"Why, what am I gonna do, burn the house down?"

"You're fourteen. In the world we live in, people your age need a certain amount of adult guidance. It's an understanding we have."

"I am so immune to that."

"Tell me something. If I could arrange for you to have your old room back at your dad's place, would you go back there?"

"No. She *hates* me. That was the whole reason me and Steph moved out of there, was because of her."

"Stephanie says you haven't been in school the past couple of days."

"Yeah, so?"

I stepped into the room and lowered myself to the edge of his rumpled bed. "Listen to me, Burt. All of us—you and I and everyone who knew Ella—we're all trying to deal with a loss we will never completely recover from. Ella was a good and loving person. I knew her my whole life. I can't tell you how sorry I am she's gone. Words don't cover it."

His eyes filled. "It's so incredible, what happened."

I nodded.

"I couldn't believe it when Mr. Daubach told me Gram got wasted. She could be mean sometimes, but still you knew she was a nice person. She cared. She let me do stuff."

"She didn't let Stephanie do stuff."

"Well, I know, but Stephanie . . . Stephanie's got some sketchy connections."

"Like the boys she went drinking with Sunday night. What were their names?"

"Yeah, Shawn Driscoll, Curt Bevins, and that dork they call Crusty, with the tattoos. His real name's Alphonse."

"That must have gotten Ella pretty angry, if Stephanie left the house against her orders."

"She wasn't here. Stephanie never would have gone with those guys if she was."

"Where was Ella?"

"You know that lady that was staying here? The wife of the plow guy that beat her up?"

"Mrs. Boisvert."

"Yeah. Gram took her in to Brooks, but when they got there they wouldn't give her her pills because she forgot to bring her ID."

"That's a shame. What happened when they got back here?"

"I was downstairs heating up some pizza, and they come in and the lady stomps up like she's mad at me, and snags her big black purse that's hanging off my chair. Then she grabs a Coke out of the fridge and she leaves the door open and Gram comes over and *whams* it shut, and . . . what's her name again?"

"Mrs. Boisvert."

"Right. Gram's like, where do you think you're going, and she goes *her house,* and Gram's like *no way,* I'm done all the driving I'm gonna do for one night. So she was already torqued around, and she finds this note that Stephanie wrote over by the phone, that says Mrs. Boisvert is not supposed to go home, and she hollers for Stephanie to ask her about it. Only there's no Stephanie. Next thing she's all over *me,* like I was supposed to tell Shawn Driscoll to get off her property? Back off, Gram. I'm just a pedestrian here."

"What happened when your sister got back?"

"Barf-o-rama."

"She and Ella got into it, didn't they?"

"In the morning they did."

"A lot of yelling and swearing?"

"I don't know, I was out in the car, but Gram was pretty ripped. She already said she had to go in, hungover or not hungover, she wasn't writing her any excuse and she wasn't leaving her home alone."

"But that's what she did."

"Well, she had to, because Stephanie locked herself in the bathroom."

"When was this?"

"After breakfast. Gram never got up when Steph got home. I heard her puking, and I know Gram heard her if I heard her. Gram wakes up if she hears a woodcock."

I thanked Burt and told him I was going to drive him to my cabin, where he could bunk on my couch. I said I'd give him ten minutes to pull together everything he wanted to take with him, because he wouldn't be coming back here.

"Wait," he said. "How about if you take me to the Olsons'? In the village. I stayed there last night."

"I'll go for that. As long as you promise me you'll do two things."

"What?"

"Go to school tomorrow and call your father, just so he knows you're all right."

We shook on the deal.

# FRIDAY

## 17

I had a miserable night's sleep, waking in pain every twenty minutes, and then the phone woke me for good a little before daybreak—the sky was graying in the windows. Black smears stained my pillowcase—blood.

"This is Shirley. You said you were going to call last night, and you didn't, so that's why I'm calling you. I have to make plans for the day, and I need to know what's happening. I'm at my niece's house. Emily. Shapiro. You have the number."

I got up and rinsed out my mouth. Inspected myself in the mirror. I looked terrible. It was a little after six. Breakfast at Wilma's in three hours. The thermometer outside the kitchen window read twenty-six. A hoarfrost had gathered in the night, silvering my dead brown lawn. Mist filled the gap between the village and the mountain. And some prematurely roaming bear had destroyed all three of my bird feeders. Not good. There was so little to eat now in the woods, he was bound to be back. I thought about getting a dog.

Vaughn didn't answer.

When I reached the West Branch Four Corners, it was still before seven. Vaughn's sedan was not here and hadn't been here the night before, by the frost along the roadside. Twenty minutes later I pulled into the gravel cul-de-sac at Mount Joe Meadows, a small complex of two-story condos set in a rolling field opposite the barred entrance to the ski-touring center. Sure enough, I found Vaughn's mustard-yellow diesel snugged into a short driveway behind a new black Lexus coupe.

Bing-bong.

Simple metal-clad door with a gimlet peephole. The peephole darkened.

Janet Fleury opened the door, sleepy-eyed in the bright-lit hall in a gold satin dressing gown and red suede slippers. "Busted," she said. Country music was playing somewhere upstairs.

"Good morning, Janet."

"You rat us out, you know, and Vaughn will lose his job."

"I don't want Vaughn to lose his job. All I want to do is to talk with him."

"What happened to you, anyway? Somebody sock you?"

"It's not serious. He awake?"

"He's getting Marc dressed. What do you want to talk to him about?"

"I'm following up on a promise I made to Shirley."

"God. You're quite the bird dog, aren't you?" She had me come in and shut the door, shivering. "Wait here. I have to go put some clothes on."

Vaughn and Marc came out of the bathroom and down the staircase, Marc first. Janet passed them in silence as they descended.

"Hi!" Marc chirped at the sight of me. "What happened to your face?"

"I broke my nose, I'm sorry to say, but other than that I'm in great shape. How are you doing this morning, Marc?"

Vaughn had halted halfway down.

"Fine! You're the police, right?"

"Yes. I'm also a friend of your Gramma Shirley's. She'd like to invite you over today for lemon pound cake."

The boy was dressed for the day in overalls and a long-sleeved striped polo shirt. He glanced up toward Vaughn and said, "I'm not allowed to go to Gram's. It's dangerous over there."

"Not Gram's. I'm talking about Emily's house. You remember

the house you went to on Monday? Where they have that trampoline?"

"Yeah, OK . . . Sure, yeah, that was fun. They have air hockey
there, and a hot tub. Actually, *two* hot tubs—one inside and one
outside."

"How would you like to drop by for another visit this afternoon? With me?"

"That'd be cool! Can I, Dad?"

Vaughn eyed me. "We'll have to discuss it. Go fix yourself a
Pop-Tart."

He came the rest of the way down as Marc scooted by me into
a small galley kitchen. Vaughn's wet hair was pulled back tight to
his head, so he looked squinch-eyed. But it was early in the day.
He had on corduroys and a canvas bush shirt with pleated breast
pockets, and that silver chest hair at his throat.

"All it would take is a phone call, and I could get a restraining
order."

"Come on, Vaughn. You and I need to talk, and you haven't
been answering your phone."

"You walk into a door?"

"Clipped a moose out on the causeway."

"Ouch. Your truck all right?"

"More or less."

He nodded. "You know, I spent a good part of the evening yesterday at the state police barracks with two of the officers who
are running the murder investigation, Brian Cahoon and Mason
Sammis."

"How did that go?"

"Surprisingly well. They seem conscientious and determined.
Lieutenant Cahoon was upset to hear how you've been on my
case."

"It's a turf thing."

"The hell it is. Delmore Osgood's the prime suspect at this juncture. Were you aware of that?"

Marc yelled, "*Dad!* I *told* you she had Cap'n Crunch! Can I have some, Dad?"

Vaughn shouted up the stairwell, "You left out that damn *cereal*!"

"Dad! Can I?"

"Yes, yes! Go ahead!" Then, more gently, "Can you pour the milk?"

"Sure. It's in a carton. Thanks, Dad!"

He looked at me. "What do you want?"

"I want your permission to pick the boy up this noon and take him to Emily Shapiro's. Where he spent the day on Monday. I can have him back to you by four o'clock."

Vaughn sighed. "Trampoline, huh?"

"Loads of fun."

"His grandmother is deranged, Hector. And she's a Baptist. Or do I repeat myself? She can't be trusted with the care of a child."

"She has drugs to control that. Come on, you know they had a good time together on Monday."

"She's taking Ativan, in fact, and as far as I'm concerned she's crazier on it than she is off it. Last spring one time Kathy went out to her folks' to pick up Marc at the end of the day, and he was very quiet on the way home, which he never is, so she asked him, 'What's wrong?' Turned out she'd taken him to the recycling station and then forgotten him. She left my son at the *dump!* The kid was traumatized. It wasn't until half an hour later that it dawned on her he was missing." He walked over and glanced into the kitchen. "You know what she's angling for, don't you?"

"What?"

"She wants to resurrect the babysitting arrangement we had

before the accident. No effing way. If you can get that across to her, you'll be doing us all a great service."

"Does that mean you're going to let me take him?"

"Look, I don't want to be a jerk about this. As long as you'll be there, I don't see a problem."

"So we're on for noon, then. Where will I find him?"

"Here."

"Here? He's been here this week?"

"It's very safe. Marc is an extremely responsible child."

"He's been here by himself?"

"Part of the time, yes. He reads."

"I don't care how smart he is, Vaughn, Marc's too young to be left alone in a strange house. Or any house. You know that."

"Hey, give me a break. Rita Brasseur's day care was ideal—lots of space, great kids, close to home. I can't replicate that situation overnight."

Janet clip-clopped rhythmically down the stairs behind him. "Marc's been doing *wonderfully well* here. He has! He is very responsible and aware. He knows how to operate the VCR and the CD player. He has his books and his juice boxes. He has Daphne's number at the office, and I pop in at noontime and get him his lunch!"

"If that's the arrangement," I said, "why don't I just take him over to Emily's now? They'll be glad to see him."

"You want him for the whole day?" Vaughn said. "Why are you doing this?"

"I'm doing Shirley a favor. You and Marc, too, by the sound of things."

"You'll be there with them all day?"

"Probably not. But Emily will be."

"I don't know Emily. Look, never mind. Come back at noon, why don't you? Janet'll have him ready to roll."

"Whoa," Janet said. She took Vaughn by the arm and pulled him close. "Let him take him. That frees me up to go to the hearing. Right?"

"Five minutes ago you weren't going to the hearing."

"I know. That was because somebody had to come back here and fix chicken nuggets, and I didn't hear you volunteering."

"I *have* to be there. Janet, I'm just surprised. I thought you—"

"I'd like to hear you testify!"

"All right. Fine. OK. It's just Marc that concerns me. That woman—"

"—is *great* with him, and you know it. We'll swing by the Shapiros' and pick him up at four on the way back though town. It'll be *fine*."

"All right, all right, all right." He lowered his voice. "Let me point out, though, Janet, that you're second-guessing me again. You're disrespecting my judgment."

"Bull. I'm speaking up for myself is what I'm doing."

"Couch it how you will."

"Oh, couch it yourself. Couch it where the sun don't shine."

Vaughn retreated toward the kitchen. "Women run my life. Always have, always will."

She winked at me. "What a wuss."

Vaughn gasped. "*Marc!* Holy moly—I thought you said you could *pour!*"

"I *can*! Only I poured too *much*!"

Janet shook her head. "I'll go get his car seat."


"I think pickups are the *best*," Marc announced when I started the engine.

"Do you? So do I."

Vaughn stood at the curb waving as I backed around into the

cul-de-sac, but Marc was already engrossed in the immediate. "I like the way you have no backseat so everybody gets to sit in the front. And you can carry anything you want in the way back. Even a bed."

"That's what's handy about pickups, all right," I said. "Put a cap on the back and you can practically live out of it. This one's getting old, though."

"I know, but so what? Everything's getting old," he said.

I glanced at him.

He leaned up to unlatch my glove box. "Wow, you got a lot of money in here."

I laughed. Under the tools and maps there was a fair amount of change.

"It's mostly pennies," he told me. "Are you saving up to buy something?"

"Not really, no."

"I am. Every time I save a hundred and sixty-five pennies, I can buy an ice cream cone at Claudette's."

"What kind do you usually buy?"

"A medium cookie dough."

"Where do you get your pennies? Do you have an allowance?"

"My dad, if he has any. I used to get 'em from my mom. But, you know, she died."

I looked at the boy again, strapped into his blue booster seat. He was watching the road, delighted with his front-row seat.

"Yes, I did know that. That's a very sad thing."

"Did you ever know my mom?"

"Not really. My mother knew her. My mother was your mother's first-grade teacher."

"Your mother?"

"Yes. My mother greatly admired your mother."

He nodded. "Is she dead?"

"Yes, she is, I'm sorry to say. Both of our mothers are dead."

"I wish they weren't, don't you?"

"Every day."

"Do you know my Grampa Marcel?"

"I do, yes."

"He might be dead, too."

"What makes you say that?"

"My Gram. She said it's like when a dog gets rabies. That's what happens. First it makes them crazy, then it kills them."

"I guess that's right."

"My dad shot a fox one time. It got in our mudroom."

"Did he? When did that happen?"

"I don't know, but it had rabies. One other time we had a drunk hunter. He wanted to use the phone, and my dad wouldn't let him. That's why he says Janet's house is safer than our house. And it's easier to get to, because Janet's road doesn't have *mud*."

"How long have you been staying at Janet's?"

"Oh, since Sunday. But we go home sometimes."

"I see. And how do you like it at the condo?"

"It's not too bad."

"What do you do?"

"Not much. Mostly I read."

"You can read pretty well, I've heard."

"Oh, yeah. I love to read. If you're reading, you're not there anymore."

"I know just what you mean."

Outside Shadboro village I had to stop behind a line of cars waiting to turn left onto the mountain road. We were held up there for a few minutes by a slow stream of vehicles coming up from the valley, heading for the end-of-season tent sale at Buster's Ski & Bike.

"Wow!" Marc said, pleased. "A *traffic jam*."

## 18

We drove up to the Shapiro residence between rows of elephant-sized rhododendrons covered in fat green buds and pulled in under an arching portico beside Emily's maroon Explorer.

Emily popped through the side door, beaming. "Oh, how fabulous! You came early!"

I lifted Marc out of his booster seat and set him down. His shirt cuffs were wet with milk. Vaughn had changed the boy's overalls, but not, for some reason, the shirt.

We followed Emily out into the kitchen, where Shirley, in a blue apron, was stirring batter in a big stoneware bowl. *"Pound cake!"* she breathed at him, bright-eyed.

"Can I lick it?" Marc said.

"Why, sure you can lick it. That's half the fun of making it."

"I have to scoot, people," Emily announced. She snapped her heels together and offered a fencer's salute, car key to the tip of her nose. "You all help yourselves to anything you need. We'll be home by lunchtime. 'Bye!"

"Where's she going?" I asked Shirley.

"Manchester. Her daughter's coming in from Chicago for school vacation."

Marc climbed up on a stool. "You know what I want to do first, Gramma? I want to jump on the trampoline."

"Jumping first? Before licking?" She stuck out her tongue. "How about licking first, then jumping?"

He giggled. "OK, sure."

"And after that you want to color eggs?"

"Yeah! Cool!"

"But right now you're gonna have to butter me a cake pan, or I can't get you a bowl to lick. Your hands clean?"

He held them out.

"Clean enough." Shirley presented him with a gob of butter on the end of a rubber spatula. "Smear it nice and even all around the inside of this pan here. Inside only, got that?"

"Same as we did Monday." He turned to me. "I *knew* this was gonna be fun if we came here."

As I rolled up Marc's sleeves, Shirley said, "Hector, guess what? Binky and Mike say I can stay in their guesthouse as long as I need to, as soon as they get it fixed up. The commode's cracked. They're putting in all new fixtures."

"Who's Binky?"

"Emily. Binky's her nickname from college. All her friends call her Binky—which, it's funny, but I never knew that."

"That sounds terrific, Shirley. Emily has a big heart."

"She was my brother's only child living here in town all these years, and we never used to have nothing to do with her. Marcel wasn't interested."

"He wasn't particularly sociable, was he?"

"Well, because he was always working, that's why. And when he wasn't working, he was hunting."

"That's it."

"Anyway, this location couldn't be more perfect. You can walk to the library and the drugstore. There's flower gardens outside. Fenced-in yard. Jungle gym. Tennis court, if you know how to play tennis. And downstairs, you should see. They have a rowing machine, a pool table, and a boxing bag. And a hot tub. Plus skateboards, Ping-Pong—oh, and *Marc*—" She bent down to him. "There's *electric trains*!"

"*Trains?*" Marc said. "What gauge?"

"Double-oh! And there's towns and tunnels and six engines! It's all been took down, but I bet we can set it up sometime, you and me. We'll ask Binky."

"But can I just see them?"

"*Sure* you can. After your nap you can."

Marc glanced at me and stopped working. "You want to butter a little?"

"No, no," I laughed. "It's all yours."

"So where you been this week, Marc?" Shirley said. "Vaughn's office?"

"Uh-uh. Janet's condo."

She gave him a sharp look. "You been at *Janet's condo*?"

"Yup. It's nice and safe."

"You mean, while her and Vaughn are up to the college, you're there all alone in her condo?"

"It's OK, Gram. It's safe. I know the rules."

I headed her off. "It's been a bad week, Shirley. Vaughn's looking for a situation where Marc can be with other children. I'm sure he'll settle on something over the weekend."

"How would you like to come *here*?" Shirley asked him. "Be with me every day? Gosh, wouldn't we have tons of fun, you and me?"

"Every day? Sure, that'd be cool!"

"Vaughn would like Marc to be with others his own age, Shirley."

"I heard what you said." She was scraping the batter into the pan. "But that's foolish. No reason why he has to be with other kids when he's got *family*. Shoot, he'll be in kindygarten in six months. Other kids—that's just an excuse. Little children are supposed to be with their family when they aren't in school. That's where they learn about love and respect, is in the family."

"You may be right, Shirley, but I doubt Vaughn's going to

change his mind on this one. My advice to you is enjoy the day. If it goes well, there'll be others."

I found a yellow telephone out on the sun porch. Information gave me Women Helping Women, and the receptionist told me she'd be happy to page Lucy Pratt. "Who should I say is calling?"

"It's Constable Bellevance, on behalf of Shirley Boisvert." I gave her the number and hung up.

I could hear the two of them around the corner in the kitchen, laughing it up. Why couldn't Vaughn let the kid spend his days here? It's four miles from the college, the home of a pediatrician . . . No better place, and it would do them good, as long as—

The phone rang.

"Hello, Lucy?"

"This is Lucy Pratt. What can I do for you, Mr. Bellevance?"

I explained where I was and why, and told her that I was hoping she'd be able to swing by, if she wasn't too busy, just to keep Shirley on an even keel while I left the house for a few hours.

"What's the problem? Is Shirley having a difficult time?"

"No, she seems fine. But Emily had to go to the airport, and I promised Marc's father that I wouldn't leave Shirley alone with the child. Now, unfortunately, something's come up that I must attend to."

"Having to do with the murder investigation?"

"Most likely, yes."

She paused. "So I'd be helping *you*, then. Not Shirley."

"You'd be helping the investigation, Lucy. And I would be grateful."

"You would be grateful."

"We'd all be grateful, yes."

She sighed. "I'm not so sure I buy this, but hang on . . ." She put me on hold for a moment, then she was back. "I can give you till noon. That enough time?"

"That's perfect, Lucy. You're a gem."

"Right, then. See you in fifteen."

The landing outside Wilma's apartment door was piled with cartons of books and papers, kitchenware, toiletries, and shoes, waiting to be carried downstairs. The door stood open.

She was backing through the living room, dragging a rolled carpet from her bedroom. The couch and stuffed chair had been pushed to one side. Dust motes swirled though bars of sunlight.

I started around her to take the other end, but she dropped hers and threw herself against me. Her heart pounded in the hollow above my hip. "You feel wonderful," she said.

"So do you." She was shivery and warm.

"Who belted you?"

We sat on the rolled carpet while I filled her in on what I'd pieced together. She listened in a sort of trance. Watching her face, the pursed bow of her lips and the concentrated scowl she fell into, made me see again why I loved her—it was all her clashing facets. She was always surprising me.

"I'm going to miss you, Wilma."

She tugged me down and kissed me.

We made love upright against the wall and then on the arm of the couch and in the chair near the open door and then slowly on the mattress on the floor of the empty bedroom. She wept afterward. I didn't have to ask why.


"How's that omelet?" Wilma was sitting down to hers.

"Delicious."

"Looks a tad bit on the leathery side."

"That's how it should look."

She took a bite of hers. "Totally edible. Pepper?" She gave me a few twists of the mill.

"When do you go back down to Boston?"

"Not right away. Monday I'm flying to Cincinnati. You'll never guess who I'm planning to talk to."

"This is for something you're writing?"

"Right."

"About what?"

"Well, you know the rash of small-town bank holdups we've been seeing all across the country?"

"I'm aware of it."

"The theory is it's because these crooks have figured out that rural areas tend to have a thin police presence and wide-open interstates."

"Sounds right."

"Remind you of anything?"

"The Granite Hills Bank job."

"Bingo! That's my lead! Rowell's beagle and the remains and the stolen vehicle in the Space Research compound. And the connection to the bank job."

"That connection is speculative at this point."

"Right, and so is Malcolm Waller as the killer of No Hands. That's where I'm betting I can score."

"How?"

"They've got him. Waller's in jail, Hector."

"Waller? Since when?"

"About a month ago. They caught him sleeping in a stolen van out in Ohio. He's awaiting an extradition hearing in Cincinnati—which may take a while to sort out, since he's wanted for capital crimes in at least two other states."

"How did you learn all this?"

"Called up the FBI. It's on the computer, big as life. Waller never had a warrant issued for him in Vermont, and so I guess nobody here got notified of his capture."

"You're flying out to Ohio to interview Malcolm Waller?"

"Worth a shot."

"Waste of time, Wilma. These hardcases never talk—especially to reporters. He has no reason."

"Sure he does. Besides, anything he owns up to, what difference will it make? He's spending the rest of his life in Leavenworth regardless."

"Wilma. Waller's a lifetime psychopath who shot his partner in the back just to see the end of him. You want to know why he won't talk? Hatred. He'll make you feel like dogshit just for begging his cooperation."

She looked grim.

"All right," I said. "Maybe it's a naive idea, maybe it isn't. But it'll make a good story either way."

"Thank you. May I ask you to consider another naive idea while we're on the subject?"

"What is it?"

"You."

"Me."

"Yes. Gabe Prescott—my editor, who is a very savvy guy—Gabe loves it. I want to profile you. Ex-BPD detective and onetime Crimson hoops star—"

"Forget it."

"Oh, Hector. Why?"

"Because I've faded from memory, Wilma, and that's how I like it."

"You have not faded from memory. Hector, down in Boston when your name comes up . . ." She stopped. "Why not think of it as a *corrective*? Come on, damn it, the paper owes you. And you know it."

"There's nothing to correct that's worth correcting."

"Sure there is! I want to *do this* for you! Why won't you let me?"

"Why won't you leave it alone?"

She put down her fork and sat back. "OK. Part of the reason I want to do this, I will admit, is for me. This'll give me a way to work through some of this stuff. That's fair, isn't it?"

"Find another way."

"I don't get it. What you went though—it's already been *written* about. With a decidedly unflattering slant, too."

"I'm past all that now, Wilma. It took a long time."

She knit her fingers under her chin. "Do you think we'll ever talk about it, just you and me?"

"Maybe. Maybe not."

"All right." Wilma set our plates beside the sink and turned to face me, her white hands behind her against the counter's edge. "I can accept that if I have to. But Hector—"

"They were working you, weren't they?"

"Who?"

"Cahoon and Sammis. Monday night."

She flushed. "They weren't *working* me! All they said was—"

"They buttonholed you before they tossed my cabin. That's why you stood me up. That's why you ran away to Boston."

"No! First, I did not run away. Second, I *vouched* for you, Hector. You and I spent Sunday night and most of Monday afternoon together, and I *assured* them that you did not act like a guy who had just blown somebody away."

"But you couldn't be positive, could you?"

She hesitated. "That's what Sammis said."

"Sure. Because I had the time, the opportunity, and the inclination."

"Yes, I know, but you didn't do it. Because if you had done it, you would never have lied about it."

"That's right."

"That's what I *told* them!" she said, in tears. "That's what I told them." She fell into me.

After a time she said in a small voice, "What are we going to do this weekend?"

"I don't know what you're going to do. I'm going to find out who killed my friends."

She dried her eyes. "I want to help you. Whatever I can do. Anything I can do, I'll do."

I leaned down and kissed her. "I'm going to remember you said that."

# 19

The American Dowsers' Society bookshop, in a corner of the rehabbed woolen mill complex, a mini-mall a mile from the convent, offered such a narrow range of merchandise—crystals, T-shirts, jewelry, incense, CDs and tapes, oils and gemstones, several types of divining tools (pendulums, willow wands, Y-rods, L-rods), and books and pamphlets on recondite subjects like standing stones and Nostradamus—that I used to wonder how the place drew enough business to stay open six days a week. Most of its sales, I learned later, were mail order.

At the far end of the store, Hugh Gebbie sat in a wing chair, a book tented on his chest, watching us over his half-glasses. A harp was plinking from the speakers.

"Howdy there," Wilma said.

"Howdy," said Hugh, rising. "You're Wilma Strong-Parkhurst, unless I'm mistaken. You wrote Agnes's obituary a couple of years ago."

She nodded. "It's Wilma Strong, nowadays."

"Aha. Delighted." They shook hands. "I'd heard you two were keeping company." Wilma blushed.

He turned to me. "Took you a while, Hector."

"I've been busy."

" 'Busy' isn't the half of it, from the looks of you. You been to a doctor?"

"I'll be fine," I said.

"A blow to the head is nothing to take lightly. You know that."

Wilma said, "We stopped by to see if you'd like to take a ride up to Tipton, help us scope out the murder scenes."

"Love to. Now?"

"Unless you're stuck in here."

"No, no. Now's perfect. But first let's step around into the office. I'd like to show you something that will intrigue you, I'm sure."

We followed Hugh into the back of the store, behind an accordion room divider, where there were several tall filing cabinets and a library table with a computer and a big, powder-blue fax machine. He switched on a high-intensity lamp. Taped down in the center of the table he had the geological survey of the North Allenburg quadrangle, which comprised all of Tipton, Shadboro, East Shadboro, and part of Tewkesville from the East Branch to the border. As a boy, I'd had the same topo map tacked to my bedroom wall.

"After our aerial tour, I decided I ought to try expanding the search to a superconscious dimension."

"You mean ESP?" Wilma said.

"Right. Clairvoyance. Remote locating. Some folks call it teleradiesthesia."

"You dowse maps," I said.

"Yes. And photographs."

"That's phenomenal," Wilma said. "How do you do it?"

Hugh picked up a reddish, teardrop-shaped stone that was fastened at the fat end to a fine gold chain. He held the chain between his thumb and forefinger, wrist bent, and let the stone dangle. "I ask questions. The superconscious responds through the device."

Wilma nodded. "You come up with anything?"

"Yes and no." He slipped a finger under the edge of the topo map and slid out a grainy newsphoto of Marcel in his pressed work clothes standing stiffly, hands clasped at his crotch, near the fender of a ten-wheeler, TOWN OF TIPTON painted on the door. "First question I asked: 'Is this man alive?' Answer? He isn't. Second question: 'Did he kill himself?' Answer? He didn't."

"Amazing. So did you ask who killed him?"

Hugh gave her an indulgent look.

"That must be the *no* part," she said. "Mr. Gebbie, you know, what you're theorizing is exactly what the police are theorizing."

"Aha. The police think he was murdered?"

Wilma looked at me.

"That's the current assumption," I said. "Based entirely on blood evidence. Would you, by any chance, have a more developed idea?"

"I wish that I did."

"Where is Marcel now?" asked Wilma.

"That's not clear. Look here."

We leaned over the table. Hugh traced his finger along a line of circles he'd made with a fine pencil. "I worked a missing-persons case once when I was studying in Wales—many, many years ago now. Ten-year-old boy named Adam Creasey had been missing for more than a week by the time I got involved, and of course everyone feared the worst. I located the body in just under five hours.

As it happened, another boy had pushed him and his bicycle into a limestone sinkhole. Adam Creasey couldn't swim."

He held both his knobby, blue-veined hands an inch above the map and let them hover, palms down. "I've invested a fair amount of time in this." We watched. After a minute he drew back his hands and flexed his fingers. "The energies run in torrents."

Wilma put her hands where his had been. "Yikes."

Hugh ignored her. "See these marks?" He pointed.

I bent over the map. A hook-shaped series of wispy loops ran from the village out along the east shore of the lake beyond the cove at Westlook.

"They represent the course of the gyrations I was able to produce. Very weak. It's perplexing."

"When you produced these gyrations," Wilma said, "what did they tell you?"

"That he's in the vicinity."

"The vicinity of what?"

"Within the area suggested by the arcs."

"That's got to be four or five square miles, Hugh."

He shrugged.

"What about Marcel's killer?"

"Nothing. Not on this map, anyway."

"That's spooky," Wilma said.

"Could his body be in pieces?" I said.

"Pieces?"

"Could he be scattered?"

Hugh looked at the map. "That didn't occur to me."

"You think he was butchered?" Wilma said. "Like Waller's holdup partner?"

"That would account for the blood. Dismembering a corpse is a tough, messy job, though. You'd need time."

"And a good sharp knife," Hugh said.

"Vaughn Higbee used to slaughter his own pigs every fall."

"God, *Higbee*?" Wilma said. "Higbee's a wimp! You're only thinking Higbee because Delmore didn't blow your brains out last night when he had the opportunity."

"Del has a short fuse, but he's no killer."

"What about Maureen? I talked to her once or twice last summer. She's got the temperament."

"Why would Maureen shoot Ella?"

"Obviously because Ella knew something."

"Why would she take the sheriff's cruiser? Why not take Marcel's pickup, if she meant to frame him?"

"Same reason she wore the red hat. If she takes the cruiser, she draws the chase and also buys time for Delmore to dismember the body and pack it up for disposal."

"No," I said. "Whoever killed Marcel killed him long before Pete ever got to the house. There wouldn't have been enough time, otherwise. The killer was cleaning up when Pete rolled in there."

"But then why go and shoot Ella McPhetres?"

"Just as you said—she knew something."

A chime sounded. Someone had entered the shop.

Hugh got to his feet. "Let me take care of this person. Then we'll scoot." He excused himself.

Wilma seized me by the wrist. "Tell me something," she said under her breath. "Witching water with a natural willow branch, that's one thing, but you don't seriously think there's a fart's worth of truth in *map dowsing*?"

"I can't promise you there isn't."

"Right. You're such a sap."

"I've got to revisit those two crime scenes. Hugh gives me some reasonable justification, if nothing else."

"Oh yeah, that'll impress 'em. We're bringing in the ghost-busters."

"We need all the help we can get."

Hugh appeared around the accordion divider. "Ready?"

Wilma hooked her arm through his. "Here's a question for you, Mr. Gebbie. If you had the hand from a dismembered corpse, do you suppose you could map-dowse the location of the head?"

Hugh glanced up at me in surprise. "You have the hand?"

I shook my head. "Different homicide." She was incorrigible.

The Tipton Town Hall offices were locked. The lone truck parked in the newly graded gravel lot belonged to Clyde Bissell, our cemetery sexton, who was burning brush and deadwood down behind the winter crypt. Gray smoke wove like pennants through the tops of the pines.

I let us into the common room. All the tables had been folded and stacked in the middle of the floor. The paint was so fresh it made your eyes water.

"Pee-yew," Wilma said, fanning the air in front of her nose.

The paneling on the walls, which used to be a yellowish custard color, was now a semigloss eggshell. The blood-spattered cork bulletin board was gone, the linoleum freshly waxed, and several of the ceiling tiles had been replaced with mismatching ones. Someone had wasted no time tackling the cleanup job, and for a second I imagined it had been Ella.

Hugh asked where she'd been killed. I led him to the doorway between the records room and the common room. He shook open a folding chair and positioned himself on the spot. Wilma and I slipped around him into the records room. Ella had given me the combination to the Mosler vault the year before, when she went in for her gallbladder operation, so that I might monitor access to the town's land records while she was recuperating.

The card file under Higbee's name directed us to page 455 of Book 67, a heavy volume bound in red leather. There we found a general description of the old farm, encompassing 380 acres "more or less," conveyed into Vaughn's sole possession by the appointed executor of Kathy Higbee's estate, an attorney in Allenburg. Book 63 held the record of the farm's transfer from the estate of Philo Boisvert to Kathy Boisvert, referring us to Book 54, page 232, where the precise description and Warranty Deed of the property were recorded. That page, it seemed, was missing.

"Now, that makes you wonder, doesn't it?" Wilma said. "Vaughn must have Kathy's copy of the deed, though, right?"

"Good question."

We looked back through the older volumes. The property was originally part of the Passumpsic Lye and Lumber Company holdings, several thousand acres covering eight contiguous town lots, most of which had been bought by International Paper after Passumpsic Lye and Lumber went bankrupt in 1920. One parcel—Lot 42, which included Greenwood Hollow—had been unaccountably dropped from the sale. In 1932 the Grand List recorded Lot 42 as belonging to Philo Boisvert, yet there seemed to be no record of the transfer. Nor was there any deed. Early land records in Vermont were often incomplete, which explained all sorts of innocent lapses, but at the same time, when a sprawling tract that had never been surveyed came up in a tax sale, it wasn't uncommon in those days for a shrewd lister to take acquisitive advantage of the situation.

"I don't see Asa Greenwood's name in these records," I said. "Asa was milking cows out there in the hollow for decades before my father started in farming. They used to hay together."

"Maybe Asa leased the place from Philo."

"Maybe. Or maybe they were relatives." Greenwood, of course, was the anglicized form of Boisvert. "This suggests it's possible Vaughn was paying taxes on property he has never legally owned."

"How possible?"

I shrugged.

"He'd be royally ripped at the town clerk if he figured that out, wouldn't he?"

"He'd be more ripped at Marcel Boisvert."

"Yeah. But smart people settle these things with lawyers, not guns."

"Most of the time."

Ella's desk had been tidied up—books and papers straightened, and her cobalt glass candy dish, gnome statuettes, and photos of her grandkids removed. The telephone was new. I picked it up and tried Rob Tierney at his office in the Federal Building. The receptionist said she'd have him call me back.

Hugh's groan drew our attention. He sat on the edge of his chair, bent over between his spread knees.

"Ooof!" He sat up straight, rubbing his palms together. "Poor Ella! My God, but she was purely *terrified*!"

"She could see what was coming," I said.

He shivered. "No way to prevent it, no chance of escape."

The ringing phone was Tierney. I asked him if he thought I could get away with a quick tour of the Boisvert property.

"Well, I don't think there'll be anybody around to object," he said. "We've pretty much gotten everything we could get out of that location."

"Where is Cahoon?"

"On his way back from Waterbury. They ran some tests on Delmore's service weapon and a couple other pistols they seized at the yard. All inconclusive."

"Where's Delmore?"

"Delmore's directing traffic around a rockslide in Shadboro. He's been pulling a lot of hours lately." Tierney paused and then added, "He says you cracked him in the head last night."

"He assaulted me, the fool. What happened, did he call you?"

Wilma excused herself, saying she and Hugh were going outside for some air.

"We had him in for coffee this morning. Back of his head's got a big fat bandage. Took a few stitches to close the gash in his scalp."

"He's not filing charges, I hope."

"No, he considers it mutual affray. You know, Hector, Delmore's got his own idea who the bad guy is."

"Oh, yeah? Who?"

"Vaughn Higbee."

"He might be right."

"Well, but Cahoon and Sammis nailed down Higbee's whereabouts last Monday morning. Seven-thirty he was up on the other side of the lake, dropping off his son at Rita Brasseur's day care. After that, he went to the mountain to pick up a student of his. That also checks out."

"Have you considered that you could be dealing with two discrete homicides? The last person who saw Marcel alive was me—early Sunday evening. He could have been killed and carried off anytime after that."

"So you're saying Higbee shoots Boisvert in the night and Delmore drives out there the next morning and shoots Pete in Boisvert's dooryard, and the two are unrelated?"

"It's a possibility."

"So who does the town clerk? Or you want to suggest three killers?"

"Higbee's farm is worth a look, that's all I'm suggesting."

"Never get a warrant. You put Higbee at Boisvert's that night, and things'd be different."

"I know."

"I know you know. You keep on like this, and Cahoon's bound to hear about it. When that happens, I might not be able to fix it for you."

"I know that too," I said.

## 20

The perimeter of the Boisvert place, from the flooded willows to the pasture fence and out to the road again, was still bounded in crime-scene tape—though there was no one here. We left my truck and Hugh's Saab out along the roadside and walked down the churned-up lane to the house as the noon whistle at Allenburg Tap and Die sounded, twenty miles up the valley.

The dooryard was a stew of mud, buckled sod, and water-filled ruts. At the east side of the house stood a great mound of shaley earth left by the backhoe in uncovering the septic tank.

Hugh found a pair of L-rods in his day pack and put himself to work.

With a crowbar and a snow scoop I was able to clear away enough of the wood-chip berm Marcel had used to insulate his foundation to expose a cellar window. I pried that free and bellied feet-first into the stone basement.

Fuel oil, clay, creosote, and mold. Wilma's penlight lit the way for me around piles of broken furniture and moldering newspapers and rags to the stairs up into the kitchen, where I unlatched the woodroom entry for Wilma.

She was appalled at the disarray. "*Look* at this. What pigs! They *trashed* the place."

"It was no *House Beautiful* to start with."

"No kidding, but I mean, look as this floor! And Jesus, cigarette butts in the sink. They didn't have to do that."

"You're right, it's bad practice." I'd seen worse, though.

The pile of white sandwich bread, the box the Utah hat had come in, and the table lamp were missing. For blood sampling, I assumed.

"See this?" I nodded toward the blood spatter on the wallpaper.

"Yikes. Is that what I think it is?"

"Marcel threw Shirley's cat against the wall." At the thought, I realized that if the police had left the cat in her bureau drawer, I'd have to take care of it now.

"Why would you do that to a helpless creature?"

"To terrorize your spouse."

"Yes, but still, you'd have to be— What are you looking at?"

Behind us against the wall just inside the room were three large cartons that hadn't been here before. On top of one, in black marker, someone had written, "Mudroom—Boisvert." On the others, "Laundry room—Boisvert" and "Front hall—Boisvert." Either the forensics techs had left them behind or they'd already returned them.

I stripped the tape from the first carton and opened the flaps.

"Are you sure you should be doing that?"

Eight boots. Two pair of cheap, Sorel-type knock-offs, rubber-bottomed outsole with felt liners. Canada Snowmaster. A pair of woman's ankle-high slip-ons with the tags worn blank. And a pair of expensive leather Wolverines—hunter's boots, steel-toed high-tops with speed laces and a deep-cleated sole. I lifted one to the light. *9M. Made in the USA.* The leather was stiff and chalky. They'd been soaked.

"What size are those snow boots?" I asked.

Wilma took out her penlight. "Well, this one's an eight and a half. And these here are . . . ten. His and hers. What are those?"

"Nine medium. Too small to be Marcel's."

"Wait—listen."

Hugh was talking to someone out in the yard.

Through the open entry to the woodroom we could see Del Osgood out there in his uniform, minus the campaign hat, giving Hugh a hard time.

When he saw me hop off the porch, he stepped back and grabbed the pistol off his belt. "Halt right there, Bellevance."

I stopped and showed him my hands. "You've got no business here, Delmore. This property's off limits to you." His ruffed-up hair with the white patch in back reminded me of a kingfisher.

"Listen to you! I'm a county law officer! Shit, *you're* the one that's out of bounds."

"You're a *suspect* in this thing, you fool."

He colored. "So are *you!*"

"Put away that gun. No one here is armed."

"Fuck you. You got no special privileges."

"Rob Tierney knows we're here. Call him."

"Tierney! Him and Holmes, they got their head up their ass. Same as you and Cahoon."

Hugh said, "I'd feel much better if you'd put away that handgun."

"Who says I want to make you feel better?" But he holstered the weapon.

"Thank you," Hugh said.

"So what the hell are you people doing out here? I seen your vehicles, so I turned in the lane, and here's this guy *dowsing*. What's he dowsing for?"

"Insights," I said. "He's a geomancer."

"Hugh Gebbie," said Hugh, extending his hand.

They shook.

"But dowsing for what? The body?"

"Noxious emanations."

"Noxious what?"

I said, "Let me talk to you a minute, Del, all right?"

"What about?"

"Come on."

He shrugged. We walked off under the trees.

"How's your head?" I asked.

"Hurts. How about you? Your nose looks broke."

"I'm OK."

"Well, that's good, because, shit, I'm sorry about the thing with Tildy. I don't know why she told me that." He sighed. "She's a cunt, what can I say?"

"Delmore," I said, "Tierney tells me you favor Vaughn Higbee as a suspect in these homicides."

"Yeah, so?"

"What's your thinking?"

"Number one, I have a piece of information that none of the rest of you are in possession of."

"What's that?"

"It wasn't *me* did these homicides!"

"Good one. But what makes you think it's Higbee?"

"What makes you so hot to persecute my family? My dad's dying, you know. If he checks out behind this harassment, you and the fucking state got a wrongful-death suit on your hands."

"Come on, why Higbee?"

"Who hated both Pete Mueller and Marcel? Who hated them two *and* Ella McPhetres? You ask anybody in Tipton. Who they gonna say?"

"Vaughn was five miles from here at the time Pete and Ella were killed, leaving his son off at Brasseur's day care."

"Oh yeah? Where do you get that? If that's what he told you, that's a lie."

"How do you know it's a lie?"

"Because. That morning when everybody was off chasing Boisvert, I got a transport assignment. Had to take Higbee's kid to a protective location. You know why? Because nobody could locate fucking Vaughn Higbee. He wasn't home, and he wasn't at work. Plus, his kid never even *saw* him that morning."

"Hold on. You drove Vaughn's boy from Rita Brasseur's day care to the Shapiro house in Allenburg?"

"That's what I just said. This kid—he's little, but you ought to hear him talk. He talks like an adult, the words he uses."

"Marc."

"Marc, yeah, Marc. OK, Higbee, his dad, is supposedly at the college where he teaches, right? So we go check out the room where his class is supposed to be, and the room's empty. He's not in his office, either. So I take the kid into town and get him an ice cream cone. That's when he tells me his dad has a girlfriend, and they been staying at her condo because the road's all broke up out into the hollow. He says his dad says he's too big to carry and too little to walk. Anyway, turns out this girlfriend was the one that drove him to day care, not Higbee, because Higbee had to go to his office. However, as I found out, *he wasn't there*."

"It was the girlfriend who took Marc to Brasseur's that morning? Not Higbee?"

"Golly, you're quick, Bellevance." He squared his shoulders. "He told me her name, too, but I forgot it."

"Janet."

"Right, Janet. So that makes Higbee *my* main person of interest. In fact, I'm about to go borrow my stepmom's four-wheel-drive and take a little jaunt out to the hollow. Ask the professor if he'll kindly clarify his whereabouts that Monday morning."

"Not a good idea, Del. You won't find him at home in the middle of the day, anyway."

"Oh yeah? Well, he ain't up at the college. The college is on spring break. Plus, when you dial his home phone, it's busy. What does that tell you, Sherlock?"

"Don't go sandbagging Vaughn Higbee, Del. Listen to me—"

"Fuck you, super-dick! It's my family that's being persecuted here, and you're the number-one reason why!" He reached for the brim of his hat, forgetting it wasn't on his head, and nodded, end of conversation. He stalked off down the lane.

I watched him as he climbed into his cruiser and roared south toward the scrap yard. Hell. Now I was going to have to get to Vaughn before Del did.

"Well, that sucks," Wilma said when I told her we had to leave. "I was getting a fascinating lesson in geopathology. Mr. Gebbie has scored a whole network of GPZs."

"Geopathic zones," Hugh explained. "I've got veins crossing veins crossing veins out here. This land is sick."

I surveyed the ground. It certainly looked sick to me.

Wilma and I headed back to the road.

"Isn't it just a little risky for you to be venturing out by yourself to some psycho-killer's lonely abode?" Wilma wondered.

"I doubt he's there. There's a hearing he was planning to attend this afternoon, but I'll have to make sure. Meanwhile, Hugh will drop you off at the cabin, and you can get the details on this hearing, all right? It's about the FCC and Howell Hill. You want to find out where it's being held and when it's likely to end. I'll call you from Vaughn's."

"Roger," she said. "Hey." She took my hand. "If it so happens that he *is* there, don't do anything . . ." she trailed off.

I waited.

"You know what I mean."

"I know what you mean, and don't worry. I can handle Higbee."

"Roger." She wasn't smiling.

As soon as I reached the four corners, it was clear that the spur into the hollow had received some long-overdue attention. Vaughn had gained that much, though the stuff they'd laid down had to be the worst of what passed for gravel in Tipton. Sand and stones, mostly. *Bony material,* Marcel would have called it. The grader operator had left the shoulders banked like pizza crust.

I stopped here and there to get out to heave the bigger stones out of the roadbed, something you might suppose Vaughn would have taken care of himself if he'd passed through, unless he was planning on calling the road crew to come back and do the job right, which wouldn't be unlike him. Along with the grader tires' heavy braid, I noted three sets of passenger car tracks weaving around the obstacles. One set was doubled: in and out. New snows.

When I pulled in around the house, I was surprised to find Vaughn's diesel here after all. I sat in my truck for a time, listening to the water drip and hiss on the exhaust, waiting for him to come to the door. He would have heard me coming. But a minute passed, and he failed to show himself. Idly, I watched a pair of mourning doves peck around under the empty pole feeder on the lawn. Grape hyacinths were in bloom underneath.

Finally I slid out and called, *"Vaughn!"*

A steer answered. Crows cawed.

The mudroom door, a board-and-batten panel suspended from a steel track, was half open, and a light shone inside.

Opposite the deacon's bench, in a long, galvanized shoe tray, were Vaughn's rubber barn boots, wet and muddy. Beside the step was a broken-down pair of insulated leather boots, also wet—worn this morning. Sandals, sneakers, a woman's Nikes and garden clogs, Marc's little hikers and his puffy blue snowboots were all neatly paired in the tray.

The kitchen door was unlatched. I stuck my head through. "Hello? Vaughn?"

I sat on the bench to pull off my own muddy shoes and went inside.

"Yo! Vaughn! It's Hector Bellevance!"

I could hear nothing besides the sizzling sound of the refrigerator's defroster. The dry air carried a citrus scent, a cleaner of some kind.

I found Vaughn's white cordless and hit Talk. Nothing but fuzz—computer modem.

I padded across the pile carpet in the dining room and sitting room—both dark, draperies drawn—and stopped at the foot of a wide flight of stairs.

"Vaughn?"

I went up.

The first bedroom on the right was the boy's. A cherry-red chest of drawers and a tall four-poster bed with a red-and-white ruffle. It had been decorated in a circus scheme: a repeating pattern of acrobats and percherons was stenciled high on the pale blue walls, and a wooden clown mobile turned over his yellow desk.

There was a television room. Two plush recliners, shelves crammed with videos. No computer.

The master bedroom was a big space and dim as the rest of the house, with two sets of curtains drawn across wide dormers. I waited as my eyes adjusted. Pair of matching wing chairs, spindly halogen floor lamps, queen-size bed, unmade. Opposite was Kathy's mirrored, kidney-shaped dressing table. It still bore her bottles and jars, her hair combs, and several photographs of Marc and Vaughn in antique frames. How could he stand it?

Through a dressing-room alcove, in an adjoining study, I could see the glow of a screensaver. I went in, clicked the mouse, and the monitor came to life—browser icon pulsing in the corner. The website he had up was called "Sing Me a Song"—a kids' music page. I disconnected the modem, went back down to the kitchen, and put in my call to the cabin.

Wilma picked it up on the first ring. "Is he there?" she whispered.

"Nope. His car's here. My guess is they went to the hearing in his girlfriend's Lexus."

"Hector, the hearing was postponed."

"You sure?"

"The hearing on the tower proposal. It was scheduled for one o'clock in Montpelier, but apparently one of the parties requested a postponement. Family emergency."

A vehicle was approaching fast over the loose road surface. I leaned up to the window. All I could see was a blue spruce wind-break, pasture, and a stock pond skimmed with ice.

"Wilma, I'd better get off. There's someone coming."

"Who?"

In the sitting room I yanked back the drapes for a view of the road. It was snowing lightly. "Jeep Cherokee Sport, dark green, about ten years old, Vermont tags. Probably Delmore. I'll see you in a little while."

I returned the phone to its charger and went back into the mudroom entry, where I waited while the Jeep rolled in and stopped behind my truck.

Delmore Osgood unfolded himself from behind the wheel.

"You keep showing up in places you don't belong, Del."

"Look who's talkin'. Where's Higbee?"

"He's not here. I don't know where he is."

"You're shittin' me. That's his car right there."

"His phone was busy because he left his computer modem connected. I think he's gone somewhere with his girlfriend. She drives a black Lexus."

"What are you doing in the house, then, if he isn't here?"

"I needed to use his telephone. Now I'm leaving."

"You got balls, Bellevance. If you can go looking around in there, I can, too."

"Del. Look. Let's say you're right and Higbee's the guy we're after. Anything you find here in an illegal search will be inadmissible in court. Do you want to be the dumb cop who trashes the evidence the state needs to convict the bastard?"

"Well, so what about you? Where do you get your search privileges?"

"All I did was borrow the telephone."

"Bullshit. I know all about you. You think you're some vigilante super cop. You . . ."

I was sitting down on the mudroom doorstep, getting into my workboots, and we both noticed it at the same time.

"What happened to your foot?" he said.

My left sock, a white cotton gym sock clean this morning, was edged with blood. "I must have stepped on something."

I peeled off the sock. My foot was fine.

## 21

"Fucking Jesus, you killed him. You *killed* him!"

"Shut up. I didn't kill anybody. Let's see what we've got."

The broad ribbon of dark blood lying across the bathroom's marble doorsill was obvious as soon as I'd switched on the lights. I had walked past it the first time, intent on shutting down the computer in the study.

The bathroom door was closed but unlatched, the room unlit. With my elbow, I gave it a push.

"Jesus fucking Christ," Delmore breathed. He reeled back, one hand pressed to his mouth.

Vaughn's jeans and safari shirt were black with blood, his crooked-toed feet splayed out on white-on-white hexagonal tiles. Shot point-blank in the chest, he'd fallen against the edge of the Jacuzzi and slid to his side on the floor.

Cordite and feces. He'd tried to get away, then turned to face the shooter, pleading, shitting.

I crouched. "This is a couple hours old. Blood pool's dry at the perimeter. And his jaw's locked up."

"No way, man."

I looked up at the choked panic in his voice.

His cleft chin was trembling. He had his big stainless out again and pointed at my head. "It was *you*, Bellevance."

I rose and sidestepped carefully into the bedroom. "Damn it now. Easy with that weapon, Delmore."

"I don't *believe* this! You beat me out here and you flat-out *executed* the fucker."

"Calm down, Del, and I'll explain why you're wrong."

"That's your rep, isn't it? You blow people away."

I shook my head. "Not this time. I don't even have a gun."

He pointed at my feet. "Where's your sock you had on? That's *evidence*. What did you do with that sock?"

I held out my arms. "Look at me, Del. Look at my jacket. If I had just walked up to somebody and shot him like that, I'd have spray all over me."

"Yeah? How come downstairs you're telling me he's not here? Shit, you knew *exactly* where he was! You led me right *up* here."

The overhead lights made the bones in my head ache. I wanted to open a window or leave the room, and all I could do was stand there, holding my face and breathing deep.

Del tapped my arm with his handgun. "I'm taking you into custody, Bellevance."

"Just hold on, will you? Give me a minute."

I massaged my scalp with my fingertips. No sense. No sense in a world where misery like this befell children like Marc. His mother and father torn from him within a year of each other, his sun and his moon, how would he find the way?

My brain felt bloated. I needed to sit for a while and think.

"You're not gonna pass out on me, are you, Bellevance?"

"No, no. I'm fine." I blinked and tried to smile. "We'd better go down and call this in."

"What *we*? You're under arrest, remember?"

"Del. Here's what you can do. You can hold me until the troopers show up. After that it'll be their call. All right?"

He paused. "Do I have to tell you your rights if that's all I'm doing?"

"I wouldn't bother."

"OK, good." He wagged the gun. "So move. Nice and easy on the stairs. You first."

Del directed me to a chair on the far side of the oak pedestal table in Vaughn's breakfast nook, where I sat while he made the call from the kitchen. The air on my back from the window behind me was cold. I was chilled. My neck felt clammy.

Del planted himself in the chair across from me, laying his shiny revolver, his lighter, and his cigarettes in front of him on a blue cotton place mat.

"What are you doing?" he said.

I had my notebook open. "What does it look like? I'm writing."

"I know, but I mean what are you doing that for? You don't have to do that."

"I'm organizing my thoughts."

After a moment he said, "You know what? I'm over here watching you and I'm thinking, if *you* didn't kill him, Bellevance, then who the hell did?"

I set down my pen and studied him. He was tapping a cigarette out of the pack. Camels, from the carton I'd given him earlier in the week. "You don't want to smoke here, Delmore. This is a crime scene."

He frowned at his place mat, rubbing the stubble under his nose with a forefinger. I thought he was going to light up anyway, but he placed his cigarette down carefully beside the plastic lighter. They jumped when he pounded the table. "*Now* I'm thinking that if you're telling the truth, Cahoon's gonna be crawling up my ass again. Fuck."

"I doubt that. It depends on what they find, Del."

"What? You mean here?" He glanced out toward the dining room. "You mean like evidence, like trace evidence?"

"Right. The killer always leaves something behind. You know that. The trick is to find it and make the connection."

"Yeah. That's the theory, anyhow. Maybe there's something on his computer. Email, something like that. Because that upstairs, that was *personal*. Who would want to off Higbee? Besides Marcel Boisvert?"

"Any ideas?"

"Shit, I don't know. His ex-wife?"

"You think she'd drive all the way up here from her horsey life in Connecticut to shoot a man she hasn't seen in ten years?"

"How the fuck do I know? That's why you investigate her, to find that out."

I sat back. "Del, would you tell me a little more about what you did at Boisvert's place Monday morning?"

"Oh, Jesus Christ. I been through this five times already."

"Was it actually you who caught up with Petey at Boisvert's that morning? Or was it somebody else?"

"Where do you guys come up with this? It was *me*. I *said* it was me the whole time. I drove down there, I gave him the hand, and I left. Biff bam boom, that was it, OK?"

"Give me a few details."

"What details?"

"You went into the Boisverts' house, right?"

"To get that bread bag. I told you that."

"You dumped a loaf of bread onto the kitchen table?"

"So what?"

"Then what did you do?"

"I left!"

"Details, Del. Think."

"OK. Shit." He shut his eyes. "OK, I got the bag and I looked around and I found this old rusty cook spoon—to put the hand in the bag with, right? And I went back out on the porch there, and fucking Pete, he *still* wouldn't take it. 'Put it in my car,' he says. So I put it in his car, in his glove box, and I left. I never saw him again. Plus I never saw nobody else at the farm. I wish I could say I did, but I didn't."

"Can you describe what you saw in the house?"

"You want me to describe what I saw?"

"Please."

"I only went in the kitchen, and it was a friggin' mess. Hot, too. Cookstove was cranking like a bastard. Lot of crap all over, dishes and whatnot, cups. Floor was dirty. It was dark. I don't know . . . Smelled like cat piss."

"Thanks. Did you hear anything while you were in the house? TV on? Radio?"

"Nope, nothing. All I heard was water running. Sounded like it."

"Where?"

"Upstairs maybe, I don't know."

"You heard water running. Like a shower, a toilet, or what?"

"Just water. I don't know. Like in a sink."

*Water,* I wrote. Somebody had been in the bathroom.

We caught the tearing sound of vehicles approaching over the new road surface. Delmore put away his gun, and together we went outdoors to greet the troopers.

Darryl Munsinger and Goomer Ainsley headed grim-faced up to the master suite to record the scene with a camera. "Watch where you put your feet," I told them. "The bedroom carpet's full of blood."

Rob Tierney pulled in a moment later. All business, he debriefed the two of us and said Lieutenant Cahoon would have more questions once he and the crime lab made it out here.

"Well, I ain't hanging around waiting for that peckerhead," Del grumbled. "I got stuff to do."

"Be easier if you didn't make us come looking for you," Tierney said.

"I'm not that hard to find. Anyhow, I got nothing to add to what I just told you. You could give Cahoon that message."

"He'll want to talk to you himself, Delmore."

"So I'll talk to him. I'm not saying I won't talk to him." Del patted his bandage. "But I'll tell you who's at the top of *my* list until they find the guy, and that's Marcel Boisvert. He fucking *hated* Higbee. Plus the guy is twice as smart as the whole bunch of you trained investigators put together."

"Thanks, Del," Rob said.

"Meaner than a damn fisher, too."

Tierney asked Munsinger to escort the deputy out to the four corners and then tape off the spur to keep out the press and the yahoos. The fresh road surface would provide excellent tire impressions, and of course the fewer the better.

We watched Del horse his stepmom's banged-up Jeep around and drive off, Munsinger right on his bumper.

Rob said, "You still think he's part of this?"

"Not anymore. Not the way he looked at that body."

"Doesn't mean he's not an accessory."

"No."

He found a tissue in his pocket and blew his nose.

"Got a cold?"

"Yeah." Perfect hexagons of snow were appearing and disappearing in his hair and on his shoulders. "What about Boisvert? Any chance?"

"Only if he faked his own murder."

He nodded. "People can surprise you."

"All the time. But what would you have to do, Rob? Bleed yourself until you'd accumulated a couple of quarts? Just so you could pour it all down the drain?"

"That's not so inconceivable. Anybody could've predicted we'd dig up that septic. Especially if you splashed a little blood around to get us in the mood. Could've been something he saw on TV one time, you never know."

"All right. Let's say it was Marcel. He'd be on foot. And he'd be keeping to the woods. Agreed?"

"I guess. So?"

"So if we take a stroll around the perimeter, we should cut his track."

"Better leave that to Cahoon. He's not happy with either one of us at the present time."

The phone started ringing in the house.

"Is he ever happy?"

"I know, but you know what I'm saying."

"Either we look now, Rob, or this weather will settle the matter in half an hour."

"Hey, Sergeant Tierney!" Ainsley shouted from the wood-room entry. "It's somebody on the phone for Higbee. What do you want me to say?"

"Jeez," he said under his breath. "I'm teaching phone etiquette now?"

To Ainsley he shouted, "Ask who's calling, tell 'em Higbee can't talk right now, and see if they'll leave a message."

The trooper ducked back inside.

"I'm going to look for a sign," I said, "just to ease my mind about the possibility."

He sighed. "Be my guest." He started off and then stopped. "You're not armed, are you, Hector?"

"Not at the moment."

Tierney unholstered his black pistol. "I wish to God you'd keep your ass out of this thing. But as long as you won't, you better take this." He pushed it toward me butt-first. "I got another one in the trunk."

"I appreciate the gesture, Rob, but I really don't—"

"*Take* it, goddamn it!"

I did. It was an expensive SIG 9-mil.

"Cocked and locked," he said. Round in the chamber, safety on.

"Thanks." I slipped it into the patch pocket of my barn jacket.

" 'Gesture,' " he growled. "Hey, you still got that vest I gave you?"

I said it was on the seat of my pickup.

"Well, put the thing on, for Christ's sake. The guy's a torso shooter, we know that much."

Ainsley came outside again. "Sergeant, this woman wants to know when Higbee's gonna come pick up his kid. I think maybe you should talk to her."

"Jesus Christ. Hang on." He rubbed the balls of his eyes with his fingertips. "I forgot we have his *kid* to deal with."

"I'll handle that piece, Rob. I know where he's staying. I'm the one who took him there."

"Yeah?" He considered it for a second. "OK, good, do it. Might keep your stubborn-Vermonter ass out of trouble."

Beyond the pea-stone parking area, the prints I could make out in the short, tracked-up lane to the barn had been left by Vaughn's rubber barn boots. The snow had turned wafery and was settling now on the pale green blades of the daylilies poking up along the fieldstone footing of the barn wall.

To approach Higbee's unseen, you'd want to come on it from the west, where the ledgy slope loomed to within twenty yards of the barn, or from the north, following the stagecoach road's traces through the hardwoods. That's where I looked first, and it wasn't five minutes before I came upon two sets of prints along the side of the road: one walker passing in both directions. Right through the oxbow snowbank at the plow turnaround, too. Clearly a Vibram-soled boot, with some considerable wear on the heel. He'd traversed the snowbank rather than skirt it. Strange that it didn't concern him to leave an obvious trail—though he would have known this snow was coming. From here it was an easy two-mile walk through the hardwoods to the shore of the lake.

I measured a full print against the edge of my notebook, and took a moment to sketch the fleur-de-lis pattern of the heel, pausing a couple of times to shake snow off the paper. I found two hard-rubber feed buckets in Vaughn's barn, which I used to cover a set of prints, one right and one left.

## 22

From the turnout below my cabin I could smell woodsmoke. Wilma had the parlor stove going. I detoured across the side of the hill to check on the greenhouse. Fifty-five inside, thirty outside. Spud had been watering for me and stoking the drum stove. And drinking my Catamount Ale, by the row of bottles on the potting bench. It was discouraging to contemplate how much I had to get done in here. In the sunspace in the cabin, too, I had hundreds of plugs in seed trays that needed to be moved into peat pots. Tomorrow, I told myself. Wilma could help.

She set her bowl of dough on the woodbox to rise beside the stove and ran up and kissed me, holding her floury hands out on either side of her like a paper doll. "I'm *so* glad to see you! The way you hung up on me, I was afraid you were—" She broke off. "What? What's wrong?"

I hung my jacket on a peg. "There's been another killing."

We sat on the couch while I explained.

Her blue eyes swam. Her freckles faded into her skin. "How can that *be*?" She buried her fingers in her hair. "What is *going on* in this place? He's stalking us! Isn't he? He's out there. He's *hunting*! And, Jesus, Heck, you could be next."

I held her for a minute, then took her by the shoulders and pushed back to look into her face. "Wilma. I've got to go in to town. Tierney's asked me to see about Vaughn's little boy."

"Oh, *God*! I forgot. Oh, Jesus, the *boy*!"

"It wouldn't be wise for you to wait for me here."

"No!" she said. "Downright *un*-wise." She jumped up. "Before we take off, though, you should freshen up. You smell like—" She grimaced.

"I know," I said. I smelled like death.

Shirley sat stiffly in the middle of a wicker love seat in the sunroom, her hands pressed together between her knees. On the other side of the louvered windows beyond her, thick flakes swarmed down. Wilma had asked Marc to take her downstairs and show her the electric trains while Emily prepared tea. Lucy Pratt had left shortly after Emily's return from the airport in Manchester. Emily's daughter's flight out of Philadelphia had been canceled, as it turned out, and Emily was going to have to make the drive to the airport again the next morning.

"Vaughn doesn't want me looking after Marc," Shirley said. "I can see it in your face. He thinks he knows all there is to know about raising kids and every other damn thing besides—"

"Shirley, Vaughn's been killed."

She squinted and tilted her head to the side. "Killed? God almighty. How?"

"He was shot."

"*Another one*? Did they catch who shot him?"

"Not yet."

"Jesus! *That's* why you come here, isn't it? You're afraid the same thing could happen to *us*—me and Marc. Isn't that right?"

"No, I believe you're safe here, Shirley. I'd like you to tell me something, though, if you can."

"What?"

"Who owns the Greenwood place?"

She stared at me, taken aback. "Why, Kathy. What's that got to do with anything?"

"You and Marcel still hold the deed to that farm, don't you? And Ella knew that. But Vaughn didn't, did he?"

"Gimme a second here. First you tell me Vaughn's been shot dead, and in the very next breath you're asking me who owns the Greenwood place? What the hell is wrong with you?"

"Where is Marcel, Shirley?"

"*What?* Jesus!"

"Now's the time to tell me. Before anyone else is killed."

She looked incredulous. "I got no more idea where he's at now than I ever did!" She drew her shoulders back. Her chin was hard. "All along I been hoping he's *dead*. Because if he ain't dead, and if he's the one you all are looking for, then I'm good as dead myself."

Emily swept in with her lacquered tea tray, the crystal honey pot, the giant strawberries in a ring around the crustless sandwiches.

"Marcel got *killed*," Shirley told her.

Emily looked at me. "They found him?"

"No, *Vaughn* got killed," Shirley said before I could answer. "He got shot. And the constable thinks it's *Marcel* that done it."

"What is it you're saying? Vaughn Higbee's dead? Is that *true*?"

"I never did believe Marcel was dead," Shirley said. "I just *hoped* he was."

"What are you *talking* about?" Emily demanded.

I told her.

"Oh my. Oh my God, no." She sank into a chair, covering her mouth with both hands. "This is the most— Oh my Lord. And you say the murderer is *Marcel?*"

"No. We don't know who it is, Emily."

"It's Marcel, all right." Shirley picked up a sandwich. "He'll hunt you down, too, Bellevance. He won't quit with me."

"Thanks."

"You haven't told Marc yet, have you?" Emily said softly.

"No, not yet. I'll talk to him," I said. "Unless you'd rather."

"Best let a woman tell him," Shirley said. "He'll need a hug when he finds this out, and it should be me. I'm the only family that boy's got left. Right, Binky?"

"I—" Emily was trying to pour the tea, her slender wrists rubbery. She stopped. "I think that makes sense." She set down the teapot. "I'm sorry . . . This has me reeling here . . . Such horrible news, I can't quite . . ."

"What's in this?" Shirley said, opening her sandwich. *"Cucumber?"*

"Shirley," I said, "think about this a minute. Do you think Marcel could have planned to make it look like he'd been killed? Just to escape blame for these murders?"

"No, why would he do that? Hell, he's a expert *woodsman*. Nobody's gonna find Marcel if he don't want to be found."

Emily looked aghast. "My Lord! You don't really think he's still out roaming the woods, do you?"

Shirley shrugged. "Nothing says he ain't."

We all sipped our tea. The squall had passed. Occasional flakes slanted down beyond the glass.

Emily excused herself to answer the telephone. A moment later she returned and beckoned me out into the hallway.

"It's for you," she whispered, handing me the yellow receiver. "Lieutenant Brian Cahoon."

I thanked her.

"Lieutenant."

"Glad I caught you, Mr. Bellevance. Look, how about you meet me at the barracks in . . . I don't know—however long it'll take me to get down there from here."

"Where are you?"

"Sorry—Higbee residence. We been having a blast out here, detailing our third or fourth homicide of the week."

"Any progress?"

"Meet me at the barracks. I'll tell you all about it."

"Fine, but before you do anything else, you're going to want to assign an officer to the Shapiro residence. If the shooter—"

"Thanks. Any further instructions?"

"Look, Lieutenant—" I stopped myself. "I protected some footwear impressions for you out in the road beyond the barn. Have you checked those out yet?"

He was silent. Then he said, "You gonna meet me or not?"

"Yes, I'll meet you. All I'm saying—" He'd hung up.

Emily pointed the way down into the spacious Shapiro rec room. Wilma and Marc were sitting in weak light on the carpeted floor, batting a big ball back and forth with Ping-Pong paddles. A green and white beach ball, ENTERPRISE printed on each white panel.

Wilma swatted it toward me. I caught it, spun it on my finger, and passed it around behind my back to a finger on my left hand.

"Bravo!" Wilma cried. "Meadowlark Lemon!"

I bowed.

"It leaks air," Marc said.

"Marc," I said, kneeling to look steadily into his luminous face, "you'll be staying here tonight with your Gram. Is that all right with you?"

"Why? Is my dad gonna be at Janet's?"

"I don't think so."

"I don't think he is, either, because they fixed our road, and we can go home now. We don't have to walk in anymore."

"How did you learn that?"

"My dad. He was supposed to come get me right after lunch, but he didn't come yet."

"He called you here?"

"Yeah. Me and Gram were gonna color eggs this afternoon, but then we couldn't. There wasn't enough time."

"Well, maybe you can do that now."

"No, because she didn't get any colors. I got this instead." He was rolling himself around on top of the beachball.

"Food coloring'll work," Wilma said cheerily. "Food coloring and vinegar. I'm sure Emily has food coloring."

I told Wilma it was time for us to pop over to the barracks. Cahoon had requested our presence.

"He requested *my* presence?"

"You're my alibi, Wilma. I may need your support."

"Your alibi for what?"

I made a nod toward Marc and shook my head.

Before we left, I told Emily she'd better keep her blinds and curtains drawn and her doors locked.

"My God. So do you think we should stay out of the sun room?"

"I would, yes."

"I see. We're in danger, then."

"These are precautions, Emily. I've urged the police to reinstate your protection."

She shook her head, lips knit together. "Hector—as of yesterday the news media were still saying the same thing you told us the other day. That the police are proceeding on the theory that Marcel Boisvert is no longer alive. Are you suggesting they're wrong?"

I told her I had no good reason to believe they were.

The Allenburg Troop B Barracks was a mile south of town just off the interstate exit, a utilitarian slab of a building plunked down on land that adjoined a state transportation department gravel pit and the fenced-in grounds of the State Regional Correctional Facility. On the seat beside me, Wilma was subdued. She didn't rest a hand on my thigh as she usually did, and she didn't speak a word until we'd turned off the wet highway into the paved lot surrounding the barracks and I'd shut off the engine.

"What is it?" I asked.

She sighed. "Nothing. Just . . . all of a sudden I'm worried about our prospects."

"Immediate or long-term?"

"Both."

"I know what you mean." I opened the door.

"But, Hector . . ." She reached over and held me there with only her fingertips pressing down on my arm. "I want the baby. I need you to know I want the baby."

"Good. I want the baby, too." For a desperate instant I wanted to be alone somewhere. On a beach. In Mexico. I waited while it passed. "If you want me to drive you back to the convent, just say so."

I could see Cahoon standing inside the glass doors at the barracks' main entry in his shirtsleeves, arms across his chest, watching through the slow-sifting flakes.

"Forget it," she said. "It's probably just a chemical thing—little crisis of confidence. I'll get past it."

I wasn't sure whether she was following me or not until Cahoon said, "Sorry, Ms. Strong, but we won't be entertaining the media this afternoon."

"I'm here only to verify that I was with Hector the whole morning, until he went up to Greenwood Hollow, which was about half past twelve."

"Is that right?" He raised his scanty eyebrows. "In that case, kindly step inside."

He ushered us through the open lobby and down a narrow hallway into a small, windowless interrogation room, where Mason Sammis was waiting for us, leaning back against the radiator with his legs spread. He liked his poses.

"The ever-effervescent Mason Sammis!" Wilma said. "So pleased."

"Go easy," I said.

Cahoon had us take seats at a long collapsible table, while he unbuttoned his cuffs and rolled them a couple of turns. He gave off a sharp, stale odor. Nodding at Sammis, he clacked a button on the tape recorder in front of him.

"Now, Ms. Strong, for the record, let me reiterate what you just told me. That Mr. Bellevance and yourself spent this morning together. Is that correct?"

"Yes. From around nine till about one o'clock."

"And exactly where were you?"

"My apartment first, in Allenburg, then the Dowsers' Society Bookstore, where we hooked up with Hugh Gebbie, then the Tipton town office and the Boisvert farm."

"The Boisvert farm? The Boisvert farm's a secured crime scene, Ms. Strong."

"That's why we were there."

"You miss my point. The Boisvert farm is a restricted area, and as such you have no right to be there. Is this understood?"

"Yes."

"Thank you. What did you go there for?"

"To gather information."

"What information?"

"We were dowsing."

Cahoon glanced at Sammis. "And you thought the deputy was pulling your chain." He smiled at Wilma. "Detective couldn't believe it. I told him, you dowsers are all-purpose ding-dongs, you can dowse for anything. So don't leave us in suspense here. What did you come up with?"

"That whole farm is contaminated by negative energy."

"Negative energy. Gee. For some reason, I'm not surprised to hear that. Are you surprised, Sergeant?"

"I'm not surprised, no."

Cahoon leaned toward her. "Ms. Strong. If you intrude on this or any other state police investigation in any way, ever again, I will arrest you, and you will be booked and jailed. Cross my heart. Are we clear on that?"

"Totally."

"Fine. All right." He turned to me. "Mr. Bellevance, why did you drive out to Vaughn Higbee's house this afternoon?"

"I wanted a word with him."

"What about?"

"Some discrepancies I discovered in the town's land records."

"And what was the nature of these discrepancies?"

"There's no deed to Vaughn's property in the file. Pages are missing. Could mean nothing. But it's possible the Boisverts originally acquired that farm illegally by seeing that it got left out of a tax sale. It seemed worth asking him about."

"So did you ask him?"

"I didn't get the chance. Someone had shot him to death two or three hours before I got there."

"Before you got there. Now, when you got there and he didn't come to the door, you thought . . . what? He was hiding from you? Or what did you think?"

"I thought he wasn't home."

"You thought he wasn't home. Regardless, you entered his residence and gave yourself a tour. Warrantless entry, police trespass. Same freelance bullshit you're so famous for."

"Not at all. Vaughn and I were friends. I went in to use the phone."

"The phone. So how was it you happened to get Higbee's blood on your foot?"

Wilma looked at me and glanced down at my boots.

"I stepped in it without noticing. The room was dark at the time."

"Yeah—*upstairs*. There was a phone downstairs. What were you doing upstairs, Bellevance?"

"I was trying to free up the phone line. You see, the problem was—"

"Fuck this *phone* crap! You know what, you son of a bitch?" He leaned down toward me from the other side of the table. "You scare me. You're out of *control*. Nobody can tell you *anything*. You're gonna do what you're gonna do and *fuck* the consequences."

"I'm sorry if I've given you that impression."

He grimaced. "You hear that? That's my problem with you right there. Sammis, what did the state's attorney say about him? What was the word he used?"

"Haughty."

"Right—'haughty.' " He shook his head. "Shitcan the attitude, Bellevance. This is the biggest homicide case in the whole damn country right now, and you—*you*—are the major dumb-ass obstacle to me running a straight-up, uncompromised investigation."

"Jeez Louise," Wilma said. "Talk about attitude."

He turned on her. "You know, Ms. Strong, you're lucky you get to tiptoe out of here right now, because that is more than I can say for your boyfriend. Sergeant?" He hooked a finger toward Sammis and jabbed it at me.

The burly sergeant produced a set of cuffs from behind his elbow. "Please rise and turn toward the wall behind you."

I didn't move. "What am I charged with, Lieutenant?"

"Obstruction. Affidavit's on the way. You're all done for tonight, Constable."

"Mr. Bellevance?" Sammis prodded, jingling the cuffs.

"You're gonna teach me a lesson now, is that it?"

Cahoon nodded. "You know what, though? I kinda hope it doesn't take."

I only looked at him, then stood to let Sammis cuff me.

Wilma shoved up to get out of our way, knocking her metal chair over backwards with a clatter. "You can't lock him up! He's *helping* you, for God's sake! He's on your side!"

Cahoon didn't look at her, but patted my back, saying, "I gotta run. Use this opportunity to reflect on your crimes."

"Hector!" Wilma squeaked. "Don't let him get away with this! You're a law officer, too!"

Cahoon paused beside her on the way out. "I hate to tell you, but as a law officer your boyfriend crashed and burned a few years ago."

"Go fuck yourself."

Cahoon glanced over at Sammis. "Feisty señorita," he said.

## 23

Sammis ushered me into a holding chamber the size of a horse stall that had a steel-mesh seat bolted to the back wall and was fitted with D-rings and shackles. I told Wilma it was nothing—the state would file charges and I'd post bail in the morning, or more likely they wouldn't file charges and I'd walk tonight. Either way, no judge was about to jail me for investigating crimes in Tipton, where I retained a certain independent authority.

Sammis shackled my ankles and took back his handcuffs, then stood by while I gave Wilma the spare key to my Power Wagon. I said I'd meet her at her apartment. Tonight? she asked. If not, I'd call. Right. Anybody she should get in touch with? Bail bondsman? Attorney? Just Spud, I said. Make sure he's keeping a fire in the greenhouse stove.

"Right," she said again. She turned to Sammis. "I trust you will at least get the constable a glass of water."

"Sure," Sammis said. "Unless he'd rather have a nice, cold, dry martini."


"Mr. Bellevance? Sir?"

A trooper was nudging my wet, crusted shoe with the toe of his shiny black one. "Sergeant Tierney here to see you."

I jerked upright on the steel seat, grunting when my back clenched. I blinked. Couldn't make out his face in the glare.

"Sorry about this, Hector."

"You warned me," I said. I cleared my throat.

"We won't be filing charges, the state's attorney has asked me to inform you."

"Thanks, Rob. I owe you."

"His idea. He says he's confident the message has been effectively communicated."

I shuffled my chains. "I'm free to go?"

"On your own recognizance, yeah. But you give us any cause to land on you again, and you'll be looking at six months' bunk time plus a five-K fine."

"I'm familiar with the statute. What did you turn up at Higbee's?"

He shook off a yawn. "Several good tire impressions. A few bullet fragments. Griswold says Higbee died before noon—fairly advanced degree of rigor, neck and shoulders."

"Soft slug?"

"Large-caliber handgun. Fired from about four feet. No brass. Shot took off half the victim's right thumb, like he was trying to grab the weapon."

"Or stop the bullet."

"He definitely saw it coming."

"What's Cahoon's take?"

"Cold-blooded whack job. Nothing missing, no sign of struggle. Shooter walked in on him upstairs and scared the living shit out of him. The professor kept a loaded shotgun up in his bathroom closet there, which was probably what he was going for. Too bad he didn't make it."

"What about those shoe prints in the road?"

"Higbee's. Clear match to the old Dunham boots in the mudroom."

"So he walked up into the woods?"

"Looks that way. We concluded he must've went up there to pay his respects to his wife."

"His wife? You mean Kathy?"

"Kathy, right. Boisvert's daughter. She's buried up there. Little cemetery about half a mile in."

"She *is*?" But this made sense, even as it surprised me. That burial ground had been neglected for decades until the Higbees took it on. They cleared out the blowdowns, the myrtle, the leaf litter, reset the posts, and patched the board fence. Kathy had been cremated, though, I was sure of that. And during his eulogy, Vaughn had told us all that he planned to carry her ashes to the lookout at the north crest of Mount Joe, the spot where he had proposed to her. From there, he and Marc and Kathy's friends would scatter the ashes to the north wind. He could have changed his mind, of course. As a gesture to Marcel and Shirley. They'd been horrified at the thought of Kathy's being purposefully obliterated, erased from the world. But, too, it would have been like Vaughn to have it both ways—scattering some, burying the rest.

Wilma's snow-covered Mazda was parked right where she'd left it that morning, far back in the dentists' empty lot, nosed into a hedge of ice-coated yews. She was off with my truck. Her windows were dark.

Rob declined my offer of chili and beer at the diner in favor of going straight to his cramped rental on the reservoir road to call his family down in New Hampshire before his wife put their boys to bed. He'd been planning on driving home to spend Easter with them, but the day's events had quashed that possibility. I felt for him.

As he drove off, I patted my pockets for my keys, forgetting that Delmore had flung them into the marsh.

The lock in the recessed back door was a basic six-pin tumbler. For years, in the back of my dilapidated wallet, I'd been carrying a small tension wrench and a few picks. I was out of practice, so I just stood in close and tried raking the cylinder a few times, and what do you know, it worked, first good thing that had happened to me all day.

Wilma's larder consisted of the morning's leftover omelet fixings, lettuce, and most of my chocolate-mocha birthday cake. I ate some sourdough bread and a wafer or two of smoked salmon, just enough to quiet my stomach, stretched out on the giant bare mattress under an unzipped sleeping bag, and fell dead asleep.

I woke to the small shock of Wilma's cold skin against mine. She'd been out at my place, she said. When she couldn't reach Spud, she decided she'd better go up and make a fire herself, only to find after she got all the way out there that Spud had beaten her to it. I thanked her and pulled her to me, her back tight against my chest.

"I never want to be without you," she whispered.

"Good," was all I said.

# SATURDAY

## 24

"Hector!"

"Hm?" I closed my eyes against the hard morning light.

"Hector! Sweetheart! Wake up!" Wilma was rocking me by the shoulder.

I sat, wincing at the knifing pain in my back, always a new and familiar thing.

"What's wrong now?" I smelled coffee.

"It's Michael Shapiro on the phone."

"It's who?"

"Dr. Shapiro—Emily's husband. He's been trying to reach you."

I took the phone from her and lay back against the pillow, waiting for my back muscles to unclench themselves.

"Dr. Shapiro?" From the angle of the sun, it had to be past eight. I hadn't slept this late in twenty years.

"Mr. Bellevance. I didn't mean to wake you. Sergeant Tierney suggested I try this number. I'm calling because Shirley Boisvert has flown the coop, and we're hoping you might have some idea where to look for her."

" 'Flown the coop'?"

"She was gone at six-thirty when we got up. The boy, too."

"Christ. Did she take her things?"

"Well, she took what she'd brought with her. A black handbag and a basket pack. Some time between eleven last night and six this morning. The trooper outside never saw a thing."

"Did she take the car seat?"

He covered the mouthpiece, relaying the question, I supposed, to Emily. "No. The car seat's here. Mr. Bellevance, I have serious concerns here. Shirley Boisvert is a person who's not in good command of herself."

"I can see that. Are the town police looking for her?"

"That's why I'm calling. Every available officer's out beating the bushes for Marcel Boisvert."

"Wait, wait." I gingerly touched my aching face. "They're doing *what*? Did I miss something?"

"Sergeant Tierney suggested that you'd be able to look for Shirley and Marc. That's what I'm asking you to do."

"That's fine. What's this about Marcel Boisvert?"

"Late last night two detectives stopped by the house with a pair of old work boots in Ziploc bags. They asked Shirley whether she recognized the boots, and she did. They're Marcel's—her husband's. The police found the boots yesterday at Vaughn Higbee's."

"You mean the old Dunham work boots?"

"Dunham, that's right. The detectives believe Marcel swapped those boots for Higbee's boots because his were waterlogged and worn out."

"Did the detectives tell Shirley where they found these boots?"

"I'm afraid they did."

"So she bolted."

"Well, as soon as the detectives were out the door, she was calling you. I overheard her. She said she wanted you to get her out of here because it wasn't safe. 'Marcel's on a killing spree,' is what she said, 'and I think we're next.' "

"She believes Marcel knows where she's been staying?"

"I don't know what she believes. She's volatile and impulsive. She's a danger to herself and to the boy."

I told him I'd be there in fifteen minutes.

"What *is* it with that woman?" Wilma asked. "She's a small-minded, selfish, twisted old coot, and I can't *believe* she's about to get custody of little Marc!"

"I doubt that will happen," I said. I gave her the latest from Shapiro as I punched in Rob Tierney's office number.

He picked it up on the first ring.

"You're a glutton, Rob."

"Do I have a choice? Hey, did Shapiro reach you?"

"That's why I'm calling. He told me you've got Marcel's shoes. You're sure?"

After a pause, he said, "Let it go, will you, Hector?"

"I can't. I'm invested in this, Rob. As much as anyone."

"That's fine, but your job right now is to find Mrs. Boisvert. OK? She took off with the kid, and they both need to be under police protection."

"Rob . . ."

He sighed. "We were a little premature on those work boots."

"How's that?"

"Somebody logged 'em in as a size ten, and Higbee's other footwear's eleven. But the clincher is we scored a match to a set of impressions we preserved on Monday in two locations—Boisvert's dooryard and out below the Prentiss Point overlook, where he ditched the sheriff's cruiser."

"And Shirley ID'd these shoes?"

"She did, and so did Ira Moody, one of the guys on the Tipton road crew. They're Boisvert's, no doubt in their mind."

"Right. Where's Cahoon on all this?"

"Same as you. Blood evidence says Boisvert is dead, but once you get past that, he looks good. He's on foot, like you said yesterday. We like him paying a visit to his daughter's grave, too."

Marcel. I was ready to believe it. Marcel. Vindictive and ruthless, never any question about that. Patient, crafty, cruel, methodical, determined. But . . .

"You have to figure he's been hunkered down close by all week," Rob said. "Problem is, this weather's taken our K-9s out of play, so it's come down to a pure manhunt. Again. We're re-canvassing the area—every caved-in hay barn, woodshed, summer camp, boathouse, chicken coop, sugar shack, and overturned laundry basket. And we're sweeping the woods between Higbee's and the border. I believe we're gonna flush the fucker this time, I really do."

I wished him luck.

The day was gusty and bitter, just freezing when we left the convent. Spitting sleet.

The green and gold cruiser we found parked at the mouth of the paved drive to the Shapiro house proved to be empty as we drove past.

Emily met us as we pulled into the carport, on her way to meet her daughter's flight down in Manchester. She looked glassy and brittle, as if she hadn't slept.

"Sorry to dash," she said, "but this time I waited till she was in the air, and so I'm going to be late. Michael's expecting you. Go on in, please, if you don't mind."

"Are you sure you're OK to drive?" I said.

She softened. "Thank you, Hector. Yes—actually, I think I need to get out of the house."

"Is your protection inside?" Wilma asked.

"Protection?"

"The trooper whose car's parked out front."

"Oh, him?" She looked exasperated. "He left with the detectives for a strategy session or something. I don't know about those people . . ."

The fresh snow in the yard looked crisp as a bed sheet—an inch or two partly fused overnight, no better mold for footprints. I sent Wilma inside ahead of me and made a loop of the grounds to intersect the course of Shirley and Marc's escape. They'd left through a sliding glass panel in the rec room, walking out around the trampoline and through the rose arbor. Two men before me— Michael Shapiro and the trooper—had also followed their tracks past the tennis court and down the old service road to the sidewalk along Palmer Street, a quiet residential drive that wound around the foot of Hospital Hill down to the brick block along Railroad Street.

Wilma and I each accepted a paper napkin and a slice of Shirley's lemon pound cake on a glass plate. Shapiro showed us to his home office. He had a fire going in a small antique box stove. We set our plates down on an inlaid mahogany coffee table stacked with periodicals. Shapiro was about sixty and thin, with a long, placid face, slightly rounded shoulders, and wisps of white hair over a splotched scalp, the image of the revered pediatrician. In fact, he'd been the childhood doctor to a high percentage of Allenburg's population. He was also on half a dozen community boards and played clarinet in the town band.

"It's not my specialty, obviously, but I think anyone can see that Shirley's suffering from a severe personality disorder. She ought to be receiving regular psychiatric attention, especially since she's developed a drug dependency that's only making matters worse."

"She's abusing her medication."

He took a deep breath. "All I can say with confidence is she should not be trusted with the care of that child. I'm afraid I made the mistake of suggesting that to her last night."

"You think that's the reason she ran off."

"I'm sure it didn't help."

"Maybe not," Wilma said, "but the main reason's Marcel, don't you think? Jesus, she ID'd his *shoes*! That must have freaked her right out, realizing he's definitely out there, armed and totally unhinged."

"We've all been a little freaked out, I'm afraid."

"Yeah, no wonder Shirley split. If I had a psycho-killer husband out there stalking me, I'd be feeling a little panicky myself."

"All the more reason for the boy to be in someone else's care."

"No question about that," I said. "How is he doing, by the way? How did he take the news about his father?"

"Never got the chance to tell him. Last night I talked Shirley into holding off until we could have a psychologist on hand. She didn't like the idea, but she agreed to wait until morning."

"Shirley left the house carrying a basket pack and her black handbag, but left the car seat, you said?"

"That's right. She didn't take anything that wasn't hers, as far as I know."

"What color is her coat, any idea?"

He shook his head. "Emily could tell you."

"Marc wears a purple and teal ski parka," Wilma said. She was taking notes.

I asked Michael to show us her room.

We followed him up a narrow flight of maid's stairs to the low-ceilinged space over the kitchen. It had its own small bath. Next to the bed on a nightstand was a glass dish of dried flower petals and a stack of *Yankee* magazines. Nothing on the maple chiffoniere but a crocheted runner and an African violet. I checked the drawers. All empty.

"What are we looking for?" Wilma said, opening the closet.

"Nothing special."

Bare hangers on the rod. Dried mud on the painted floor.

"Where did Marc spend the night?" I asked.

Dr. Shapiro led us back down the stairs, through the kitchen, and down into the rec room. In the video nook, a sofa bed had been made up. Marc's small sleep had hardly disturbed it. Emily had given him a stuffed flamingo for comfort.

"Here's a thought," the doctor said. He was gazing out across the patio to the snow-crusted crocuses along the border, hands in his pockets.

"What?" Wilma said.

"The Boisverts lost their first child. Did you know that?"

"Yes," I said, "a boy named Philo. He was about my age."

He nodded. "Shirley's present condition has me wondering whether that child might have been autistic. There's a connection. Back then, of course, that kind of thing was never diagnosed."

"What happened to him?" Wilma said.

"He was sent away," I said.

Dr. Shapiro turned to me. "You remember Dabney Granger."

"I remember the name. He was my mother's doctor."

"Dabney was my first partner. Took me on right out of medical school, God rest his soul. Dabney always maintained that that was a euphemism."

"What was?" Wilma said.

" 'Sent away.' "

"A euphemism," I said, "for a more drastic solution."

He came away from the door. "Dabney saw the boy from infancy. There was precious little help medicine could offer in those days. And Marcel had no money for special care in any case. It was a tragic situation."

"You're suggesting that they offed their baby," Wilma said.

"Well, the child must have been close to five, but yes, it happens. Even today."

"You sound almost cavalier about it."

"Don't mistake me. I don't condone such killing. I do, however, sympathize with the anguish that parents often feel. Along with the humiliation. And the rage. Especially in men like Marcel Boisvert."

"So that's mitigating to you? Their humiliation?"

"In a way, yes, it is."

Wilma was amazed. "So, you mean no one has ever officially determined what became of little Philo?"

Dr. Shapiro shrugged. "He was 'sent away.' "

"That's hard to believe," Wilma said. "But I suppose the prosecuting attorney must have felt he didn't have a case."

"This was thirty-five years ago. Back then when it came to such family matters, rural communities often looked the other way."

"So what are you thinking? That little Marc has taken the place of her own lost boy?"

"Well, she wants to make sure he isn't taken away from her, I have no doubt of that."

All at once the big chilly rec room seemed oppressive. But at six-six I never have felt comfortable for long under a dropped ceiling. The soundproofing tiles held thumbtacks and leaflike scraps of yellow and pink crepe where streamers had once been festooned above some kid's birthday party.

I said, "If that's the central reason she left, to keep Marc to herself, then she wouldn't have had to go far."

Dr. Shapiro nodded. "Last night when she was ranting about how the police dumped her in our fishbowl of a house with a one-eyed deputy keeping lookout, she said the least the state could do was get her into a safe house."

"A safe house?"

"That's what she said."

"That was the offer her women's counselor was pushing last Sunday. Shirley wanted nothing to do with it at the time." I excused myself and went upstairs to telephone the Women Helping Women hotline.

In less than a minute, Lucy Pratt was calling back.

"I heard the news," she said. "It's just unbelievable, it's horrendous. How're Shirley and Marc holding up?"

"That's why I'm calling, Lucy. They've disappeared on us."

"*What?* What is that supposed to mean?"

"They left the Shapiros' early this morning, the two of them. Tell me, did Shirley say anything to you yesterday about needing another place to stay? Like a safe house?"

"No. No, she was happy as a clam! They were having the greatest time, jumping on the trampoline, playing with the model trains . . ."

"When did Professor Higbee call?"

"About an hour after you left. His plans changed, and he was going to pick Marc up early. When Shirley got off the phone, she started raving about him shacking up with some tramp, her not being allowed to see her grandson . . . She was in a tizzy."

"How was Marc?"

"Marc? Marc was so *sweet*. She was sitting in an armchair all agitated, rubbing her hands on her knees, and Marc went over and took her by the hands and reminded her that they still had to color eggs. Well, she looked at him and looked at him—it was like she was bringing the world back into focus—and *ding!*—it's like the clouds part, Bible beams start coming down, and she says, 'You're *right,* little guy,' and five minutes later she's out the door."

"She left the house?"

"She went to the Shop 'n' Save to pick up the eggs and the Easter colors. Problem was, she didn't realize that two years ago that store got moved all the way out to the damn mall, so it took her *forever*."

"She walked to the mall? By herself?"

"I'm *sorry*. She was so *breezy* about it—I never for a minute suspected her husband was out there stalking her, or obviously I never would've let her go! I had no idea she was going to walk to the damn *mall*. She could have gone down to Brooks Pharmacy right down the hill on Railroad Street, five minutes away. They have eggs."

"Were you angry at her?"

"No, I was angry at myself. And I was angry at *you*, if you want to know, for sucking me into a babysitting gig when I had a hundred other things I should have been doing."

"So did you color eggs?"

"No. There was no time by the time she got back. Marc was watching out the window for his dad's car, but he never showed up—" She choked. "I'm sorry . . . I'm sorry . . ." She swallowed. "I'm just so *upset* about *Marc*."

"We'll find him," I said. "But if Shirley happens to get in touch, Lucy, you'll call Dr. Shapiro, won't you?"

She would, of course she would.

## 25

Wilma and I crossed the Shapiros' crusty yard to Palmer Street's root-buckled concrete sidewalk. A layer of fine grit splashed up from the sanded pavement covered its broken sections in ribbons and fans. Given that, I was sure we'd find a print of Marc's heel, small as a doe's hoof among the dog-walkers' and joggers' tracks, to suggest their direction. But we didn't—neither uphill, toward the senior housing complex, nor down toward the center of town. Whatever time they left, though, it would have been easier walking right out in the middle of the empty, unlit street.

After St. Stephen's School and the Aubuchon Hardware parking lot, Palmer joined Railroad Street between Dunkin' Donuts and Brooks Pharmacy. None of the register clerks in either place had anything to offer about a small boy with curly blond hair and a wiry older woman with a black handbag.

It was nine-thirty. At the far end of the block, opposite the VFW hall, was the Vermont Transit depot, really more of a Gas 'n' Go than a bus station. A row of blue fiberglass scoop chairs bolted to a chrome frame opposite the coffee counter and a rack of magazines and real estate flyers—that was it for the bus travelers. The ticket agent was behind the lunch counter, spooning macaroni salad into a serving tray.

No, no one fitting those descriptions had been through the depot. Yes, she assured me irritably, she was sure she would have remembered.

A couple of baggy-pants college boys with backpacks and lacrosse gear at their feet, trading swigs from a liter of Sprite, were waiting for the next bus south to White River. And there at the far end of the row sat Stephanie McPhetres, cross-legged, eyes shut, wool cap pulled down tight over her chocolate dreads, nodding to hip-hop in her headphones. I recalled that she'd been planning to spend spring break with her cousins in Hartford, which, she'd told me, was the reason she was going to miss the memorial service—

Damn.

"What's wrong?" Wilma asked.

"Hell. I forgot all about Ella's service." I looked back out into the street. "It starts in twenty minutes up in Tipton."

"But don't you think they postponed it?" she said. "You know—considering the manhunt and everything?"

I nodded. She was right.

All Stephanie had for luggage was a black and yellow day pack. She was wearing black jeans with the cuffs rolled to midcalf and a pair of large, untied, thick-soled leather boots—the ones she'd had on Sunday night when she'd gone tromping through Ella's dining room, sending nuggets of mud everywhere. Same as the Wolverine boots I'd found yesterday in the evidence box in the Boisverts' kitchen.

I took Wilma's elbow and nodded toward the seats. "That's Stephanie McPhetres," I said.

She pursed her lips. "Yeah? Husky thing. Quite the grunge, too."

"Do you recognize those Wolverine boots?"

Her mouth fell open. "Holy mackerel. But they *can't* be, can they?"

"Get yourself a cup of coffee. I'll check it out."

"Stephanie," I said softly, tapping her knee.

She jerked herself straight and pulled off her knit hat. Woolly clots of hair fell around her face. "What? Shit, what do *you* want?"

"I'd like to ask you where you got your boots."

"What boots?"

"Your new Wolverines."

"Why, what do you care?"

"Please answer the question, Stephanie," I said softly.

She straightened herself in her seat. "Gram got 'em someplace, I don't know where she got 'em. She gave 'em to us last Christmas. But if you really wanna know, these here aren't mine. They're my little brother's."

"Ah. These are Burt's?" I knelt down and pulled back the tongue. *10M. Made in the USA.* "They're a tad big on you, aren't they?"

"So? 'S it make any difference to you?"

"Yesterday, as it happens, I came across another pair of Wolverines just like these. Size nine."

"Yeah? Where'd you find them?"

"How did you end up with your brother's boots?"

"How?"

"Come on, Steph."

She rattled her dreads. "I *took* 'em. OK? He left 'em at my dad's. Why, am I under arrest?"

"Why did you take them?"

"Because I wasn't gonna wear my sandals out in the fucking rain, all right? And she *confiscated* mine."

"Who did?"

"Gram!"

"How come?"

"For wearing 'em in the house, which, *I'm* the one that vacuums. What does she care? Right? Gram was *always* pulling shit like that. You wouldn't believe all the stuff of mine she confiscated."

I nodded, feeling a sudden hot prickling in my armpits and groin. "Safe travels to you, Stephanie."

"Yeah, you, too."

I motioned for Wilma to follow me outside.

"What's the deal? What did she say?"

We sat on a split-rail bench set out for the smokers in the shelter of the eaves between the men's and women's. I wrote for a minute, until Wilma's restraint ran out.

"Come on! *What's the deal?*" she demanded.

"Shirley," I said.

"What about Shirley?"

"It's Shirley."

"Shirley?" she whispered.

"She had no shoes when Marcel ran her off the farm Sunday morning. Just her house slippers. After she got to Ella's that night, Ella let her wear Stephanie's Wolverines when they went in to the drugstore. Shirley wore them later that night, too, when she hiked back to the farm. On Ella's snowshoes, straight down the lake and across the flooded pasture. She got back home sometime before dawn, wet and cold. Took off her waterlogged boots there in the kitchen, and when she turned on a light, the first thing she saw was her cat dead on the floor."

Wilma grabbed my arm. "Oh . . ."

"She went upstairs, got a gun, and shot Marcel right where she found him—in the bathtub."

"Which explains the blood."

"The knifework explains the blood."

"She cut him into pieces?"

"She's been putting up deer for years. She probably would have gotten away with it, too, if Pete hadn't walked in on her while she was cleaning up."

"Pete went into the house?"

"Sure he did. Pete went all the way upstairs and seized Marcel's guns. But he must have suspected something wasn't right. Marcel's truck was there. Where was Marcel? However it played out, Shirley ended up backing him right out into the dooryard and then killing him."

"But why would she shoot Ella, too?"

"Shirley believed Ella was the only person who knew she'd gone back home. That's why Ella called Pete early that morning—because she thought Shirley had put herself at risk."

"My *God.* That's horrible!"

I pushed up and Wilma followed, holding a Price Chopper flyer over her head. Sleet flickered around us like tinsel.

"So then, when she left the farm, Shirley put on Marcel's boots instead of Stephanie's."

"Looks like it," I said.

"On purpose. As a sort of a ruse—same as the red hat."

"Right."

"Then yesterday she left Marcel's boots at Higbee's. Very smart. But wait, if she was trying to put Pete's murder on Marcel, why didn't she take his truck? Taking the sheriff's rig makes no sense."

"I hope we'll get the chance to ask her that question."

"And how in the hell did she get all the way out to Higbee's?"

"That one's easier. Yesterday when we saw Marc, what he was playing with, do you remember?"

"A ball. A beach ball."

"And what did he say about it?"

"He said it leaked."

"Didn't he say, 'We're not coloring eggs. I got this instead'?"

"So?"

"Shirley brought it back for him. That beach ball was a give-away—a promo item." I looked at her.

"*Enterprise!* That's *right.* The rental car agency out by Ridley Motors! That's where we're headed?"

"First let's get my truck. I'm not walking out to the highway in this garbage."

"OK. But, Hector, come on, if Shirley's got a car she could be *miles* from here by now."

"She could, but this is all she knows. Besides, she has no reason to run. She's got her prize."

"So where would she go?"

"Not far, not in this weather. She'd go someplace where she wouldn't be recognized. And where she could keep Marc happy."

"OK. Jesus." She moaned. "How in the hell is that kid *ever* going to be happy?"

"He has time. Don't write him off, Wilma."

"No, I know. I know. All right." She wiped her eyes with the back of her wrist. "He likes trains, and he likes trampolines . . ."

"Yes. And he likes swimming pools."

The Enterprise Rent-a-Car office shared a double-wide trailer with H&R Block out on the state highway among the car dealerships and the fast food places. The bow window near the door framed a spare display of sand and seashells and four green-and-white paneled beachballs. GO SOUTH, YOUNG LOVERS was spelled out in cotton skywriting on blue poster board above the hazy ocean horizon.

A youthful, roly-poly go-getter named Brad was running the shop. He was delighted to see us, and yes, he'd been there the day before as well, bright and early, he commuted up from Barre six days a week, left at five-thirty in the morning, didn't get home till seven, eight, and yes, he certainly remembered Mrs. Boisvert, very nice lady, very nice, a little unusual, but not in a bad way. She had no credit card! Never run into that one before. But it wasn't a problem—just put in a call to her bank, local bank, Allenburg Savings, talk to a manager just to see if she had some kind of—

"*Brad*—" I leaned into his smooth face. "What is she driving?"

He lost traction. "Uhhh . . ."

"What kind of car?"

"Grand Vitara! See, she had to have four-wheel drive. I was just fortunate I had something in that category, because normally, by the weekend—"

"Thanks. Color? Plate number?"

He riffled through a sheaf of pink sheets while we waited. Burgundy. New York State tags, YTG 394.

Brad let me use a phone to call Rob Tierney's office, while Wilma sat and flipped through a *Newsweek*. He was out. I left a message. *Call immediately*. The receptionist would make sure he got it.

I sat there. I picked up a *People*. The cast of *Friends* was on the cover. I threw it down.

Three or four minutes was all I could stand. There was no way around it, I'd placed the boy in Shirley's care. Against his dead father's wishes. I had done that. His plight was all my doing.

I scribbled a clipped message for Brad to give Sergeant Tierney, and we plunged out into the weather.


If she'd rent a car, it seemed a safe bet she'd rent a room. And the room would be in a hotel with an indoor pool. That meant there were two nearby places to check, the new Excelsior Inn, south of Allenburg at the first interstate exit, and the pricier Vanderhof Inn and Resort, out toward Shadboro on the mountain road.

We tried the Excelsior first, since it was closer, and as soon as we eased down into the glazed parking lot off the highway, Wilma spotted the burgundy Grand Vitara with the New York tags parked near the inn's main entrance.

I parked right alongside.

"That was too easy," she said. "What now?"

"Now we go liberate Marc."

"Would you perhaps enlarge on that just a little bit?"

"Marc comes with us. That's our main goal here."

"We want to separate Shirley from the kid."

"Yes. Though first we'll want to separate her from that big black handbag of hers."

"I can see the wisdom there."

"As soon as she releases him, you whisk him out here to the truck or wherever seems safest."

"What are you going to do with Shirley?"

"Hold her until Tierney arrives. You take Marc back to the Shapiros'."

"You really think Shirley'll just let him go?"

"I do. As long as we put it to her the right way."

"Seems like she's been a step ahead of you all along, Hector. If she figures out you're on to her, we're burnt toast."

"Scooch forward, will you, please?" I pulled the seat back out and groped behind it for the heavy glove with Rob's 9-mil inside of it.

"You *are* worried, I hope," Wilma said.

"I'm always worried."

"That's reassuring."

I took the gun out of the glove and checked the clip and the chamber.

"That isn't," she said.

"Wilma. If you'd rather wait here in the truck, it's all right with me."

"No, no, no. I'm with you, Hector. You need me, right?"

"I may. Thanks."

Out in the rain, I took off my barn coat so I could fasten on Rob's body armor. It was a tight fit on my frame but lighter than anything similar I'd worn before. I tucked the handgun underneath the vest at the small of my back.

The Excelsior Inn was quiet, no one in the lobby. The desk clerk was a prim Asian woman—Su, by her name tag. Su had no Boisverts, sorry. I waited while she took a call, then explained that this was a police matter involving a kidnapping and possible homicide. I invited her to call Dr. Shapiro.

With that, she checked her register. "Room 238. Shapiro. That's the name they checked in under. Second floor, turn right. It's almost to the end."

Shapiro. I thanked her.

I gave a jaunty knock on the door to 238. No answer. I knocked again and called in, "Shirley? Marc? It's Hector!"

Nothing.

I knocked again. "Shirley? I'd like to talk to you."

There was no sound in the room.

"Try the pool?" Wilma said.

"Not just yet."

If they'd gone down to enjoy the pool, it seemed possible that Shirley had felt safe enough to leave her weapons behind in the room. And if she had, our next steps would be uncomplicated. It was worth checking.

A Hispanic woman not much taller than her linens cart was working the far end of the floor. When she glanced up at me and realized I meant to speak to her, she sucked in her breath.

"Miss, if you don't mind, my wife and I have locked our keys in our room. Will you help us?"

"No Inglees." Eyes downcast.

"*Soy policía, señorita. Y necesito su llave maestra.*"

"*Si, si.*" She fumbled her key card out of her apron and surrendered it to me.

"You know, Cahoon's right about you," Wilma said. "You're *terrible.*"

The green light stuttered in the lock, I pushed, and the door swung inward.

"I'm *serious,*" she was saying behind me. "How do you know the psycho-killer's not on her way up here this very second?"

We stopped dead.

There they were, looking at us.

# 26

At the other end of the narrow room on either side of a small round table framed by the sliding glass doors behind them, Marc and Shirley were eating Cocoa Puffs out of coffee cups.

"Shirley!" I said. I smiled at them. "I'm glad to see you're both all right. Forgive my barging in like this, but there are a lot of people who're very worried about you."

Marc was sitting on his doubled legs. He rose on his shins and whispered something across the table. Shirley shook her head.

"May we talk for a moment?"

"We're not going back there," she said. "If that's your agenda."

The door swung shut behind us. The close, humid air had a strawberry scent. Neither of the beds looked slept in. I didn't see the basket pack on the luggage stand or in the open closet space, and guessed she'd left it in the car. Should have thought to look.

The black satchel purse stood on the floor at Shirley's ankle.

"Why not? A couple days ago you were saying Emily's was perfect."

Shirley scanned our faces. "It was. Up until there was doctors involved. Doctors is where I draw the line."

"What's wrong with doctors?" Wilma said.

"Nothing, long as there's a call for 'em."

We stopped in the middle of the room, at the foot of the first double bed.

Intent on me, Shirley said, "Them doctors all got the idea they can tell you what to do. Even if they don't know the first thing about you."

"They're not out to do harm, Shirley. They only want to help."

"Don't need help." She flicked her eyes toward Marc. "I told him what happened, and sure, he was upset, but we worked through it. He didn't need no mental wizard to sort it out for him. Just look at him. He's doin' fine."

"We're our own family," Marc chimed in, as he shook out more Cocoa Puffs. The tabletop was strewn with them. "Me and Gram. We're the only one the other one's got left."

"That's a sad thing," was all I could think of to say.

"Everybody dies sometime," he said.

"See?" she said. She laid the big handbag on the table and opened the clasp.

Wilma looked at me.

"I'm an orphan," Marc said. "But not the same kind of orphan as I'd be if I didn't have a grandmother."

"You're luckier than a lot of orphans," I said.

"The good thing is me and Gram can move back out to the hollow. Right, Gram?"

Shirley's lips made a whistling sound. "Won't be soon, though, not the way things're goin'."

"They got to find Grampa first," Marc explained.

"They might never," Shirley said. "He's awful good in the woods."

"We're never gonna forget this, are we, Gramma?"

"Nope. No matter how we try."

Wilma drew a breath as Shirley reached into her handbag.

She pulled out a large plastic pill bottle, unscrewed the top, fingered out three capsules, and set them beside her eyeglasses. She poured milk into her cup and swallowed the pills.

"Shirley," I said. "Here's what's going to happen now. Wilma and I are going to take Marc back to Emily's, where he'll be safe. It's only temporary, of course—keep that in mind."

She didn't reply.

"Sound OK to you, Marc? You and I can set up that model train. How would that be?"

He looked searchingly across at Shirley. She said nothing, her eyes on me.

"We can't go back there," Marc said finally. "Too many windows. That's why we came here, right, Gram?"

"That's right." Her voice toneless.

"We're just like two honeybeezzz," Marc added quickly. "Snoozzzing in a warmmm honeycomb." He pressed his hands together and held them against his ear.

Shirley smiled faintly and said, "I been caring for him his whole life. I never let nothing bad happen to him, and I ain't about to start now." With the tips of her fingers she teased a blued sixgun out of the handbag onto the table. Short barrel, fat cylinder. She placed her palm on the grip.

"He doesn't *have* to go," Wilma said. "Not immediately. Does he, Hector? All we really basically need to know is that he's *safe*."

Should have left her in the truck, Bellevance.

"Marc and me, we'll get by," Shirley said, "one day at a time.

Nothing else you can do when you lose a loved one." She patted the gun. "You just got to take things one day at a time. That's normal behavior. We don't need nobody's help."

"Gram?" Marc said.

"What?"

"Is it OK if I turn on the TV?"

"No, honey. Nothing's changed, you know that."

"I want to just see if they put my dad's picture on again."

"Hon, now, remember what I told you? I got about fifty-eleven pictures up to the farm."

"I know, but I want to just *see*."

Wilma flashed me a hard look that I couldn't read. She stepped up to the hulking television console and jabbed the On switch. Nothing happened.

"You need the remote," Marc said, waving it. In the next second, when he slid off the chair to hand it to her, and Shirley's attention went to Wilma, I cut behind the boy, a guard coming off a pick, and in a stride I had Shirley's bony knuckles clamped to the gun and the gun pinned to the table.

"*Jee*-zus!" she hissed.

"Relax your hand and let the gun go, Shirley."

Her eyes blazed.

"Relax your *hand*!"

She rammed her forehead into my broken nose.

I grunted and staggered backward, toppling onto the bed.

Wilma let out a short scream.

I shook off the first wave. My hands were bloody. I held my nose and coughed and spat onto the floor.

Shirley sat straight up with the chunky handgun pointed at me along the tabletop.

"Marc!" she yelled.

The boy darted into the cove of her knees. She drew him to her with one arm. He was pale and openmouthed, Shirley's long face burning above his, the blade of her jaw flattening his curls. "I'm not lettin' him go. So you can forget that. Not after what I been through to get him back."

"Why did you hurt him?" Marc whimpered.

She turned the boy around and pulled his face into her shoulder. "Don't you worry. You're safe with me. I ain't about to shoot nobody."

"You can keep him!" Wilma said. "We'll just leave. We'll get out of here." She didn't budge.

I spat again. Wiped my face with my coat sleeve. You always were a sucker for finesse, Bellevance.

I looked toward Wilma.

She grimaced at me. "What do you say, Constable? Amscray?"

"Constable's staying right here," Shirley said.

"He is? No, he isn't. What for?"

"This won't work," I told Shirley. "Not a chance in hell."

"Oh, it'll work," she said. "Got to work. I'm all out of guns."

"Killing more people won't fix anything."

"Your truck a stick?" she asked.

I nodded.

"Hector?" Wilma said. "What's happening?"

"You drive a stick?" she asked Wilma.

"I what?"

"A stick. Stick shift!"

"She doesn't," I said.

"Wait— I do!" she said. "Standard shift?" She looked from me to Shirley. "Sure I do!"

"That's good. We'll be taking his vehicle, and you're the designated driver."

"That's very funny." She was white.

She turned Marc around by the elbow. "Go in the bathroom now and get your clothes on. Us honeybees got to fly."

"You're coming, too, aren't you, Gram?"

"Course! Sure I'm comin'. You remember what we said? About the back stairs?"

"I go down first?"

"There's my smart boy. You wait where I told you. By the fire hose. I'll be along after."

He scooted past Wilma and shut the bathroom door. The fan came on.

"Which pocket's your car keys in?"

"Right coat," I said.

"Reach in slow and toss 'em on the other bed there."

Wilma said, "Listen, Shirley, if you actually believe that I'm going to drive you somewhere at gunpoint, you are sadly mistaken. I—"

Shirley stood abruptly and swung the gun around on Wilma. Smith .357 Magnum with a three-inch barrel. I'd owned one for years. "Shut your mouth," she said. "You're gonna do what I tell you."

Wilma cringed. "OK! All right, all right, all right . . ."

Shirley directed the gun at me. "Toss 'em. Easy."

I did. My spare set. She took them.

The bathroom door opened. "Gram? My pants are wet. My underpants."

"That's OK, hon. Just don't wear 'em. Hurry now."

I had propped myself up on the bed and was trying to work my right arm behind me for Rob's auto. "Shirley. Think this through carefully now, Shirley. There is nowhere for you to go. There is nowhere to hide. They'll find you."

"Who? Who's gonna find me? Nobody's after me except you."

"You're wrong. I've already notified the troopers, Shirley. You won't make it. There's no chance."

"Huh. I got a better chance than you got right now, I'll tell you that much."

"Your rental car left clean tire impressions all the way out to Vaughn's."

"So? I went there. I went and got Marc some clothes. I never seen Vaughn Higbee."

Her forearm was tiring. She pulled the gun in a little closer to ease the strain, flexing her wrist from side to side. The Sig was wedged up underneath my vest. In this position I'd need both hands to work it free.

"You know what I'm thinking?" Shirley said. "What if Marcel was to find you here? He wouldn't leave you to tell the tale, that's for damn sure."

The bathroom door opened and Marc stepped out. "We're coming back later, aren't we, Gram?" he said. He was crying.

Shirley glanced at him. "Grab the boy's parka," she told Wilma. "The stairs is to your left. Marc'll show you where to wait. Don't get no ideas, either. You try and run with him and he'll fight you like a wildcat."

Wilma didn't move.

"Tell her, Constable," Shirley said, her jaw hard. "Tell her to take him down and wait for me."

"Do what she's asking, Wilma."

"But, Hector—"

"Or I'll kill you. Tell her."

"Or she'll kill me," I said.

Wilma's anguish blazed in her eyes.

"You'll be fine," I said. "I'll meet you later at the convent."

The second the door clicked shut, Shirley strode toward me and stopped a few feet from the bed, her right arm rigid again, her hand a squeeze away from delivering the end of everything.

"Don't," was all I could get out. I coughed. The blood was making me queasy.

She backed off a step and sneered. A welt had risen on her forehead. "Troopers can't hold me to account for these murders. You ought to know that. Not while they got Marcel's shoes but they don't got *him*."

I cleared my throat. "Are you confessing, Shirley?"

"Hell, no."

"Where is Marcel? What did you do with him?"

She tossed her head. "He's wherever they ain't looking for him. They won't never find him."

"He killed your Celeste, didn't he, Shirley?"

This got to her. Her eyes narrowed, and the gun dropped a foot. "How'd you know about Celeste?"

"I found her lying in your bureau drawer. At first I thought Marcel had put her in there for you to find. But he wouldn't have bothered to do that. You're the only one who would have laid her out like that."

After a moment she said, "Ground was froze."

"Marcel never heard you come in, did he?"

"He couldn't tolerate her hissing at him. Every time he stepped in the house. She cat-sensed the nature of him and he couldn't stand it."

"You carried Celeste upstairs, and Marcel was there in the bathtub. You placed her in the drawer and then you went and got a gun from the bedroom and you walked in and you shot him."

Her right arm twitched, remembering the recoil.

"Then you drained him and dressed him out. Didn't you, Shirley?"

She nodded.

"What did you do with him after that?"

She pursed her lips. "They was howling for him the whole time."

"Who was?"

"Pack of coy-dogs out in the intervale."

"Coyotes?"

"We been hunting them animals for years. They're just too smart. We tried trappin' 'em and baitin' 'em, and I don't know what we did. You can't fool them bastards."

"You fed Marcel to the coyotes?"

"No more'n what he deserved."

"For what he did to Celeste? Or to Philo?"

She tipped her head, and the Smith sagged a few inches more. "What did you say?"

"Philo."

The lines in her face deepened. "You don't remember Philo."

"I remember that he was a troubled child."

She shook her head. "He wasn't troubled. Philo didn't have all his faculties. That's all it was. He couldn't listen. He didn't have no *language,* no sense of *where he was at* . . ."

The Smith dropped a little more. Still, there was scant chance I could heave up and close on her without getting shot. Then again, I was going to get shot anyway, heave or not. As I elbowed myself straight on the bed, my main concern wasn't whether the vest would stop a .357 Magnum slug at four feet, but whether she would hit the vest.

"Get up," she demanded. She'd felt me gathering myself. "Stand up now, I'm telling you."

I squared my shoulders. *Now. Go.*

She had the gun on me again, nostrils flared. "It's gonna look like he found you here. And me and Marc escaped."

"No, Shirley, no. This is *pointless.* You won't—"

Her lips stretched into a grimace, I rose, she fired.

The roar and shock sent me back into the heater housing. I slumped to the floor.

The door to the room slammed shut behind her. Seconds passed. The shock ebbed as pain bloomed like fire in my chest. For a few seconds I lay still, doubled up on my side, waiting for the damage to register.

The dent in the middle of my vest was hot to the touch. And wet. Blood—I was bleeding underneath. The slug had cupped the fabric, but the layers felt intact.

You're stunned, Bellevance, that's all. Or mostly all. Pretty serious blunt-force wound to the breastbone. But I could function, I could definitely function, with all these endorphins flooding in. At least until the blood loss overtook me.

I drew my legs under me and pushed, holding my chest with one hand, working the Sig free with the other.

I'd never catch Shirley on the stairs, and there was no time to phone for help—not if I meant to keep them from taking my truck and trying to make a run for it on these roads.

I unlatched the sliding door and stepped onto the small balcony. It overlooked a utility area. The drop appeared manageable—fifteen feet down to a mulched slope studded with shrubs. I scissored over the railing and stepped off.

My right heel shot out from under me when I hit the wet mulch and pitched me sideways into a rugosa, which is what kept me from rolling further. The pain felt like a separate phenomenon, something almost outside of me, like some desert sun pounding down on my consciousness.

I got up and thumbed the safety off the Sig.

When I reached the corner of the building, I peered around toward the parking lot. No one in sight. A tractor-trailer swished by on the state highway.

Out in the main lot, my truck and Shirley's rental were parked side by side in the first row beyond the covered entrance. Shirley and her hostages were still in the building, then, taking their time. If they left the inn by the main doors, I'd have to run hard to intercept them before they would reach my pickup. But it made more sense for Shirley to avoid the lobby, so she'd likely choose the nearer exit—and if she did that, I'd have her.

A pushbar squeaked. Twenty yards from where I stood, a door swung out.

I drew back. Shirley came marching fast down a walkway bordered with crumpled narcissus. She was alone and rigid with panic. So Wilma had followed the plan—as soon as she'd gotten Marc out of that room, she'd taken off with him. If the boy had struggled with her, he was no match for Wilma, not in the state she was in.

Shirley turned away from me, toward the inn's main entrance, and I darted out to the parking lot and ran along in a crouch under cover of the first rank of glazed cars, the rain at my back. She had the black bag over her shoulder, but it looked as if she still held the handgun hidden inside her open wool jacket.

When I'd gained a clean line across the roof of a black SUV, I leveled my gun over the luggage rack and shouted to her. *"Shirley!"* She was ten yards from me.

She whirled and looked behind her.

"Throw down the gun! Do it! *Now!"*

She stiffened and quartered toward my voice, raising the Smith.

I let a round go. It bent her in two.

She sat and bounced, firing a chalky burst into the concrete. I stepped around the car and shot her again. Her head slumped toward her lap and she fell over sideways. Underneath her, the ground went crimson.

Somewhere nearby, Wilma was screaming.

Bile filled my throat. Sleet whispered on the cars.

*"Gram! Gram!"* Marc. He came running. The inn's dark glass doors flashed behind him.

*"Marc!"* Wilma cried. *"Marc, stop!"*

I stepped up to block the boy's view. "Marc— No, Marc. You can't help her." It was all I could say.

He spun around. Wilma dropped to her knees and Marc threw himself against her. He wailed into her breast as she rocked him back and forth.

She was staring at me.

"I had to do it."

"I know." Tears ran down her pale cheeks.

My head felt airy. My lungs ached. I could hear a siren. Someone shouting. The front of my trousers was an apron of blood.

I stooped to try to connect with Wilma, to touch them both, but I couldn't trust my legs. I had to straighten up, undone by the conflagration in my chest. When I opened my eyes, Wilma's orange hair and plaid coat were the only colors I could see. The world around her went from white to gray to black.

When they first got a look at me, the EMTs thought I had a bullet in me. The impact had cracked the sternum. Significant raw trauma, but no ballistic penetration. Though, penetration or not, a couple of inches right or left and I would have compromised an artery and bled to death in ten minutes.

As soon as I was patched up and stable enough to sit through a debriefing, Cahoon, Sammis, Holmes, and Tierney trooped one after the other into my curtained recovery area. "Best do this sooner rather than later," Cahoon explained, "as long as you're up for it." Now was as good a time as any—unless I wanted to have an attorney present. I didn't.

Cahoon, gruff and obsequious at the same time, began by urging me to seek the services of a violence and grief counselor, placing in my lap a short list of candidates. After I gave them a brief account of the shooting, Nezzie Holmes laid into me, about how my interference in the state's investigation had not only nearly gotten me killed but had also put innocent lives in danger—

*"Enough!"* I growled with all the force I could muster. "Sergeant Tierney asked me to find the boy. I found him." I coughed. It brought tears to my eyes.

Holmes was right, more or less, but I was in no mood to lie there and listen to him. The only surprising aspect of the aftermath was that once the pieces had fallen into place, all of Shirley's machinations struck none of them as extraordinary. The hero of the hour was Sergeant Tierney, for his foresight in making sure the constable had what he needed to save his stubborn-Vermonter ass.

I was glad to see them all leave.

Five minutes later, however, Cahoon was back, peeking around the green curtain. "Psst! Bellevance! OK if I hide in here?"

"What is it?"

He chuckled. He was feeling pretty chipper, I realized, now that his big multiple-homicide case had reached a solid, if untidy, conclusion. "Hey—I forgot I had a few personal items to give back to you." He held up a Filene's shopping bag and set it on the bed.

Inside were my Colt auto, its empty magazine, and my Chippewa work shoes in separate plastic bags.

"Thanks."

He nodded. "Sure thing. There's a pack of yipping media I got to go talk to down in the lounge, but I wanted to just say one thing to you now that I got you alone. Yesterday, if I insulted your integrity, you know, in front of your girlfriend . . . Well, I'm sorry if you took that the wrong way."

"I didn't take it the wrong way, Lieutenant."

"Good." He looked at the floor. "No, because I have this deep respect for your gut, you know—your animal instincts." He looked up. "Trouble was, right from the beginning of this thing, you been exhibiting the same lone-ranger mentality that you went bust behind a few years ago. That's where this whole thing started. You know what I'm saying? If you had let us in right at the beginning, you wouldn't be in here all busted up like you are, and nobody else would have gotten executed, and you woulda been spared the burden of taking another human life."

"Hindsight's twenty-twenty."

"I'm saying you could've stood back and waited. You could've waited for Tierney."

"It was my mess, not his. Anyway, you're lucky it all went down the way it did. You would have had a hell of a time getting a conviction with Marcel unaccounted for."

Cahoon shrugged. "You think? Nuts crack, in my experience."

"Not that one."

"Never know now, will we? Plus, that's no justification. Not that you needed one. Considering your past history."

"You're a sadistic prick, you know that?"

"I'd rather be me than you."

"Good. I guess we both lucked out there." I patted the shopping bag. "Thanks for the items."

"Sure thing. Can I ask you one question before I go?"

"What?"

A tall, bleached-blond nurse glanced in at us. Cahoon leaned in a little closer to my cranked-up bed.

"You ever see the movie *Lawrence of Arabia*? Peter O'Toole?"

"Long time ago."

"One of my top ten. You remember the part where Peter O'Toole's talking to this other officer, and he's telling him how he had to execute a guy? He says there was something about it that disturbed him. And the other officer says, 'That's to be expected,' and O'Toole thinks for a second and then he says, 'No. I *enjoyed* it.' "

"I'd forgotten that."

"That's something I always wanted to ask somebody like you. Do you *enjoy* it?"

I had a bruise on my hip the size of a flank steak, a padded dressing covering the wound in my chest, and my spine didn't want to bend, but I reared back and threw my fist into the side of his head anyway, ripping out my IV.

He toppled into my tray table and landed the floor with a *woof.* My water cup went rolling across the linoleum.

The nurse yanked the curtain aside. "Judas Priest. What the blazes is going *on* here?"

Another nurse appeared behind her.

Cahoon pushed himself to his feet. "This fella needs a course in anger management," he said lightly. His comb-over was hanging off his head like a broken wing.

I fell back in a fog of pain.

A nurse bent over me. "Get that jerk off the floor," I heard her say.

# SUNDAY

## 27

Easter morning a frigid wind was gusting out of the south, and the low clouds were spitting snow. When Wilma came walking up the path from the road, the collar of her bird-hunter's jacket up around her ears, I was outside in my own personal haze of painkillers, watching Spud spread manure on my upper gardens. She brought me a green basket with marshmallow chicks and jellybeans in it, which she set on the ground at her feet.

"OK if I hug you?"

"But gently."

She stood on my toes to give me a kiss.

"He's doing fine," she said over the noise of the tractor. She'd stopped by the Shapiros' to check on Marc. "He's eating and talking. Jane Uhlen is there—the shrink he's been seeing since last summer. She seems excellent."

"Did you ever get through to Vaughn's sister?"

"Inky. Yes, we had a long talk late last night. She's flying in this afternoon. Turns out she and her husband have a girl Marc's age. They'll be taking him back to Utah in a couple of weeks."

"Glad to hear it."

"How are you?" she said.

"I'll mend."

Spud shut down the tractor. "That gonna do ya? Or you want another load?" He jumped to the ground, holding his cap on.

"I love that smell," Wilma said.

Spud laughed. "Country girl at heart."

"I wish!"

"*He* wishes," Spud said, with a nod toward me.

Wilma looked into my face. "He's gonna have to take me as I am."

"Yeah, well, that's a saw that cuts both ways," Spud said. Then, embarrassed, he chopped his heel into the sod and changed the subject. "That Shirley," he said. "Who ever woulda suspected? Hell of a nasty old she-bear, wasn't she?"

"She sure was," Wilma said. "The thing is, though, now that she's dead, there's no hard proof that she killed anybody, is there?"

"Oh, there's some," I said. "The lab found traces of blood inside her basket pack. If they're Marcel's, as I don't doubt they are, that'll say a lot."

"OK, but I mean, officially, doesn't it all have to remain in the realm of conjecture? You have no confession, no murder weapon, and no body."

"That is problematic. Though I have a hunch he'll turn up."

"You don't really think she fed him to the coyotes, do you?"

I shrugged. "I'm meeting Hugh Gebbie at the town garage in half an hour. Come along if you want."

"What's at the garage?"

"Don't know. Maybe nothing. You want to join us, Spud?"

Spud climbed back up into his open cab. "I got shit to do. But give old Hugh my regards. What are you gonna look for?"

"Marcel."

"No, we're not," Wilma laughed. "Are we?"


Hugh was waiting for us outside the town garage's wire mesh gates. They were locked with chain against unauthorized vehicles, but we were able to walk around into the yard through the trees.

I crossed to where the town's heavy equipment stood in a row just before a brushy incline some twenty feet above the lake shore.

Hugh and Wilma followed. Between the Quonset building and the bluff, the road crew had staked out two parallel lengths of red plastic snow fence to try to keep the prevailing winds from stealing too much of the sand pile. Out over the ice, shafts of sun were slanting down through the overcast all the way up the length of the lake.

We circled around the snow fence. The wind was sharp. Hugh went on ahead of us with his Y-rod, apparently getting a series of tugs.

"I have no problem with her dumping him here," Wilma was saying. "It's close to the house. And she figured nobody would stumble on her—especially with the Lake Road closed off in the village. But coyotes? I'm sorry, that's *wacko*. You can't count on coyotes. Soon as summer rolls around, pieces of him're gonna start turning up—just like the hand out at Space Research."

"Not if they're small enough."

"What's small enough?"

We stopped at the end of the row next to the GMC ten-wheeler, and I unhooked the rubber cargo straps that held a woven plastic tarp over Marcel's sturdy orange gas-powered Altec Direct Drive Whisper Chipper, new last year. The town had purchased it with the aid of a conservation grant, now that the standard practice of burning cut brush was frowned upon.

"My God!" Wilma said. "The spout's aimed out over the lake. Right? It is, isn't it?"

"Gruesome image," Hugh said.

Wilma stared off toward the mountain. The cloud cover had brightened a little. White wisps flew across the dome. "I am *never* going swimming down there again."

"Do you happen to remember all the herring gulls crowding this end of the lake the first part of the week?" I asked.

"Herring gulls?" she said. "No."

Hugh threw up his arms. "The gulls! My God, you're right! They're *such* opportunists."

"First-class scavengers," I said. "Much more efficient than coyotes."

"Oh," she said.

I peered into the discharge chute.

"You see any residue?" Wilma said.

"Looks like she fed sand into the hopper before she shut the machine down. That would scour it out."

Later that afternoon, though, forensics techs using chemicals would have no trouble bringing up traces of Marcel on the knife blades and the chute, and the next day a hands-and-knees search of the shingle below would recover shreds of plastic, a few teeth, a toenail, more than enough for Marty Griswold to pronounce Marcel Boisvert among the deceased. Method, cause, and time of death unknown.

Wilma took my arm. "How in heaven's name did you make this connection?"

"I had an inkling yesterday, as I was crawling into Marcel's basement. You know how people in these parts will bank an old foundation with spruce boughs? Last winter Marcel used wood chips."

"OK. That's quite a leap, though, isn't it, from wood chips to people chips?"

"Early this morning I couldn't sleep. As I was lying there in the dark mulling everything over, it simply came to me. I'd heard it."

"What, this?" She rapped the Whisper Chipper's silver muffler.

"Sure. Last Monday morning out on the front porch at Sullivan's, I was sipping coffee, trying to make myself slow down and stop thinking about you and Boston and all the rest of it—you know, trying to just enjoy the sunshine and the soft air, listening to the kids over on the playground, the birds, the water in the storm drains, and I heard the sound of some machine I couldn't identify, something loud and shrill, like a circular saw. Out in this direction."

Wilma shuddered.

We walked out to the brow of the bluff and looked down at the shore. Everything—the boulders, the shale, the pier-stumps (all that was left of the hotel's shoreline promenade), and thirty years' accumulation of driftwood and trash—was pearled with rime.

Wilma poked around in her tote bag until she found a yellow warbler's contour feather. She smoothed it between her fingers and held it out to the wind in her upturned palm.

"Spirit of the lake, grant him peace."

"Amen," said Hugh.

"Peace to the living while you're at it," I said. It seemed a more practical request.

A gust took the feather. It fell for a moment, spinning, then caught an updraft and sailed out over the lake, disappearing finally in the ivory depths of the sky.

# ACKNOWLEDGMENTS

I owe a great debt of gratitude to many generous professionals in law enforcement, social work, and education for the time they took to help shape my inventions by patiently answering all of my questions, however clumsy or obvious they may have been.

Vernon Geberth's invaluable *Practical Homicide Investigation* is the most comprehensive text I know on the subject. Other law enforcement officers, current and retired, whose insights and information were critical to the story-making process are: Sid Adams, Tom Buckles, Gerry DeLisle, Mark Henry, Teddy Miller, Gaylon Smith, and Herbert Spellman.

Many good friends and neighbors also played supportive and inspirational roles during this story's long development. They include Denise Boland de Gramajo, Chris Braithwaite, Craig Dreisbach, Zoe Gascon, Tom Glines, Alejandro Gramajo, Deborah Greenman, Tony Ganz, Paul Lefebvre, Gary Moore, Humphrey Morris, Susan Morse, Howard Mosher, Steve Parker, Carol Rossi, Curt Sjolander, Michelle Trottier, and Bob Waldinger, whose book, *Effective Psychotherapy with Borderline Patients,* contains a wealth of provocative analysis.

As ever, the guidance and care offered by my wonderful editor, Shaye Areheart, have made this book a much better work of fiction than it would have been without her. Last, the love and bottomless encouragement of my good wife, Eileen Boland, have made just about everything better. I'd be lost without her.

# READER'S GROUP GUIDE

*Set in a small town in northern Vermont,* The Fifth Season *is a gripping story of a rural community swept into unimaginable violence when pride, grief, and deep-seated resentments collide.*

Hector Bellevance has returned to his hometown of Tipton, Vermont, after his marriage and his career as a policeman in Boston ended badly. He works as the town constable, a job that requires little more than "light peacekeeping," and he has settled into an easygoing love affair with Wilma, the ace reporter for the local paper. The simple rhythm of life in Tipton is brutally interrupted when a body is discovered on the site of an abandoned weapons factory.

With the sheriff and the state police occupied with the murder investigation, Hector receives the unwelcome task of informing the town's road commissioner, Marcel Boisvert, that his wife, Shirley, has gotten a relief-from-abuse order against him, so Marcel must vacate his home. Marcel is known for his uncompromising nature and merciless grudges and prejudices. But even those who know him best could not predict the consequences of Shirley's act of defiance. Within twenty-four hours, two more bodies are found, Marcel has disappeared, and Shirley is only one of several village residents who begin to fear for their lives.

Melding the quirky flavor of cozy mysteries and the tight pacing and forensic detail of police procedurals, *The Fifth Season* captures the dark side of small-town life and exposes the destructive power of thwarted hopes.

1. How do the descriptions of Marcel Boisvert and Vaughn Higbee [p. 7] establish the antipathy between the two men? What specific details bring out their differences? Is their enmity purely personal or does it reveal something about the social structure of the community as a whole?

2. How does Marcel's status as a descendant of Tipton's first settlers shape his attitudes about his role and importance in the town? Why does the author present the Boisvert and Bellevance family histories [pp. 33–37]? How does the past help to shed light on present relationships in the village?

3. What do Vaughn's threats, as well as the tone he takes with Hector, demonstrate about how he sees himself in Tipton? Are you more sympathetic with him or with Marcel?

4. How did Kathy's death affect Shirley and Marcel as individuals? What do their reactions reflect about their psychological makeup? What impact did it have on their relationship? Given what you know about them, do you think that the deterioration of their marriage was inevitable?

5. Shirley offers a stinging indictment of the way children are raised today [p. 30]. Is her point of view compatible with her own experiences and decisions as a mother? To what extent is it motivated by anger, remorse, and/or guilt?

6. Discuss Hector's mother's explanation of Marcel's treatment of Hector [p. 36]. Do you agree with Hector that "it sprang more from her forgiving nature than anything else"? Is Marcel's behavior understandable and forgivable, or is it motivated by mean-spirited anger and bitterness? What evidence is there that Marcel is capable of genuine love?

7. Is Vaughn a good father? Does his need to be "the witty, irreverent, party-going prof" [p. 89] take precedence over his responsibilities as a parent? Do you think he should have made an all-out effort to convince Marcel that Marc needed

his grandparents in his life? What part do pride and stubbornness play in how the two men regard each other?

8. Does Hector's familiarity with the community aid his investigation? To what extent is it a hindrance? How does his history as a hometown boy who made it in the big city only to come home in disgrace affect his relationship with the local sheriff's department and the state police? Why do they exclude him from the investigation? Are their suspicions about him [p. 104] justified by the evidence, or do they stem from personal animus?

9. In what ways does the murder investigation differ from traditional police-procedural novels or television shows?

10. What role does the romance between Hector and Wilma play in the novel? Do Wilma's pregnancy and the decisions she and Hector face enhance some of the novel's themes?

11. Bredes sets a series of gruesome events against a cozy, seemingly benign setting. How does he make this juxtaposition both believable and intriguing?

12. Did *The Fifth Season* change your ideas about small-town life? What aspects of life in Tipton appealed to you? Compare the problems faced by families in Tipton to those found in urban or suburban communities.

13. As you read *The Fifth Season,* which character or characters did you suspect of the murders? Does the narrator present the story in a way that encourages readers to work out the solution on their own?

14. Were you surprised when the murderer was revealed? In retrospect, did the narrative point toward the culprit's identity? What incidents or conversations held clues to the character's growing desperation and alienation from reality?